Second Wind

AIMEE NICOLE WALKER

Second Wind
Copyright © 2018 Aimee Nicole Walker

ISBN: 978-1-948273-03-9

aimeenicolewalker@blogspot.com

Cover photograph © Wander Aguiar—www.wanderaguiar.com
Cover art © Jay Aheer of Simply Defined Art—www.simplydefinedart.com

Editing provided by Miranda Vescio of V8 Editing and Proofreading - https://www.facebook.com/V8Editing/

Proofreading provided by Judy Zweifel of Judy's Proofreading—www.judysproofreading.com

Interior Design and Formatting provided by Stacey Ryan Blake of Champagne Formats—www.champagnebookdesign.com

Copyright and Trademark Acknowledgments

The author acknowledges the copyrights and trademarked status and trademark owners of the trademarks and copyrights mentioned in this work of fiction.

Dedication

To Gary Lacasse,

I've waited for the right characters to come along to tell a story worthy of a dedication to you. Thank you for reminding me that love doesn't always come easy, early, or without risk. Gary, you work hard to make the world a better place, and I'm proud to call you my friend.

Second Wind Playlist

You're My Best Friend—Queen

Fly Like An Eagle—The Steve Miller Band

Right Here Waiting—Richard Marx

Can't Fight This Feeling—REO Speedwagon

The First Time—U2

End of the Road—Boyz II Men

Who Let In The Rain—Cyndi Lauper

I Want To Break Free—Queen

Better Things—The Kinks

The House That Built Me—Miranda Lambert

Begin Again—Taylor Swift

Second Wind—Maren Morris

In Your Eyes—Peter Gabriel

Stay A Little Longer—Brothers Osborne

Pillowtalk - Zayne

So You're Saying—Joe Nichols

No Place That Far—Sara Evans

Sweetest Goodbye—Maroon 5

Lights Down Low—Max

Whatever It Takes—Lifehouse

Believer—Imagine Dragons

Time After Time—Cyndi Lauper

A Thousand Years—The Piano Guys

Yours—Russell Dickerson

With Arms Wide Open—Creed

1—You're My Best Friend

Rush Holden

“I CAN'T BELIEVE YOU THINK A FLEA MARKET IS A SUITABLE place to buy your niece a birthday present,” my boyfriend, Travis, said snootily. At least he said it low enough that only I heard him. I tried hard not to roll my eyes for fear that the vendors would think I was maligning their goods.

“Some of us come from humble beginnings, Trav. Not everyone needs an iPad or the next best gadget to feel loved.”

“I didn't get her an iPad,” he said defensively. “It's a middle-of-the-road tablet for her to read on. I think it's good to encourage her love of books. I don't think Jules will be upset with me this time.” According to my sister, Travis tried to buy Racheal's affection rather than pay attention to her. It was the easy way out, and Jules didn't like it.

I turned and looked into the pair of blue eyes that had pulled me out of months-long despair when we first met. Ten years ago, I thought Travis was the answer to my lonely heart's prayers, but somewhere along the way, we seemed to have drifted apart. It felt like both of us were just going through the motions in our relationship rather than take a chance on finding someone new.

"And I agree with you, but I saw the Kindle you bought her, and it's *not* middle of the road. It's that new waterproof version, and I think it's a bit fancy for a seven-year-old girl. Besides…" My words faded off when my eyes locked on the perfect gift. "Oh my God! There it is!" I bounced on the balls of my feet and ran over to the faded pink bike with a banana seat and a dingy white basket attached to the handlebars. "It's just like the one that Jules had when she was a little girl."

"You can't be serious, Rush." Travis didn't bother hiding his derision. I glanced up at the seller and caught the narrow-eyed look she gave him.

"It's a classic," the woman said in a voice that stated Travis must be daft.

"How much?" I asked her. I didn't care what Travis thought, I knew Racheal would love it.

"One hundred," she told me. "It's in mint condition."

"Dollars?" Travis sputtered. "You want *one hundred dollars* for that? Mint condition? You can't tell what color the paint used to be and don't get me started on that filthy basket? What are those woven into the plastic? Flowers?"

I put my hands on my hips and turned to face him. I gave him a look that said, "You better shut the hell up if you want me to give you head in the near future."

Travis threw up his hands and took a few steps back. "I'm not going to say another word. It wouldn't do any good, so I'm not going to waste my time or energy."

I handed over five crisp twenty-dollar bills then wheeled my prize to my charcoal-gray Volvo XC60 with my head held high. My SUV was another thing Travis disapproved of, but I needed the room to haul camera equipment, and sometimes people, to locations for shoots. I refused to budge on buying a bigger vehicle, but I did let him sway me toward German engineering. I passionately loved the luxurious feel that my Diva afforded me while providing the much-needed room and all-wheel drive during Chicago's harsh winters.

"I guess I can understand the nostalgic appeal, but can I at least make a suggestion?" Travis asked as I pushed the button on my fob to open the hatchback.

"I'm listening," I told him.

"I know a guy who restores a lot of things. Maybe he can jazz the bike up a bit for Racheal."

"You mean completely overhaul it?" I asked suspiciously.

"No," Travis replied. "I'm talking about shining up the paint, replacing the torn leather seat, and maybe trying to clean up that basket." I busied myself putting the bike in my SUV so Travis didn't see how tickled I was over his distaste for the basket. "He can also make sure the mechanics are in working order. That rear tire looks flat."

"It is flat," I confirmed. I couldn't fault Travis's practical logic. What good was it to buy Rach something she couldn't ride? "I only have a few weeks. You think he can work me in?" I never bothered to ask how Travis knew such a diverse group of friends. Yes, Chicago was a diverse city, but as an investment banker, I expected him to rub elbows with others like him—the one percent crowd.

"All we can do is ask," he replied practically, looping his arm around my shoulders and kissing my temple.

It must've been my lucky week because I met with Jack St. James a few days later and found out that he was able to work me into his schedule. "I haven't seen one of these in ten years," he said excitedly. "Where'd you find this gem?"

"Flea market," I told him. "It's just like the one my sister got for her birthday when we were kids, and I want to fix it up nice for her daughter's birthday."

"That's a cool gift, man," he said. "What do you have in mind?" There was a glint of something extra in his golden-brown eyes, like maybe he'd offer up additional services if I were interested. I wasn't. *Was I?* No!

"I don't want it to look brand new," I told him, pretending I didn't notice his interest. "I just want it to look clean and be safe for Rach to ride."

"That's doable," Jack said then went over the cost and timeframe to whip the bike into shape. "Does that sound fair?"

I was surprised by how much he planned to charge me, but nothing was too good for my princess. "I can live with it." If I wasn't a faithful man, I might have offered to blow him if I thought it would save me some cash. Jack sure was magnificent to look at, but I'd never cheat on Travis. "Call me when it's ready, and I'll come pick it up."

"I look forward to it," he practically purred.

Would he have been so flirty if Travis had come with me? I think the better question to ponder was if Travis would've even cared. My man had run hot and cold with me the past six months, and I grappled with what I should do about it. I knew the answer didn't lie in a stranger's bed, so I thanked him and kept it moving.

Racheal had perfect April weather for her birthday party two Saturdays later. Jules and Will purchased and beautifully restored a home in the Forest Glen neighborhood of Chicago fifteen years prior, creating the perfect home to raise a family in. It just took them a lot longer to get their little miracle than they had planned. My sister had suffered several miscarriages and had all but given up when she decided to try one last time. They were blessed with a perfect baby girl nine months later. Racheal was the apple of our eye, especially mine since it didn't look like I would ever have kids of my own.

"Let me guess," Jules said when I walked into her house alone with Travis's wrapped gift tucked under my arm. "Business trip? Important lunch with a client? Too busy? Doesn't give a fuck about your family or feelings?"

"Something like that," I said, kissing her cheek. My sister pulled no punches when it came to Travis and the lack of effort he put into his relationship with my small family, which consisted of my sister, Will, and Racheal. Jules had always welcomed him with arms wide open, but Travis could never get used to her bold, unfiltered personality.

"She'll take some getting used to," Travis said after meeting her. It didn't take me long to realize that he either couldn't, or wouldn't, get used to her.

To be honest, I was glad he didn't come. He'd look down his nose at the barbecue feast my sister prepared, refuse to eat the sugary cake and ice cream, and rush us out of there as soon as he thought we spent sufficient time there. I liked to linger after everyone else went home and spend time with my three favorite people.

"Try not to take it personally," I told Jules.

"Pffft," she said, waving her hand. "I couldn't care less what that asshole thinks about us. I just hate to see you settling for someone who doesn't make you happy. You deserve a home filled with love and children."

"I am happy." I forced a smile on my face to prove how happy I was, but I could see that it fell short.

"Stop badgering Rush," Will said, entering the kitchen with a platter laden with grilled burgers, hot dogs, and sausages. "There are like two dozen hungry people outside, including one impatient birthday girl who wants to open her presents but can't until after she eats."

Jules approached the counter and finished arranging the platters of burger and hot dog toppings that she was working on when I arrived. I pitched in, grateful for the interruption. My love life might not be worthy of a romance novel, but it worked for me. I sometimes got tired of defending why I stayed with Travis. It didn't matter my reasons. I chose him, and I wanted that to be respected.

"I'm sorry, Rush," Jules said when we returned to the kitchen to clean up the mess after everyone devoured the food. "I have no right to judge you or criticize your life." She held her tongue while we loaded the dishwasher, but just like when we were kids, her words started flowing the minute she stuck her hands in the warm, soapy water to wash the platters that didn't fit in the dishwasher.

I sensed a *but* was coming. *Wait for it. One... two... three...*

"But, I—"

My laughter interrupted her, and she elbowed me hard in the stomach. My breath left my body in a *whoosh*. "Vicious," I said, placing my hands over my abs to protect myself from another blow.

"You deserve better than Travis's cold indifference," she said then pinned me with the same glare she gave me when I annoyed the hell out of her as a kid. "Even though, I'm not sure why I think it now."

"Because it's true," Will said, joining us. "Look, why don't we rehash this again for the two hundredth time *after* the birthday girl opens her gifts and eats her cake. How much longer do you think I can hold her off?"

"Fine," Jules said, drying her hands and tossing the towel on the counter. "We're not finished, Rush."

Will and I fell in several steps behind her. "Don't worry; I'll distract her so you can get the hell out of here whenever you're ready," he said in a conspiring tone.

"You're a keeper, Will," I told him. I couldn't have loved him more if he was a blood relative.

"Come sit by me, Uncle Rush," Racheal hollered when I walked down the deck stairs.

I crossed the lawn and took the seat beside her, but that apparently wasn't enough because Rach climbed onto my lap. My heart squeezed tight in my chest when she aimed her megawatt smile at me. How much longer would I be my angel's favorite person on earth? How long before someone else replaced me? I shoved the worrisome thought aside and hugged her a little tighter.

Rach remained on my lap while she opened each gift and thanked everyone. Of course, Jules made a list of who gave her what gift so that she could help Racheal send thank you cards later. When we were kids, my mother always told us we were never too young to learn impeccable manners. Jules was passing along those teachings to her daughter.

"What did you get me, Uncle Rush?" she asked. "That," Racheal pointed to the Kindle, "is definitely a gift from Travis." Not Uncle Travis, just Travis. She seemed to like the tablet, but she certainly didn't respond in the way that Travis predicted.

"I think the gift tag said it was from both of us. What makes you think I got you something else?"

"Because I'm your favorite person on the planet," she replied, sounding seventeen instead of seven.

"True," I said. "Loop your arms around my neck." As soon as she complied, I rose to my feet with a giggling princess clinging to me. "Maybe I do have a surprise for you." I looked at my sister and nodded my head toward the house. "You won't want to miss this either."

Jules seemed as excited as Racheal when we took a shortcut through the house to reach my SUV parked in the driveway. I set Rach down on the pavement and said, "Close your eyes." I laughed when both special ladies in my life eagerly complied. "No peeking."

"We won't," they said together.

I popped the hatchback and pulled the bike out, setting it in front of them. I closed the door and waited until I thought the ladies had squirmed long enough. "Okay, open your eyes!"

"Wow!" Racheal said when she saw her new bike.

"Oh my God!" Jules said before briefly covering her mouth with her hands. "It's just like the one I used to have when I was a girl. Oh man, you loved that freaking bike as much as I did."

"I sure did," I replied.

Our father had decided when I was seven years old that I was man enough to learn how to ride a bike. All the other kids had already learned and Butch Holden's kid was just as good as those other boys. I wanted to ride Jules's bike, but dad had said only sissies would want to ride a girl's bike.

"My boy will never grow up to be a sissy."

I didn't know what my dad had meant at the time, but I could tell by his tone of voice that being a sissy was a very bad thing. I didn't want to be bad, but I loved that bike so much. Jules even had these streamer things that dangled from the ends of the handlebars and floated on the breeze whenever she rode her bike. I didn't get streamers and a pretty basket; I got some dark-blue, boring bike that I hated.

"Guard your bike, baby girl," Jules said. "Uncle Rush stole mine one afternoon with the help of his friend."

"He did?" she asked in wide-eyed wonder.

Memories I spent decades trying to forget rushed through me, making my eyes tear with both joy and sorrow. Jules bit her lip nervously when she realized what she had said. I saw the regret in her eyes, but she'd already picked the scab off my wound.

"I did."

"Wow! I want to hear all about it," Racheal said, throwing her leg over the banana seat.

"Wait a minute," Jules said. "You have to wear your protective gear. Bad things can happen if you don't, right, Uncle Rush?"

"Very true."

"Oh man, I want to know what happened."

I waited for my niece to put her helmet, knee pads, and elbow pads on before I gave her the G-rated version of the day I couldn't resist temptation any longer. Of course, I never knew if it was the bike or the boy who pushed me over the edge. Once I was in the privacy of my car heading home, I let myself remember the full version of events.

"Do it, Rush," Lincoln Huxley said. "Who cares 'bout them."

I looked into his dark-brown eyes and believed I could do any-thing. Even at seven years old, I knew he was special. We were the same age, but Lincoln looked much older because of his unusual height. I loved Lincoln with all the pure innocence of a child, especially when he acted as the lookout so I could wheel Jules's bike out of the garage and down the driveway.

"I don't know how to ride," I said fearfully. "What if I fall?"

"You get up and go again," he replied without pause, sounding like an adult. "You can do it, Rush."

Lincoln was the only one besides Jules who believed in me. Mama wanted to, but she was too afraid of what Daddy would say if she stood up to him. I recognized the whipped-dog expression in her eyes, even if I didn't know what it was. I wanted to please Lincoln so he would love me like I loved him. I'd heard my cousin Nancy say that she wanted to kiss a boy named Derrick. She said she loved him the minute she saw him and knew they would get married someday. I loved Lincoln from the moment he moved into the house down the street from mine two years before, and even though I didn't know what it meant, I wanted to kiss him and marry him too. I hated any day that didn't include him in it. I would tell him someday, perhaps after I rode the beautiful bike.

"Climb on," Lincoln said, holding the bike steady for me.

"Okay."

The bike started to wobble to the right, to the left, and back to the right again, so Lincoln placed a confident hand on the back of the seat to steady me. "I'll hold on and run beside you. That's what my daddy did when he taught me to ride."

"Okay," I said nervously.

"I won't let go 'til you say so."

"Okay," I said, sounding a little braver.

"You have to pedal."

This was it! The moment I'd been waiting for since Jules got the bike for her birthday. I was seconds away from seeing those streamers blowing in the breeze and earning Lincoln's approval. I pedaled slowly *at first, trying not to squeal when the bike felt like it was going to tip over.*

"I got you," Lincoln said, jogging alongside me. "You can do it."

"I can do it!" Feeling braver, I began pedaling faster.

"Go, Rush!" Lincoln cheered.

"Don't let go, Lincoln," I said fearfully.

"You're so good, Rush. Don't stop."

I felt it, the moment that he let go. The bike wobbled and shook, but I kept it upright as I gained more speed. I rode into the wind with the breeze stealing my breath, but I was too excited to be scared. I was riding a bike! A pretty bike with a basket and streamers. My attention shifted to the pink and silver streamers floating on the breeze, wishing my hair was long enough to flow behind me when I should've been pay-ing attention to the cracked, uneven sidewalk in front of me.

"Rush!" Lincoln called out from behind me, snapping me out of the daydream, but it was too late to avoid disaster.

I hit the huge gap in the sidewalk and flew over the handlebars, landing on my back awkwardly. The impact knocked the air out of my lungs, and I gasped in panic, trying to pull air back into my body.

"Rush! Rush!" Lincoln said, dropping to the pavement beside me. He cupped my face tenderly and looked at me with worried, dark eyes. "Are you okay?"

I tried to answer him but couldn't. Lincoln shifted his gaze away from my face to see if I was hurt anywhere.

"Oh no!" he said at the same time I felt a horrible, burning sensa-tion in my arm.

The pain was so severe that I wanted to scream, but I couldn't manage even a squeak. Mrs. Johnson rushed out of her house to see if I was okay.

"Oh, honey," she said tenderly, running her hands over my buzzed hair. "Lincoln, you run back to his house and get his parents. Tell them to bring the car. Rush needs to go to the hospital."

Hospital? I raised my head to look at my arm, but Mrs. Johnson wouldn't let me. "Don't you worry, little lamb. You'll feel better soon."

I was too scared to cry, or at least that's how it felt. My dad was going to be mad at me for stealing the bike. I heard the car pull up and the doors slam shut as my parents raced over to my side. My mother started to cry, but Dad told her to be as brave as I was. For the first time in my life, my dad looked at me with respect. All because I was too traumatized to cry over my broken arm. "He's showing what a strong man he's going to be someday, Alice."

"He's just a child, Butch," *my mom countered, then cowered when my father pinned her with a stern look.*

"Sorry, Rush," *Lincoln said, kneeling beside my head.* "I shoulda held on."

I shoulda held on. I shoulda held on. I shoulda held on. The words played on an endless loop as I walked inside the quiet brownstone home I shared with Travis. Maybe my life lacked the sense of adventure that I'd once had, but it was safe and reliable. Maybe Travis didn't make my heart pound and blood race through my veins like a certain dark-haired boy once had, but neither did he have the power to hurt me. Lincoln Huxley was my best friend, my first love, and the boy who broke my spirit in ways that hurt far worse than any broken bone.

2—Fly Like an Eagle

Lincoln Huxley

"**A**RE YOU READY FOR TODAY?"

I looked up from my computer screen to lock eyes with the woman who I'd shared my life with for more than twenty years. Her eyes were the same guileless blue they'd always been, but lately, I noticed that worry replaced the twinkle I expected to see in them. Ophelia Jenkins-Huxley leaned casually in the doorway, but the frown lines around her mouth contradicted her pose.

"I was born ready," I said with a flippancy I didn't feel. I was the king of faking it until I made it. One could even say that *I* was fake, an absolute fraud. I offered her a reassuring smile, but the grimace on her face said that I'd failed to hit the mark.

"We don't have to go through with this deal, Linc. We haven't signed any documents, nor have we given a verbal agreement,"

Ophelia said softly. "It's not like the universe needs another country club."

The deal she was referring to was the biggest one of our careers. If we succeeded, it had the potential to introduce us to the wealthiest clients California had to offer. If we failed, it could ruin us and destroy everything we had worked so hard to build. Every decision we ever made led us to this deal, and I wanted it so bad I could taste it. What kept me up at night was my concern that I wanted it for the wrong reasons. Did I pursue Maxim Detwiler because I wanted his business or was it because he made my dick impossibly hard, and I couldn't stop imagining what he would look like naked over me or beneath me? I would never betray my wife by acting on the physical attraction I felt to him, but what if I was following my dick to certain financial disaster?

I scrubbed my face with my hands to push the images away and focus on the conversation with my wife. "The Oasis is everything I dreamed of since we first stepped foot on California soil, Phee. Yeah, I'm stressed. We would be risking everything on this deal, but I want it bad." *The deal or the man?*

"There's something about Detwiler that I don't like," my wife said. Ophelia had probably detected that the wealthy man returned my attraction. But unlike me, I saw in his heated gaze that he was more than willing to act on it.

"Do *you* want to back out, Phee? Is that what this is about?" I would be disappointed if it didn't happen, but I would never choose business over Ophelia. She was my wife, best friend, business partner, and mother of our two children. There was no one on this earth I respected more than Phee, and her business instincts were unmatched by anyone I'd ever known.

"Back out? No. More like take a few steps back and reassess that this is the best fit for us. We've always been able to navigate the changes in the real estate market, but what he's proposing is way out of our depth. This isn't just us brokering a deal between two interested parties and collecting our commission. This project would require us to give up a huge chunk of our life savings to be a part of a deal that I'm not sure fits us. We've come a long way since our college days, Linc, but we've never forgotten who we were or where we came from. What is it that we told our kids all these years? If something seems too good to be true, then it probably is."

Truer words were never spoken. If I had been able to forget who I was or where I came from, we wouldn't have built a life together. I would've most likely made different choices that led me down a completely different path with someone else. I can't say that I would've been better or worse if I'd made other choices, because you can't comprehend what you've never had. I was completely happy with the decisions I made and the person who shared my life. I had no regrets. I clenched my jaw when a tiny, but persistent, voice in my head called me a liar.

"Is there something specific about the deal that's bothering you, or is it just an impression?" I asked Phee, focusing my energy on her question instead of the doubt I couldn't seem to stifle any longer.

"Why us, Linc?" she asked. "I'm not trying to undermine our success, but there are far more successful real estate brokers and developers Detwiler could've chosen. Why us? I can't help but think that he has less to lose if he destroys our life, where the heavy hitters would hit back and take him down too."

She made an excellent point. The initial investment money should've been easy for Detwiler to come up with, so why did he even want partners? He'd said it was to introduce us to people who could change our lives, but there wasn't anything wrong with our lives. Phee was right about the country club not being our thing. Why invest in something that we wouldn't enjoy?

"Okay," I agreed. "We'll view the evening's activities through cynical eyes, and we'll walk away if we don't like what we see."

"Deal."

My phone vibrated on my desk, and our twenty-year-old

daughter's face smiled up at me from the picture I saved as her contact photo. It was a selfie she took of the two of us on graduation day. My heart swelled with pride and love. Kennedy might've been an independent young woman living more than two thousand miles away in Chicago, but she still called her old man almost every day.

"Hey, baby girl," I said into the phone. "How'd your exams go?"

"Tell her that her *mother* loves her too and would like to hear from her sometime also," Ophelia said loud enough for our daughter to hear her.

"Put me on speakerphone," Kennedy said. I heard the humor in her voice.

"Hello, my baby girl," Phee said after I pushed the button on my phone. "How are things going? Are you ready to come home for the summer? You haven't given me a date to buy your plane ticket." Kennedy was finishing up her second year at the prestigious Loyola University. We couldn't wait for her to come home.

"About that," she said hesitantly. My heart sunk. "I didn't want to say anything to you until I knew it was a sure thing, but I was offered an amazing opportunity to intern at Wright Creations in D.C. this summer. I'm going to miss you guys like crazy, but I can't pass up this offer. It's a once in a lifetime thing."

"As in our nation's capital?" I asked.

"That's on the other side of the world," Ophelia whined.

"More like the other side of the country, Mom, but I know it feels farther." Kennedy giggled. "I hear your fingers clicking on the keyboard. Let me guess; you're looking up Wright Creations online."

"Damn right I am," I replied without shame. "If you're going to miss your summer with us then I want to make sure the opportunity is as good as you say." Phee rounded the desk and read the screen over my shoulder.

I immediately clicked on the "About Us" tab because I didn't care about their list of clients or their testimonial. I wanted to know about the CEO and what his company stood for. When the page loaded, I was stunned. Two brothers, Grayson and Preston Wright, were the founders. The bios weren't the typical ones you saw on most corporate sites. Sure, there was the usual data dump about when they began the company and some of the awards that they'd achieved. I knew nothing about marketing, but even I recognized they had achieved a lot in a fairly short period. That wasn't what stood out to me though. It was the pictures of the men that accompanied the bios. Preston posed beside his wife and two children, as did Grayson with his husband and two children.

"Oh, honey, this company sounds amazing. Look at all the charities they support," Phee said.

"I haven't met them in person," Kennedy said, "but I enjoyed talking to them during our Skype interviews. Grayson conducted my interview from his home office while his kids played with their toys on his lap until his husband came and wrangled them out of there. Apparently, they took advantage of Chase's distraction when he signed for a delivery and let themselves into Gray's office."

It was nearly impossible for me to swallow past the lump in my throat.

"Daddy, you're too quiet."

"I'm just going to miss you so much," I said after clearing my throat.

"Please don't be upset. I'll still be home for the family vacation in Cancun. I told the Wrights about our plans, and they wouldn't dream of making me miss it."

Of course I let her think it was her absence that stole my breath and made my heart race. There was no way I could describe to her, or anyone, what I felt at the moment because I didn't fully grasp it myself.

"I'm not upset," I assured her. I could never be that selfish and squash her dreams like that. "When do you move, and where will you be staying?"

Phee and I listened as our daughter laid out her detailed plan.

"I'm going to live it up next week with my friends before I pack up and move to D.C. for the summer."

"Live it up?" Phee repeated.

"Not booze and boys," Kennedy replied wryly. "I want to spend as much time as I can at Navy Pier. May is perfect weather in Chicago, and you know how much I love the pier. I'm going to miss that Ferris wheel."

I did my best to stay engaged in the conversation, but the mention of a Ferris wheel took me back to a place that I tried my damnedest to forget.

"I don't know, Linc," Rush Holden said from beside me. I looked down at him and noticed the difference in our height. I'd hit another growth spurt over the summer and left Rush behind me. "That Ferris wheel looks really high."

"I'll go with you, Rush. It will be okay."

"Like the time you taught me how to ride a bike?"

"Better than that," I promised him.

Rush looked over at the guy operating the carnival ride. He looked like he hadn't bathed in a week, his clothes consisted of dirty jeans and a concert T-shirt from some band that was too small to cover his belly. The man belched loudly and rubbed his stomach with a cigarette-stained hand before he returned Rush's stare.

"I changed my mind," he told me. "Let's go find something else to ride."

"You say this every year when the carnival comes to town," I reminded him. "Every year you regret not riding it. What happened to you wanting to fly like an eagle?"

"I know," he said softly. Rush bit his lip while he looked up at the ride as it whirled in a big circle. He swallowed hard then turned and looked up at me again. His green eyes were wide with excitement and fear. "Let's do it." He nodded as if to convince me, but I knew it was really for himself. Then he looked at me with the same determination as when he stole Jules's bike.

Excitement flared in my chest at the knowledge that something big was about to happen. I thought it was my reaction to seeing one of Rush's dreams coming true and happiness that I had a part in it. I just hoped that things went better than the last time I gave in to my urge to make Rush the happiest kid on the planet. It didn't seem like anyone else cared about making Rush smile, but I did. In fact, I made it my mission to earn one of his beautiful smiles every day. I returned his nod and simply said, "Okay."

It seemed like we waited forever for our turn. The wheel just kept spinning and spinning, never slowing down. I started to think that maybe the thing was broken or something, but then it started to slow down. When it came to a stop, the ride operator unloaded and reloaded one passenger car at a time. We were in the middle of the line, and I expected that Rush would change his mind before we reached the front, but I was wrong.

Rush was nervous, I could tell by the way he tapped the toe of his right foot while we waited, but he slid into the car when it was our turn, sitting proudly and as tall as he could. He let out a little giggle when we rose high enough for the next car to unload and reload.

"Oh man," he said when we reached the very top of the ride. "It's so beautiful up here." Rush placed his hand over mine and squeezed before he slid his fingers between mine.

I glanced around at the majestic Great Smoky Mountains, but they didn't hold my interest like the boy who sat next to me. I looked down at our joined hands and felt that same fluttering in my stomach that I always got when Rush was near, but it was more intense after he touched me. Not even the roller coaster I rode the previous summer compared to the thrill Rush gave me. I was terrified of feeling that way about another boy but even more scared that it would stop. Rush gasped and clutched his stomach with his free hand when the ride started again, but by the time we circled back up to the top, he'd thrown his head back and delighted laughter shook his body.

Rush released my hand and threw his arm around my shoulder.

Then he leaned into me and said, "Thank you, Linc."

My stomach stopped fluttering because it fell to my feet. My heart thumped so loud that I was sure everyone could hear it when Rush looked up at me like I was Superman. I wanted the ride to last forever, but good things never lasted. All too soon, the ride ended. The greasy, gross guy opened the door of our car and looked down at the way Rush still leaned into me. The disgust I saw in his eyes made me feel bad. Dirty, like his clothes.

"Let's go," I said, jerking out of Rush's embrace and climbing off the ride.

Rush, unaware of the hateful look the operator gave us, scrambled to follow me. He was talking a mile a minute about flying like an eagle and that I was a much cooler superhero than Superman. "Hey! Wait up! Are you mad at me, Linc?"

I was trying to get as far away from the hateful man as fast as I could, but I didn't stop to realize how it might look to Rush. I jerked to a stop so he could catch up to me. "I could never be mad at you, Rush. I just didn't like that creepy guy."

"Forget about him," Rush said, shrugging. He threw his arms around me, hugging me tightly. He was always so giving with his affection, but never quite like that day at the carnival. I knew by the look the guy gave me that I shouldn't like Rush hugging me, but I liked it a lot. I couldn't stop thinking about it for days afterward and decided I would find ways to earn daily hugs to go with those smiles.

"It sounds like you have an excellent plan, baby girl. Daddy and I approve. Right, Linc?" Ophelia asked, nudging me.

I blinked back to the present, but the first thing I saw was Grayson and Chase Wright smiling at me from the computer screen. I hadn't let myself think about Rush in a long time, but it seemed like *what could have been* flooded my brain at seeing the picture of the happy gay couple.

"Absolutely," I said to both of my girls. "Kennedy, I'm going to miss you like crazy, but you make Mom and me proud every single day. We love you, kitten."

"I love you guys too. Talk later." I sat there looking at the phone for a minute after Kennedy disconnected.

"Honey, are you sure you're okay?" Phee asked, running her hand over the back of my hair. I leaned into her touch as I had been doing for more than two decades. She was my comfort zone, my safe place. She deserved so much more than I could ever give her.

I tipped my head back and looked up at her. "Just disappointed. I'll be fine though."

Phee leaned down and gave me a quick kiss on the lips. She never let on if she noticed the lack of spark between us, but how could she not? "I have some calls to make before we leave." She looked at the watch on her slim wrist. "Give me an hour?"

"Sure," I said nodding.

Sadness filled my heart as I watched her walk away. *My life is good. I'm happy. We're happy.* I repeated it in my head over and over, doing my damnedest to convince myself that it was true.

The memory of smiling green eyes and joyful laughter mocked me and called me a liar.

3—Right Here Waiting

Rush

I LOOKED AT MY WATCH ONCE MORE. DAMMIT, TRAVIS. WHERE the fuck are you?

"Mr. Holden, would you like me to pour you another glass of wine to enjoy while you wait for Mr. Dennison to arrive?"

"Just bring me the bottle, Walter. I'm not driving."

"Right away, sir." The kind, silver-haired man offered me a small smile before he left the table to retrieve the bottle of wine. Thankfully, I only saw sympathy and not pity in his smile because there was only room enough for one at my pity party.

"And more bread," I called after him. Why the fuck should I care if I ate too many carbs? Would Travis even notice if I gained weight? He sure as hell couldn't find time in his busy schedule to meet me for dinner. I'd made the reservations six months in advance and had been looking forward to the night. Apparently, I was the only one.

"Here you go," Walter said when he returned to the table. "I'll check back to take your order when Mr. Dennison arrives."

"You know what? I'm just going to order now," I told him. "I'm starving, and I don't feel like waiting any longer, Walter."

My favorite waiter looked momentarily stunned but blinked away his surprise to take my order. "Of course, sir. What will you have tonight?"

"I'll have the filet, medium rare, with sautéed onions, mushrooms, and risotto."

"Excellent choice," Walter said. "I'll have that out to you soon. Would you like an appetizer while you wait?"

"Fried calamari," I told him. *Go big, or go home.*

I glanced around the restaurant and noticed how pretty the twinkling, white Christmas lights and elegant decorations looked. Christmastime in Chicago was pure magic, which was reflected in the smiling couples and laughing friends dining all around me. I instantly regretted checking out my surroundings because it made me realize just how lonely I'd become. I could've called Travis's assistant, Sylvia, and asked her to remind him that he was late for our reservation, as I had done too many times to count over the past few years, but I would've been just as lonely if he'd shown up for dinner. I just wouldn't have looked as pathetic.

I glanced at the overpriced watch he bought me for my birthday last year and saw that he was forty minutes late. *Fuck! I hated waiting.* It gave me too much time to think, and thinking about my past was all I seemed to do since I gave Racheal the bike for her birthday the previous spring. Waiting for Travis reminded me of all the times I waited for Lincoln to finish football, basketball, or baseball practice so he could hang out with me. I waited to see his smile and hear his laughter. Waiting. Waiting. Waiting.

My entire life, it seemed like I'd waited for someone to arrive or something bad to happen. Growing up in eastern Tennessee in the eighties, I was at the mercy of the world around me. One slip and I would've lost everything I loved, including my home. There was no way in hell Butch Holden would allow a gay son to live under his roof. The words written in his precious bible were more important to him than Jules or I ever were. According to Butch, homosexuality was a sin, and he didn't tolerate sin in our home. I shudder to think what he would've done to me. Homelessness would've been the kindest form of punishment.

So, I waited for fate to deal me a cruel blow. I waited for my parents to reject me. I waited to be bullied in school and scoffed at by my teachers. Worst of all, I waited for Lincoln to miss me as I had missed him. I didn't know what happened to cause the rift between us, but it was there. One minute we were best friends, and the next thing I knew, he didn't have time for me anymore. I became a distant memory in junior high once he became king of the gridiron and discovered girls.

I knew that Lincoln would never love me the way I loved him, but I at least wanted to be his best friend again. I missed the sleepovers where we stayed up playing video games until the wee hours of the morning and the campouts in the back yard where we read comic books by the glow or our flashlights. I hated that I was no longer the first person he told his secrets to, hell, he didn't even acknowledge my existence once we hit high school. I wish I could've avoided him altogether, but he sat behind me in homeroom. Every morning, I kept my eyes on my desk and willed my body not to shake when he walked by me. I would catch a whiff of the soap he used in the shower that morning, and it was all I could do not to sniff the air. Fuck, why did he have to smell so damn good? I just wanted to nestle under his armpit and feel the weight of his arm around me again.

I hadn't realized how much of my happiness was built around Lincoln until he was gone. He might've been physically present, but he was emotionally closed off to me. The joyful gleam in his eyes was gone, and he only aimed that crooked smile at the cheerleaders. The last fond memory I had of us together was the sleepover we had at my house. My mom had made a big deal of us boys going into junior high and insisted that we celebrate the end of an era while welcoming in another. If I'd known that it would be the last time Linc would willingly spend time with me, I would've done things differently. I would've cuddled into the side of him longer because he didn't seem to mind it. Maybe I would've stayed awake longer to watch him sleep while fantasizing about feeling his soft lips against mine. Did he know how I felt about him? Did he see the way he made my pulse race? Did he know that those little accidental touches weren't an accident at all? Was he disgusted by me?

That had to be it, but what could I do about it? How did a sixteen-year-old boy apologize to another sixteen-year-old boy for loving him? How awkward would it be that I waited four lonely years to approach him? Would he understand that it took that long for me to find the courage to seek him out after he shut me out of his life? Linc had always been the one to motivate me to take on the things that scared me, but this time, just talking to him was the thing that scared me. How would I even start the conversation? Did I assure him that I was just confused and it wouldn't happen again? Lincoln wasn't stupid; he'd see right through my bullshit apology and know the truth. He'd know that I loved him. What then? Would he tell my parents? Would he make fun of me in front of all the kids? I didn't know, but I was desperate to have him back in my life and had to try something.

I knew where to find him after school. I hid beneath the bleachers on the visitor's side of the field and watched practice. Did I approach him afterward when they walked back up to the school to shower? No, that would look weird in front of the team. I sure as hell wasn't going to approach him inside the locker room and risk my body reacting to his partially clad or naked body. I ended up waiting for him in the hallway outside the locker room.

I slid down the wall to sit on the cold linoleum floor, but I needed the chill to keep me from getting overheated when I couldn't stop my overactive imagination from running wild with images of Linc in the shower, soaping up his body. I tried to think of the math homework I had waiting for me or the essay I had to write for English lit, but it didn't work. Nothing was going to stop me from popping wood right there in the hallway outside the boys' locker room.

I closed my eyes then begged and prayed to anyone who would listen to spare me from humiliation. My answered prayer came in the form of the two players coming out of the locker room carrying on a conversation they hadn't intended for me to overhear.

"Did you hear that Jana let Lincoln touch her tits beneath her bra?" Skip Hastings asked.

"He's so lucky," Joey Baughman said. "How long before she lets him—Oh, hey, Rush! Didn't know you were out here," he said, jerking to a stop. "Are you waiting for your dad?"

I couldn't let on how badly the guys had hurt me with their words. How would I explain bursting into tears? "Uh, yeah. I stayed late to work on a project and needed a ride home." I needed a ride home all right, but not because of any sanctioned after-school activity. My dad definitely wouldn't have approved of the thoughts I'd had about Linc in the shower.

"He won't be too much longer," Skip said.

"See ya around," Joey tossed over his shoulder as they walked away from me.

"See ya," I returned with a casualness I didn't feel. Being forced to fake everything from me being straight to them being kind had its advantages. The football players didn't like me, but they were decent to me out of respect for my dad. All of that would change if they learned the truth.

"She's going to give it up to him. I know it," Skip said when he thought they were out of earshot.

I waited long enough for them to turn the corner at the end of the hallway before I shot to my feet and ran the opposite direction toward the door that accessed the staff parking lot. I paced alongside my dad's car while trying to calm myself down, but I couldn't get my emotions under control before my dad came out. My ability to fake it had suddenly abandoned me, and I knew I had to get as far away from everyone as I could.

Instead of waiting, I hitched my backpack on my shoulders and started to jog home. I knew my dad would see me once he finally left the school, but I decided to worry about an excuse then. I just needed to clear my head from all the clutter inside it and running was the only thing that helped. My inability to play football was a huge disappointment to my dad, but he had high hopes that I'd be a state champ in cross country or track and field.

I hadn't made it very far down the rural road before the overcast sky opened up and released a torrent of rain on top of me. I wanted to shake my fist at the universe and curse the sky, but I didn't waste the energy. I concentrated on putting one foot in front of the other, listening to the pounding of my heart and the slapping sounds the soles of my sneakers made against the pavement. I was so focused on those things that I didn't hear my dad's car approaching until it was right beside me.

I got the shock of my young life when I stopped and turned to my dad's Buick. Lincoln was sitting in the passenger seat staring at me with a gaping mouth and wide eyes that slowly roamed up my chest until they locked on mine. I saw a desperation and wildness in his dark eyes that I didn't understand. The window in front of Lincoln's mouth started to fog up from his hot breath, and the rain fell faster, distorting his image through the rain streaming over the glass.

My dad honked the horn, snapping me out of my daydream. I jerked the rear door open and climbed in behind Lincoln. "What the hell are you doing, Rush? Are you trying to make yourself sick?"

"I didn't know it was going to rain. I just thought I'd treat the jog home as training for cross country."

"It's November, Rush. Where in the hell is your coat? Your mama is going to kill us both."

Hearing about Lincoln and Jana destroyed me to the point that I

26

didn't realize I left the school without a jacket.

"At least it's unusually warm outside. Makes for some great foot-ball, right, Linc?" my dad asked.

"Yes, Coach," Lincoln answered in a voice barely above a whisper. Why did he sound so breathless, strangled even?

"I'm not sure how you can be so damn book smart but completely lack common sense like putting on a jacket when it's cold, son." My dad chuckled like he was saying something funny instead of insulting me. "But the perfect solution came to me just now, Lincoln."

I was staring at the back of Linc's head, so I saw him stiffen. "What's that, Coach?"

"You need serious help in math, and my son is a math whiz," my dad said cheerfully. "Starting tonight, Rush is going to tutor you in math until you get your grades up. One more shitty grade in that class and I'll be forced to bench you until you get your grade up. That would pretty much be the end of our season, Linc. We could kiss our dreams of a state championship goodbye." The pressure on my former best friend was so heavy that I don't know how he kept from bowing beneath the weight of it all.

"Um, yeah," Lincoln said hesitantly. "If that's okay with Rush."

"Of course it's okay with Rush," my dad scoffed. "I think it was a blessing that your parents weren't able to pick you up today. You can call your mom at work when we get to our house and let her know that you're staying for dinner and studying with Rush." He didn't even both-er to check if it was something I wanted to do. He'd made his mind up, and the two of us were to obey him without question.

"Yes, sir," Lincoln said.

My father was too busy congratulating himself to notice how un-happy Linc sounded. That hurt way more than hearing about him with Jana. He couldn't help it if he didn't like me the way I liked him. I un-derstood that much, but I couldn't comprehend why Linc hated me so much.

I chewed my bottom lip the rest of the way home to keep from *crying and went straight upstairs to take a shower and warm up. Only in the privacy of the shower did I silently release the tears of sorrow, heartache, and regret, pressing a washcloth to my face to muffle the sound of me crying. I wasn't in there long before Jules knocked on the door and told me that dinner would be ready in ten minutes.*

I shut the water off, wrapped a towel around my waist, and headed to my bedroom. At least I'd have a few more minutes of quiet in the sanctuary of my room to pull myself together before I had to go downstairs and face my family and Lincoln. When I opened my bedroom door, Lincoln rose off my bed and stared at me with wide eyes. His mouth fell open, and a soft sigh escaped his mouth.

"What are you doing up here?"

Not that long ago, it was his favorite place in my house. It was our little refuge from the world. Suddenly, the room didn't seem big enough for both of us. I couldn't understand why Lincoln kept raking his eyes over my chest and bare legs peeking out from beneath the towel.

"Rush," he whispered raggedly. What I saw in his dark gaze snatched the air from my lungs. It wasn't disgust that had kept Lincoln away from me. It was fear. The same fear of discovery that I'd battled the past few years.

"Here you go, Mr. Holden," Walter said, setting the deep-fried calamari on the table. "Anything else?"

It took me a few moments before I was back in my favorite restaurant with Walter instead of my old bedroom with Lincoln. "This looks great, Walter. Thank you."

I savored the calamari followed by my entrée, sipped wine, and ordered dessert for one to go. It was nearly eight o'clock when the Lyft driver dropped me off in front of the home I shared with Travis. All the lights were off, which meant he hadn't made it home yet either. A good man would worry about his partner's safety when he was more than two hours late for a celebration dinner, but I was too angry to worry. It wasn't the first time he'd left me high and dry and humiliated by his callousness. I just wasn't sure what, if anything, I was going to do about it.

I put my dessert in the refrigerator, stripped naked, and took a hot shower. As always, my cock responded to the touch of my hand, which was about the only action it had seen lately. Why deny myself pleasure? I closed my eyes and let my fantasies fly, stroking my cock fast and slow, hard and teasing until I was right on the verge of climax. Just as I was about to shoot, Travis jerked back the shower curtain. He stood there fully dressed in his five-thousand-dollar suit and his eyes zeroed in on my hands.

I didn't bother to stop. I closed my eyes and went back to the dark-eyed stranger in my fantasy, not caring that my partner was watching. I could feel Travis's annoyance radiating from him, and it only made me hornier.

"What are you doing, Rush?"

In my head, a dark, deep voice said, "Come for me, Rush."

And I did. Loud and proud as I spurted cum all over the shower floor. Once the last drop fell from my slit, I turned and looked into Travis's eyes. "That was my anniversary sex."

"Fuck!"

"No, thanks, Trav. I'm no longer in the mood," I said, gesturing to my spent dick that lay against my thigh.

"I'm sorry, babe. I—"

"Save it, Travis." I jerked the curtain closed and finished washing my hair and body.

After I toweled off and redressed in sweats and a T-shirt, I found Travis sulking on the living room sofa. I ignored him and retrieved my six-layer chocolate cake from the refrigerator. I wasn't a bit hungry, but I wasn't about to let him find it after I fell asleep either.

"Where's mine?" he asked with a pout.

"In the restaurant where I left my dignity."

"Why didn't you call me?" he asked, insinuating that his insensitivity was my fault.

"I shouldn't have to call and remind you that it was our

anniversary. We made these plans together. You entered them into your phone. I know your assistant hands you a printed itinerary every-single-fucking-day, which would have included our reservations. You saw it this morning when you reviewed your day then forgot about it. Forgot about me," I added. "Now I'm going to eat this cake, go to bed, and forget about this fucking disaster of a day."

"I'm really sorry, Rush."

It was too little, too late.

4—I Can't Fight This Feeling

LINCOLN

"THANK YOU FOR AGREEING TO MEET ME, LINCOLN," Maxim Detwiler said. "I understand that the country club development didn't appeal to you last year, but I have another proposal for you to consider. One that I think will be mutually pleasing." I'd run into Maxim numerous times since Phee and I rejected his offer, and he never once gave me a hint that he was considering another business arrangement with us.

I studied the way the billionaire reclined in the restaurant chair. He wanted his casual pose to put me at ease, but I could tell the way he propped his elbow on the back of the chair was contrived so I would see the way his biceps bulged beneath the fine cloth of his expensive dress shirt. The semi-turned angle of his torso also gave me a glimpse at the smattering of dark chest hair exposed by the gap from the buttons he'd undone at the top of the shirt. I supposed the way he stretched out his long legs beneath the table could look like a man having a relaxing dinner with a potential business partner, but I suspected he just wanted to tap his foot against mine. Why? To let me know he wanted to fuck me. Hell, he'd made that quite obvious, even though I pretended not to notice. Or was it to establish dominance?

He might've pulled it off had it not been for the calculated look in his eyes and the tense lines forming commas around his lush mouth when he smiled seductively. Yeah, I admit I noticed those plump lips and even imagined having the billionaire at my feet servicing my cock. Imagining and acting on it were two different things. The momentary pleasure he would give me would evaporate before the last drop of cum fell from my dick. Besides, the more time I spent in his company, the more I disliked the man. I would not ruin the life I built with Ophelia for a quick fuck.

"Well, Maxim, you would've also invited Ophelia to dinner if you wanted to discuss business. She's my partner in all things." I gestured around the extravagant private dining room in the four-star restaurant he'd chosen. "You also wouldn't have ensured that we were secluded from the other diners if you merely wanted to discuss another business arrangement."

"Right you are, Lincoln," Maxim said, straightening in his chair. He leaned forward, placing his elbows on the table and dialed up his seduction by teasing the corners of his mouth with the tip of his tongue. "I didn't bring you here to discuss a building project."

"Then why?" I knew the answer, but I needed to hear him say it.

"You know why, Lincoln. We're both too old for coy games." His words were short, his voice hard. "I didn't invite the lovely Ophelia here because I'm not interested in extending this offer to her. There's only room for two for what I have in mind."

"Stop." I held up my hand for additional emphasis. "That's never going to happen."

Maxim threw his head back and laughed wickedly. "If that's true, then why didn't you bring your darling wife with you? You could've played it off that you assumed she was invited, but you showed up here alone."

"I…"

"Because you feel the attraction between us, even if you won't admit it. You want me to pursue you. It makes your dick hard. Are you hard right now?" Maxim propped his head on his fist. "Tell me, does she know that you're into cock?"

I pulled the napkin off my lap and tossed it onto the table. I would've risen to my feet, but the erection tenting my pants would've proved Detwiler's point. Yes, it flattered and aroused me that such a sexy, powerful man obviously wanted me, but I hated that my body physically reacted to what my mind rejected. He was misjudging my strong will and moral code. "Maxim—"

"Tell me, Lincoln, have you ever had sex with another man. Or even kissed one? There's nothing quite like it." He licked his lips like he was picturing those things with me right then and there.

"I will not discuss my sex life with you." The parts of me he wanted to reveal were memories I buried so deep that no one could unearth them. I never wanted them excavated and exposed to anyone, especially not him.

"Your shaking hands and voice give you away, Lincoln. Does Ophelia know? Do you think of men when you—"

"Shut the fuck up," I snarled as I rose to my feet. "This meeting is over. Don't you ever contact me again, or I'll go public with your harassment."

"I'll go public with just how much you liked it." Detwiler nodded at my hard cock pressing against the outline of my thin dress pants. "There's no need for this anger. We can be discreet. Your secret will be safe with me."

Humiliation was the ice bucket of reality I needed to douse my ardor. "Fuck you!" I told him before I turned and walked away.

"I was trying to," Detwiler called out to me. "Maybe next time."

There wouldn't be a next time. I prayed that I looked more composed than I felt when I walked through the restaurant and retrieved my car from the valet. I wouldn't let myself think of the way the evening unfolded or recall the words Maxim spoke as I navigated through heavy San Diego traffic. I held my shit together until after I exited the interstate and neared the gated community where I lived. My body quaked, my eyes burned with unshed tears, and guilt clawed at my gut. I couldn't go home in that condition, so I stopped at a park a few minutes from my home and tried to gather myself.

I put my car in park but left it running since I didn't expect to be there long. I tipped my head back, closed my eyes, and willed my heart to stop racing and my lungs to pull air in at a normal rhythm. The commands to calm down and find my center went unheeded, and I felt hot tears of misery and self-loathing slide down my cheeks as one repressed memory after the other flooded my mind. It was like an invisible dam had broken, and I could no longer pretend. Was it Maxim's words that triggered the flashback of me marching across Rush's room to kiss him when he returned from the shower and found me standing in his bedroom? Or was it just the fact that I'd never really gotten over my first love and heartbreak?

It felt like I stood there for a thousand years while my eyes cataloged every inch of bare skin exposed to me. A drop of water clung to the tip of Rush's shaggy, blond hair, and I watched as it lost the battle and fell in slow motion to his shoulder. I tracked the droplet as it cascaded down his lean body and disappeared beneath the towel at his waist. His body was so different from mine—lean to my bulk, pale to my tan. It was like the contrast that our photography teacher talked about in class.

I jerked my gaze upward and finally looked into vibrant green eyes that had always looked at me with such adoration. God, how I had missed Rush during my self-imposed exile from his life. He made me feel things I'd never experienced before, and he scared the hell out of me. One false move and my life—our lives—would be over.

"Rush," I managed to say between dry, shaking lips.

I couldn't put a name to the things I felt, but whatever they were, Rush was feeling them too. It felt an awful lot like love. I couldn't fight the feelings any longer, and the tenuous control that remained snapped.

I crossed the room, cupped his face in both my hands, and kissed him with all the pent-up frustration I'd felt the past few years. Rush gripped my biceps in surprise, and I clumsily backed him up against the door. I wasn't quite as experienced as I led my friends to believe, but I had at least kissed Jana. It felt nothing like kissing Rush though. I mean, their lips felt similar, but the emotions inside me were completely different. My heart pounded in my chest in a way I had never felt before, and I thought it was fear of having someone look at me the way that carny did years ago. Then I realized my greatest fear was never knowing how Rush tasted. The need to slip my tongue past Rush's lips overpowered any thought that discouraged me from having what I craved. Need rose swift and hard, grabbing me by the throat, threatening to choke me.

I pulled back slightly, smiling at the wonder and awe that bloomed across his face in a sweet, pink blush. "Linc," he said between ragged breaths. "I didn't know…"

"Now you do. We both do."

Rush's mother called from the bottom of the steps to let us know that dinner was ready just as I leaned in to kiss him again. We both groaned softly in frustration then smiled at our similar reactions. Yeah, we both felt the same fire in our bellies and even further south.

"We can resume this after dinner," I told him.

"You mean after you finish your homework?" Rush asked brazenly with a raised brow.

I assure you that there has never been a better incentive issued. Coach thought the threat of getting benched was enough to get my head out of my ass, but it turned out I only needed the promise of Rush's sweet, soft lips to buckle down and pay attention to the equations and formulas in my text book. Gone were the questions of why the skills were necessary and when I'd ever use them. Instead, I was determined *to learn all the sensitive places on Rush's body.*

I learned that Rush had a lot more control than I did. His voice didn't shake when he explained the problem and how to solve it, even though we lay on our bellies on his bed while sharing his math book. His breath only slightly hitched when I crossed my leg behind me to run my toe up his calf. He just pointed to the math problem with the eraser end of his pencil and continued to explain the unexplainable to me.

Rush eagerly rolled onto his back as soon as we finished our homework. Leaning over him, I got lost in his luminous eyes and happy smile for several heartbeats until the urge to taste those tempting lips again became too much for me to resist. I pressed my mouth softly against his a few times before teasing his lips open enough to slide my tongue past them. He tasted of cinnamon and apples from the pie his mom baked for dessert and something else even sweeter that was unique to Rush. I became addicted to his sweetness and found every excuse to taste it greedily.

We were both too young and innocent to know how to barter for the things we wanted, but over the next few weeks, that's what we did. I became the most dedicated pupil while Rush became the most eager teacher. Rush taught me algebra, and I showed him how his body reacted when I kissed his neck, nibbled on his ear, and pressed my hard-on against his. We both wanted more, to cross the line that wasn't supposed to be crossed by two boys, but something held us back. I suspected that something was fear. Still, we knew the sound each other made when we spilled inside our underwear after rubbing against each other, and I knew there would never be a kiss sweeter than the one that Rush always placed above my heart right before we pulled away to clean up.

Rush's parents left us alone because they wouldn't suspect that the brainiac and jock were grinding erections and making out after our study sessions. Coach was just happy my grades were improving and that I seemed to be even more focused on the football field. My parents were just happy I wasn't around so they didn't have to pretend to be a happy family. Those few hours up in Rush's room each night meant so much more than horny groping and kissing. They were about freedom and spending time with someone who truly understood me and loved me.

As wonderful as it sounds, my time with Rush wasn't free of anger, suspicion, and fights. It hurt him to see me with Jana the day after our first kiss. He logically thought that I would end things with her right away. When I arrived at his house for our second tutoring session, he asked me about the stories the guys on the team were talking about, and I told him the truth. Jana had let me kiss her, and that was all. I admitted to Rush that I pursued Jana because of her ultra-religious beliefs that mandated she save herself for marriage. My dad kept busting my balls over not dating girls, and I gave in to get him off my back, just as I made up stories about what Jana and I got up to on our dates to make the guys happy.

Rush wanted to believe me; I saw that in his eyes. It was also evident how much he longed to be the one holding my hand in the hallways at school and proudly wearing my varsity jacket, but in his green gaze too was the heartbreaking acceptance that it would never happen.

"I wish it could be you, Rush," I said when silent tears slid down his face. I begged him with my eyes to see the truth and hear it in my words. "I only want you."

He said nothing for several moments, so I closed my book and rose from his bed. Rush's hand snaked out and grabbed my wrist. "Don't go."

I sat back down and slowly tugged my arm until his hand slid down to mine. Then I curled my fingers protectively around his like I wished I could protect our hearts. I knew no good would come out of the love building between us, but I was powerless to stop it. Only Rush could stop me from hurting him by sending me away. Instead of telling me to go, he leaned into me and pressed his mouth against my throat.

"Promise me that you'll only give this to me," he said, placing his hand over my wildly beating heart. "I'll share your time if I have to, but I won't share this. Tell me it's mine, Linc. Please."

"Only yours, Rush," I easily promised.

I knew it was hard for him, but he never mentioned it again. Guilt lashed at me, leaving me feeling battered and bloody. I tried to carry on the charade with Jana, but knew it wasn't fair to her, to Rush, or to me. I kept finding excuses not to be with her so that I could secretly spend it with Rush. In the end, she got tired of waiting for me to return her calls and her affection. She issued an ultimatum over Christmas break that I either spend every free minute with her or it was over. I couldn't be mad at her for being upset, but she gave me the push I needed. I drove away from her house and straight over to Rush's.

His parents were out doing some shopping and Jules was at her boyfriend's house, which meant we had the place to ourselves for the first time since we started exploring the feelings brewing between us. That night we didn't go all the way, but for the first time, no clothes separated us when our combined releases mixed on Rush's stomach and chest. I had given my heart to the boy I loved more than any person on the planet and knew it was only a matter of time before I shared all of me too.

My cell phone rang, snapping me back to the present. I saw Ophelia's name on the screen and wiped away my tears and cleared my throat before answering.

"Yes, dear," I said in playful exaggeration.

"Is everything okay? I started to worry that Maxim Detwiler kidnapped you or something," Phee said.

"Um…"

"I can see that the man wants you all to himself, Lincoln. He doesn't bother to hide it."

Please don't ask me why Maxim thinks it's okay, Phee. Please don't ask questions. "It won't do him any good, Phee. I made that very clear."

"So he *did* invite you out to fuck you." I could imagine her nodding her head as she realized that she was right.

"Yes," I replied, unwilling to lie about that at least. *Please don't ask questions.*

"Well, I can't blame him. You are a beautiful man, Lincoln Huxley." I heard the smile in her voice. "What are you doing now?"

I put the car in reverse and backed out of my parking spot. "Coming home to you, of course."

Ophelia was my safe place, and I'd always choose her.

5—The First Time

Rush

"SIGN HERE, HERE, AND HERE," MY ASSISTANT, NIGEL, SAID.

"You mean where those little stickers say, 'sign here' next to the signature line with my name typed beneath it?" I teased.

"Yeah, those are the ones, smart ass." I knew if I turned, Nigel's brilliant blue eyes would be rolling up inside his head as he battled patience. I loved to give him a hard time, but my photography business wouldn't be nearly as successful without him. I was the creative force, and Nigel took care of everything else, even though I had an MBA. "Do you want your incredible images featured in the most famous fashion magazine on the planet or not?"

"Hmm," I said, pretending to think about it with my pen hovered next to one of the X's that marked the spot.

"Idiot," Nigel said, but his chuckle softened the heat in his words. "I should've just forged your name as I do on all the trivial things I don't want to trouble you with."

I looked over my shoulder and found him smiling with wicked mirth. "What trivial things do you forge my name on?"

"Little things like invoices and receipts," my assistant said then shrugged. "Oh, the prenuptial agreement that Travis sent over last week."

"*What*? We said there wouldn't be a prenup."

"I'm kidding!" Nigel rubbed the tension out of my shoulders. It was his fault, so it seemed only fair. "I can't believe he finally is making an honest man out of you." Nigel didn't sound at all pleased.

"Me either," I said honestly.

For the six months that followed our disastrous anniversary evening, Travis went out of his way to make things up to me. He started coming home earlier, and we cooked meals together like we did when our love was new. We both ignored our phones and paid attention to one another. There were nights when we didn't even turn the television on, choosing to talk over a shared bottle of wine or snuggle on the couch while reading. Our tastes in books were the opposite end of the literary spectrum, but it never bothered me that I loved wild adventures found in fiction while Travis preferred more serious non-fiction books. He couldn't relate to my love of treasure hunts, and my eyes glazed over when it came to biographies and historical retellings of wars and events that happened decades before my time. Sure, I knew they were important, but they weren't my idea of entertainment. What mattered to me was how hard we both tried to fix our relationship.

Travis surprised me with a weekend trip to Sister Bay, Wisconsin in June for my birthday where he rented the cutest cabin. The quaintness was so unlike him, but he knew how much it meant to me. "I know it's not the Great Smoky Mountains that you love so much, but I thought this cabin on the lake would be a nice substitute."

"I love it, Travis," I said, looking around the pretty bayside cabin. It was so different than the mountain cabins from my youth but beautiful in its own right.

"Good, because I love you."

His words stunned me because Travis was not a demonstrative man. I answered him with a passionate kiss that I hoped would chase the doubt out of my heart and mind forever. That night, I lay in bed staring at the ceiling as Travis snored softly beside me. Instead of seeing the whitewashed wood planks, I saw rustic ones belonging to memories I didn't want to relive. Instead of feeling sated after a few bouts of sex, I felt antsy like my skin no longer fit. One false move and I would shatter apart into a million pieces. My pulse kicked up as my heart raced from the memories pressing against my consciousness. I closed my eyes and willed my mind not to take me there again because it hurt too bad. *Just let me rejoice in what I have now. Please.*

Too bad my heart didn't listen. It said *remember what love really felt like, Rush.* Behind my closed eyes, I was seventeen again and had slipped away for a birthday celebration with my first love. We told convincing lies to our parents, and Lincoln took me to his grandparents' secluded cabin. We both knew what would happen that weekend. I would give Lincoln Huxley every part of my body, and he would give me his. I didn't want to remember, but I couldn't seem to control my thoughts.

Lincoln dropped our duffle bags on the floor and looked around. "What do you think?"

"I think it's amazing," I said, looking at his big, strong body. I swallowed hard, suddenly nervous about what would happen between us.

As always, it was like he could read my mind. "Nothing has to happen, Rush. I just want you all to myself for the weekend. No lies, no pretending. It's just us."

No matter how much it hurt, I wasn't leaving that cabin without feeling him inside me. True to his word, Lincoln didn't press me. We ate the food he brought and played board games for hours before I worked up the courage to whip my shirt over my head. I didn't think much of myself when I looked in the mirror, but it was plain to see that Linc adored what he saw.

"Come here," he said, sounding a little intoxicated. We were both a little drunk on the hormones rushing through our bodies.

I felt how much Lincoln wanted me, but he never pushed. He left me in charge, and I became braver and needier with every kiss and touch. I was the one who undressed us and prepared his dick for my body. I shivered beneath Lincoln as he stretched me open with his fingers, kissing me and capturing my cries of both pain and pleasure. The first time was understandably short and messy since we were both virgins, but what we lacked in finesse was made up with eagerness tenfold.

We stayed naked for the rest of the weekend until it was time to go home. I tried not to be sad but lost a little more of the battle with every mile that took us closer to reality. I bit my bottom lip to keep from crying, because I wanted to be brave and not ruin the beautiful memories we made by whining about things neither of us could change.

Linc pulled over at a rest stop a few miles from our small town. "I love you, Rush."

"I love you too, Linc." The dam on my control broke, and I lost it.

I could tell he wanted to hug me, but we couldn't risk someone driving by and recognizing us. "Keep remembering that I love you no matter what happens. Keep thinking that someday, we won't have to sneak around."

"I want that so bad." It was torture looking at him in school or around town and not being able to touch him or tell people that I loved him. I had to stay alert all the time and let no one see the way my heart lit up when he walked into a room."

"We just have to bide our time, Rush. Keep waiting for someday."

I held onto that hope as long as I could, even when cold reality tried to creep in and ruin our happiness. The better Lincoln played football, the more girls he attracted, and worse—college scouts.

"University of Michigan, Wisconsin, and Ohio State are all after

Lincoln," my dad said happily at the beginning of our senior year of high school. "That's just the beginning. I wouldn't be surprised if the West Coast schools show interest in him before too much longer. When one of the scouts for the big schools zooms in on a prospect, they all follow." I wasn't sure how the hell my dad knew this since none of his high school players ever made it to a big school like the ones he mentioned.

I expected my dad's enthusiasm, but I didn't expect Lincoln's. I somehow thought football was just something that he did, and that I was his real passion. He disavowed me of that notion later that night when he came over and got the news from my dad.

"I can't believe it," he said excitedly, pacing the floors of my bedroom. "It's what I've been working for all these years."

"It is?" He'd never talked about wanting to play college football.

"It's my way out of this damn town. You're coming too."

"I am?" The dread I'd felt moments before turned to pure joy. "You want me to come with you?"

"Of course," Lincoln replied like I was daft. "With your grades, you can get into any school that I can. Where do you want to go? What's your passion?"

"Photography," I replied. "Not that I can make a career out of it."

Lincoln smiled, and I knew he was thinking about the box of Polaroid photos of us that I kept hidden. I became obsessed with the camera when I received it for Christmas when I was ten. I worked odd jobs around the house to pay for the film, and Lincoln was my favorite subject. In high school, I took photography classes as an elective and fell deeper in love with it. My mom gave me a Nikon for my birthday and let me turn a small closet in our basement into a dark room so that I could develop my pictures. My father thought it was a complete waste of time and money, but my mom supported my hobby at least.

"Why couldn't you, Rush? Someone is getting paid for all those photos in the magazines you look at all the time. Where would you need to go to school? Maybe one of them would also offer me a full ride to play football so we can be together."

"I don't know," I answered honestly.

"Ask Ms. Saunders. She will know," Linc said, referring to our guidance counselor.

The next day, I did just as he recommended. I thought Ms. Saunders would be enthusiastic when I asked for help finding a good photography school. Instead, she slid her glasses down to the tip of her nose and looked at me over the top of them. She blinked a few times in confusion before she asked, "Why would a smart boy like you want to do a silly thing like that?"

"What do you mean?" What did my IQ have to do with it?

"Rush, you're capable of so much more than taking silly pictures."

I thought of the picture I took last year when Lincoln scored the winning touchdown in the state championship football game. I had submitted the picture to the local paper and it appeared in almost every publication throughout the state. That photo didn't seem silly to me, but maybe because it featured my favorite subject. When most people looked at it, they saw a football player, but I saw my best friend and the person who encouraged my dreams the most. I mean, he helped me steal my sister's bike, convinced me to conquer my fear of heights, and even made me feel like I was soaring on the wind when he touched me.

"Have you talked to your parents about your goals?"

"No, ma'am."

"I think you better speak with them before we discuss this further." She used the same tone of voice I'd expect had I shown interest in going to clown school.

"Yes, ma'am."

For the rest of the day, I tried to convince myself that my parents would support my decision to attend the college of my choice. I mean, couldn't I just keep my major a secret for a while? The important part was that Lincoln and I would be together at college; nothing else mattered to me. Linc sensed my mood but couldn't ask about it until we were studying in my bedroom. He had become good at tanking his grades just enough to need tutoring but not enough to fail a class and jeopardize football. I was shocked my dad hadn't found him a new tutor.

"I'm sorry Ms. Saunders was a bitch," he said, dropping a sweet kiss on my forehead.

"Ms. Saunders wasn't a bitch. She just didn't see the merit of going to school for a degree in photography." Unfortunately, she'd talked to my father, and I received a forty-minute lecture that night when he came home from school. I didn't tell Linc that part because my time with him was limited, and I didn't want to waste it talking about things I couldn't change. It felt like a cloud of doom was hovering nearby just waiting to rain down disaster on our heads.

Lincoln rolled me onto my back and slowly lowered his head to mine. I forgot to be worried when his mouth was so close to mine. He'd just pressed a kiss to my lips when my bedroom door flew open. We both jackknifed into a sitting position and stared at my sister who'd strolled into the room. Jules closed the door quietly and approached the bed.

"You need to be more careful," she hissed. "I heard one of you knuckleheads moaning when I walked by." Jules was a few years older than me and knew the sounds of two people making out. "Not only that, I saw the picture of the two of you hanging in your little dark room. It looked like you turned the camera around to aim it at your faces and snapped the picture. It was a cute, creative thing, but it's obvious how much you love each other when I look at it. It's a good thing I found it and not Mom."

"What were you doing in there?" I demanded to know.

"Mom wanted me to look for a box of fall decorations and that was the last place she remembered seeing them." Jules blew out a long breath and said, "Look, I adore both of you, and I don't want to see you hurt. You know what Dad will say if he finds out, Rush. Stop being careless." She shoved my shoulder playfully. "Dinner is ready, morons."

Lincoln hadn't said a word the entire time that Jules spoke. I turned to look at him after she left, and my breath froze in my chest when I saw that fear had paralyzed him. Linc's eyes were wide and afraid, his mouth gaped open and shut repeatedly as he tried to suck air into his lungs.

"Lincoln." I softly touched his arm, but he recoiled from me like I had burned him. Linc rose to his feet and walked to the window that overlooked the back yard. I could see his shoulders sharply rising and falling as he breathed choppily.

I went to him, certain I could make it right. I placed my hand on his shoulder, and he jerked away from me for the second time. "Don't," Lincoln said, sounding both angry and miserable. "I need to go home."

"Lincoln, please don't..."

He said nothing else as he grabbed his bags and left my room. Despite what he said about loving me and hoping we had a future together, his actions said otherwise.

I hated that I lay beside my lover in a cabin he rented to make me happy and thought of another man—well, the boys we used to be anyway. I shoved all thoughts of Lincoln Huxley aside and focused on the life I had, instead of the one I'd lost. I woke Travis up and made love to him like it was our first time all over again. I felt the difference in both our reactions.

The next morning, Travis proposed to me over a brunch he prepared. I said yes without thinking it through because he was offering me the future I had dreamed of for so long. I guess a part of me still doubted Travis's motives and expected him to drag out our engagement for another year or longer, but he surprised me again when he said that he wanted to get married in September.

"That's quick," I'd told him.

"You have connections. Use them," he had replied coolly.

And so I did.

"The dates for this photo shoot aren't going to work," I said to Nigel after really looking at the document for the first time. "Travis and I will be on our honeymoon."

"Are you really going to pass this up?" Nigel asked in shock. "Travis would change the honeymoon around his career, why shouldn't you?"

"Nigel, that's no way to start off our marriage. They'll need to change the dates for the shoot, or they'll have to find another photographer. I'm willing to rearrange everything on my calendar for them *except* my wedding and honeymoon."

"Okaaaay," he said dramatically. "You're the boss, so it's your funeral."

"Wedding," I corrected.

"Same difference in this case, if you ask me," Nigel mumbled as he left my office.

From my shattered heart as a young man, I learned a few important lessons that I used as guiding principles as an adult: never say something I didn't mean and never break a promise.

I told Travis that I wanted to marry him, and I would. I planned a fucking spectacular honeymoon, and we would go. I wanted my chance at a happily ever after, and how many more chances would a man in his forties get?

6—End of the Road

LINCOLN

TWO FAMILIAR SAYINGS COULD BE THE TAGLINES OF MY LIFE: All good things come to an end, and you don't know what you've got until it's gone.

I first learned those lessons my senior year of high school when I let fear drive a wedge between Rush and me. I pushed him away after his sister barged into his room one afternoon, and there's nothing I regret more in my life than how I behaved during the months that followed. I doubled down on trying to make myself into something I wasn't with a vigor that shamed me every time I looked into Rush's eyes. He was like a ghost drifting through the hallways of our high school, hauntingly beautiful and alone. Rush wore his hurt and betrayal openly, avoiding me every chance he could. I understood how bad it hurt him to see me back together with Jana, and I only hoped that one day he could forgive me.

The months between fall and spring were somehow both fast and slow. There were days when it seemed like an entire month passed in the blink of an eye, and others felt like the world was moving in slow motion. I chose a college to commit to and prepared for the next chapter in my life. I saw the end of the school year barreling down on me and wanted to slow things down. Although I was excited about a fresh start at college where no one knew me, it would be without Rush by my side. On the other hand, without Rush's laughter and love, the days seemed to drag on endlessly. One week felt like three, one month without his lips pressed against mine felt like a year. I was a powder keg waiting to blow as the days ticked closer and closer to graduation, to the day that I'd say goodbye to Rush.

Our senior prom was the week before graduation, and Jana had been hinting that she was ready to take things to the next step in our relationship. I knew it wasn't because she was so in love with me that she wanted to throw caution to the wind. It was because she didn't want to let go of the prized tight end who'd achieved something no other athlete from our high school had: a Division I scholarship to play football at The Ohio State University. Columbus, Ohio didn't sound like the most exotic place to play football, but the Buckeyes were a true powerhouse in college football. I thanked my lucky stars every single night before I fell asleep.

"Besides, everyone thinks we're already doing it," Jana said.

What a turn my life had taken. I made up all that shit about Jana to keep the guys from guessing how much I loved the boy who'd been my best friend since I moved to our town. It had come back to bite me in the ass big-time. Of course, all I'd heard since we got back together was how she wanted our senior prom to be the best night of our lives. All I wanted to do was stop time and hold onto the boy I loved with my whole heart, or transport us to a place where we could be ourselves and not have to worry about what anyone else thought.

On prom night, I donned my tux and pasted a fake smile on my face. I laughed when all the kids in our group did and pretended the night was everything I had dreamed it would be. I tried not to be obvious as I kept an eye on the double doors of our gymnasium. I couldn't tell you what the decorations looked like or even what Jana wore, but I remember every detail of how Rush looked when he showed up at our prom wearing a classic black tux and a look of misery on his face. I wanted so badly to go to him and kiss the frown line marring his forehead, but I stood still.

"I see Rush brought his usual date."

I didn't care which girl said it from our group, none of them mattered to me. I couldn't help but smile a little because that Nikon camera he wore around his neck was his constant companion. I knew watching the happy couples dance and show affection to each other made him miserable, but Rush took his duties for the school newspaper and yearbook seriously.

The worst part of the night came when they crowned Jana and me prom queen and king. Rush's heartbreak was a palpable, breathing thing as I walked out to the center of the gym floor with her. Our classmates formed a circle around us and watched as we swayed to the music. Jana cried happily; I cried internally for the boy's heart I crushed with every step I took. I don't even remember the song that played, but I recall the look on Rush's face when I locked eyes with him after it ended. He stood just outside the circle with his beloved camera held in front of his face. I knew the second our eyes connected through the viewfinder. Rush slowly lowered his Nikon, and the sorrow in his eyes nearly brought me to my knees.

Rush turned and exited the gym, as if he couldn't take it for another second. Jana was so busy squealing and jumping up and down with her friends that she didn't notice my lack of attention. I used the distraction to quietly leave the gym and seek out the only person I had wanted to bring as my date. I knew where I'd find Rush too. He would go to the one place in that school that brought him peace and happiness; it's what I would've done too. Except, I would've gone to the weight room while I knew I'd find Rush in the photography lab.

Just as I suspected, the red light was on, indicating that photo developing was underway. I knew Rush hadn't been in there long enough to start, so I yanked the door open. He jerked his head up and gasped when he saw that I'd followed him. Tears streamed down Rush's face, and I had never hated myself as much as I did at that moment.

"I'm so sorry, Rush." The words were lame but true. I could see in his eyes that he needed more from me, and I'd give it to him no matter the cost to myself. "I wish it could've been you. I know you don't believe me, but I'd give anything to be able to dance with you."

Rush closed his eyes and nodded his head.

Music from the gymnasium floated up through the floor of the journalism and photography classroom. The lyrics and melody were hauntingly perfect for our situation. Rush opened his eyes, and I saw the same awareness in his liquid green gaze.

"End of the Road." I could barely hear my voice over the music and the pounding of my heart. "Dance with me, Rush."

We wouldn't have forever, but we had that moment. I refused to be denied. Rush walked out of the photo lab and into my arms, and I forgot to be afraid. I only thought of the wonderful memories of us that I'd cling to until my last breath, our only dance would be my favorite. The song went by too fast as we slowly danced in a circle, staring into each other's eyes and crying bittersweet tears of both sorrow and joy for our last embrace.

"I'm never coming back here, Lincoln. I can't live a lie for the rest of my life. I know it will be scary and hard, but I feel like I'm suffocating."

"You're the bravest person I know, Rush." He scoffed, but I meant it.

"I'm afraid of everything. I was terrified of learning to ride a bike or getting on the Ferris wheel. I only did those things because of you, Linc."

"You did those things, Rush. I only encouraged you. I'm going to encourage you one last time. Leave here and don't look back. Live *openly and happily for both of us. Just don't forget me, okay?"*

"I could never forget you."

When the song was over, we shared one last, long kiss. The saltiness of our tears mixed with the special sweetness that was unique to Rush Holden. Fuck, I couldn't imagine never tasting his kisses again. The anguish of knowing it was truly the end of the road for us was almost crippling. Our good thing had come to an end, and I truly didn't know what I had with Rush until it was gone.

Fast forward twenty-five years and a few months later, those same two phrases come back to haunt me as I sit across from my wife at the dining room table in the dream home we built together. It was supposed to be a dinner to celebrate the next phase in our life: empty nesters. Ironically, both of our children chose Chicago for the next stage of their lives. Kennedy finished her internship in Washington D.C. and completed another year at Loyola before Holden joined her for his first semester at School of the Art Institute of Chicago. The tuition could see us eating ramen noodles before long, but our children were ecstatic.

I just wished I could say the same for their parents. Without the kids, I was suddenly at a loss for things to say to the person who knew me best in the world. Ophelia didn't seem to have the same problem although it was hard to figure out what she was saying between the body-wracking sobs. She buried her face in her hands, which slightly muffled her anguished cry. I was grateful we decided to eat at home rather than go to a restaurant.

"Honey," I softly cooed, dropping to my knees beside her chair. "They'll be all right, and so will we."

Phee shook her head vehemently. "No," she said.

"Sure we will."

My wife slowly raised her head and looked at me with an expression I would describe as defeated. "We're not okay, Lincoln," she finally said between gasps. "We haven't been okay for a very long time."

My heart sank when I realized that I was the source of her

sorrow, not the kids. I seemed to have this effect on the people I loved most. I did this to her; I made her miserable. My beautiful wife who deserved the absolute best in life had streaks of mascara running down her angelic face. Each new tear felt like someone had taken a razor-lined strap to my battered soul.

"Let me fix this," I pleaded with her from my knees. "I'll try harder, Phee. I love you."

"I love you too, Linc." Her words should've eased the panic swelling inside me, but the devastated look in her eyes told me that it was no longer enough for her. "But I'm not in love with you. I think you feel the same way too."

"No." I shook my head in denial. "That's not true, Phee. I—"

"Haven't voluntarily touched me in so long that I can't remember. You reciprocate after I initiate sex between us, but you never take that first step." Her tears slowed a little, and she let out a cute little hiccup like she did when she cried after Kennedy and Holden were born. "I watch the way other couples who are *in love* behave, Lincoln. They reach for each other and turn into one another. When was the last time you reached out to hold my hand while we walked in public or did more than give me a quick goodbye or hello kiss?" She tipped her head to the side and narrowed her eyes. "Come to think of it, when did you ever do those things?"

"I can do those things, Phee. Please don't give up on me. I don't know what I'll do." I lay my head on her thighs, and she ran her hands through my hair, giving me comfort. "I can't lose you." A thought suddenly occurred to me. I raised my head and asked, "Or is it too late? Have you already met someone else?"

I saw the answer in her eyes. "I haven't acted on the attraction," she said quickly. "I'd never hurt you like that, Linc. I've tried to ignore these feelings for more than a year, but they're getting stronger. If you and I were truly happy, there is no way I could feel like this about another man."

"Who is he?" I asked. "Who's taken my Phee from me?"

"That's not important right now," she said then smiled sweetly. "No one could ever take me from you. I know it will be hard, and I know this sounds selfish, but I still need you to be my best friend. It's not about the business or even the kids; it's the fact that no one has ever made me feel as safe as you did. You've loved me the way I was, never asking me to change. I could tell you anything, and you'd never judge me."

"Except that part where you'd fallen in love with another man," I said. "You didn't trust me with that." The bitterness that had crept into my voice had more to do with the blow to my pride than anything else.

"I'm trusting you now, Linc. I'm begging you not to hate me."

The only thing that mattered was assuring Phee that I could never hate her. I'd come to terms with the rest later. "Never that, Phee."

We held each other and cried over the loss of our marriage and the fear of the unknown. Our focus turned to when and how to tell our kids, but we didn't make immediate decisions. Phee and I thought it was best to sleep on it and talk more once the shock had worn off.

That night, I slept in the guest room. Well, I tried to sleep anyway, but I mostly stared at the ceiling and berated myself for ruining the lives of everyone I ever loved. I tried to grasp onto anger, but it eluded me because I most likely deserved everything that happened to me. No matter how hard it was for me, I would put Phee and the kids' needs before my own. I wouldn't wallow in self-pity and try to hold her back for my selfish reasons.

That was exactly the biggest problem too. I would still have my best friend and business partner, but I was losing my safety net. Without Phee, I was free to explore a part of me that caused goose bumps of terror to pop up all over my skin. Without her as an excuse, what reason would I give for denying my urges. I still risked losing my family and my clients if they found out the truth.

I rolled over onto my side and curled into a ball. The chill began to fade from my body and sleep started to sneak past the edges of consciousness. I dreamt of two boys sharing a dance in a quiet classroom, but this time around, they looked at each other with hope instead of desolation.

7—Who Let in the Rain

Rush

I KNEW IT WAS A BAD OMEN WHEN I WOKE TO POURING RAIN ON my wedding day. It was supposed to be a sunny and unseasonably warm September day, and not an end-of-days kind of monsoon. It might've been a little more tolerable if I'd woken up beside my soon-to-be husband, but Travis wanted to spend the night before our wedding apart to pay homage to traditions I didn't observe. I wanted to make him happy, so I caved. Travis stayed in a Hilton hotel near the venue while I stayed in our home. We spoke on the phone before bedtime and expressed our mutual joy in beginning the next part of our journey together. I was thinking babies all the way, but Travis just chuckled when I brought it up. *Baby steps, Rush. Baby steps. You're finally getting your guy to say, "I do."*

I had felt light and happy when I drifted off to sleep, but that feeling evaporated when I opened my eyes the next morning and saw the rain cascading down my windows. I was so disappointed that all my plans for an outdoor photo shoot were ruined, but I pushed it aside to look on the bright side.

I received an early-morning phone call from my sister and niece, text messages from Will, Nigel, and Kent, as well as others who wanted to wish me luck before the ceremony. I even received a *welcome to the family* text from my soon-to-be mother-in-law. It was a bitter reminder of the family I'd lost when I decided to come out before leaving for college. I was dead to them, as was Jules for not abandoning me along with them. Travis was far luckier than he could ever realize to have a mother and father who loved him without condition.

I refused to be maudlin on my wedding day and give my parents the power to hurt me. There were many times I wondered if they thought about me, or perhaps heard about my success as a photographer, but I wouldn't allow my wedding day to be one of those times.

I showered and dressed in my classic black tuxedo with the utmost care, knowing that later *my husband* would remove it from my body. I wanted everything about me, and our first night as husbands, to be perfect. I quirked up a half smile when I thought about all the times my drive for perfection drove Travis mad. That thought led me to wonder what he was doing at that precise moment at the Hilton.

We had agreed not to text or talk before the ceremony, choosing to reveal the emotions we felt in person as we stood holding hands and staring into each other's eyes. I blew out a nervous breath once I was fully dressed. All grooms were nervous, right? The unease I'd felt building inside me all day was just wedding day jitters and that's all. I wanted to reach out to Travis and let his calm voice settle my nerves, but I stuck to our agreement.

I turned and faced the full-length mirror to inspect myself from head to toe, smiling because I liked what I saw. Then memories of another time I dressed in a black tuxedo slammed into my psyche hard enough to make me take a startled step back. I remembered how much I wanted to find a viable excuse not to attend that prom and see Lincoln dancing the night away with Jana. I would've welcomed a car accident and hospital stay over the pain of seeing them together. I'd heard Jana talk on and on about the *special night* she had planned every morning in English class. She either didn't know that I could hear her or didn't care.

I sucked it up and went to the stupid prom. It was as horrible as I expected, but then, something bittersweet and beautiful happened. Lincoln followed me upstairs to share a private dance. I held on tight to him, hoping that moment would glue the shattered pieces of my heart back together. I urged my brain to remember everything about the moment from the way he smelled to the sound of his ragged breathing that said he was every bit as destroyed as me. Nothing was more painful than watching him walk away after our final kiss.

One thought helped me get through that night and the painful summer that followed after I left eastern Tennessee for good: Lincoln Huxley thought I was brave.

I wasn't sure why my brain reminded me of one of the most painful memories from my past on what should've been the happiest day of my life. Was it to show me how far I'd come, or a reminder that the passion I felt back then was still unrivaled to that day? But it was normal. I'd always heard that your first love stayed with you for the rest of your life, and Lincoln had been so much more than just my first love. I wiped at the tears that fell from my eyes, chastising myself for my ridiculous stroll down memory lane. What happened to my resolve to avoid maudlin thoughts? It seemed I had been doing it an awful lot lately, and it was time to put my energy on my future, not the past.

"We're here, Uncle Rush," Racheal hollered from the living room. Caught up in my thoughts, I hadn't heard them arrive to pick me up.

There was a knock on my door. "Come in."

Jules entered wearing a regal, strapless dress in a vibrant purple hue that looked beautiful against her fair skin and made her eyes look greener. My sister suddenly halted when she saw the evidence of my tears. "Rush?"

"I'm fine, Jules. Who isn't emotional on their wedding day?" I crossed the room and hugged her tight. "Thank you for standing beside me, today and always."

"Damn you, Rush," Jules said in a tearful voice. "Now you had to go and make me cry. I'll always choose you." Those were the same words she told me before I came out to my parents. Oddly enough, the monsoon on my wedding day was eerily similar to the day that Jules and I said goodbye to our old life and boarded a Greyhound bus headed to Chicago.

"Why are you upset?" Racheal asked from the doorway. "Travis isn't *that* bad. At least he's handsome." Her bluntness was just the thing we needed to dry up our sentimental tears and laugh.

"It will be Uncle Travis in a few hours," I reminded her.

Racheal screwed up her face and tilted her head to the side like she was thinking hard about that. "We'll see," she said using the same tone as her mother when Jules said no without really saying it.

"I adore you, kid," I said, dropping to my knees in front of her. "You look so beautiful today that no one will even notice me up there on the altar."

"You think so?" My precocious niece spun around in a circle, her lavender organza skirt billowing and swirling around her legs.

"I know so," I assured her.

"We're going to be late," Will said, leaning lazily against the doorframe. I noticed that he only had eyes for his wife. He looked over at me as if just realizing his place and purpose. "Thanks for making my wife cry, asshole."

"I'm her brother; it's my job."

"It's *my* job to get you to your wedding on time, so let's go," Will said.

I sat in the back seat of Jules and Will's car with Racheal, trying my best not to let the weather bring me down.

"The Crystal Gardens will still be beautiful in the rain," Jules said from the front seat. She looked over her shoulder at me and offered a sweet smile. "The sound of raindrops on the glass windows will be romantic."

"Or put all your guests to sleep," Will added dryly.

"You're not helping," Jules said to her husband.

"The meteorologist used the phrase 'of biblical proportions' when discussing the amount of expected rainfall today. Rain makes people sleepy," Will told us. "Of course, this was the same jackal who originally said it would be in the high sixties and sunny."

"Don't listen to him, Rush. You're going to have a beautiful day." I couldn't help but notice that her smile didn't quite reach her eyes. I knew she didn't care for Travis and thought I was making a mistake, but she didn't say anything because marrying him was what *I* wanted. *Right?* Of course, it was.

I didn't think it was a big deal when Travis was fifteen minutes late. When was he ever on time? There were many reasons, namely traffic, that could cause his delay. It wasn't like he could walk from his hotel in the torrential downpour. After a half hour passed, I started to worry that he was involved in an accident, because who was that late to their wedding? Sure, he'd missed our anniversary dinner and was late to countless other events I wanted to attend, but he wouldn't leave his colleagues and esteemed guests checking their watches and questioning his character or capabilities.

Will checked the local news app for any alerts about a traffic accident that would've tied him up so long. Jules threatened to start calling hospitals. Racheal slipped her small hand into mine to comfort me while I stared at the phone in my other hand. I'd called Travis's phone every five minutes, silently begging and pleading for him to answer my calls or reply to my texts. So many horrifying scenarios floated through my mind, and I just wanted to know that he was okay.

The response I was waiting for finally came an hour after the time we were supposed to commit our lives to one another. It was a simple text with three words: *I am sorry.* My hand went suddenly limp, and my phone fell to the floor with a loud clatter.

"Is that him? Is that Travis?" Jules rushed over and picked my phone up off the floor. I closed my eyes and braced myself for her reaction. "*He* stood *you* up?" my sister asked in disbelief. "That son of a bi—" She stopped and looked down at her darling daughter who copied every little thing Jules said and did. "Sweetie, why don't you go with Daddy so I can have a private word with Uncle Rush."

"Okay, Mommy." Racheal squeezed my hand once more before she walked away with her dad.

"I'm going to gut that fucker like a fish," Jules snarled as soon as they were out of earshot. "Then I'm going to do something else equally vile, like set his remains on fire." She shook her head vehemently then walked to me and put her hands on my cheeks. "I know right now it might not seem like it, but that arrogant bastard did you the biggest favor by walking away. He just did it in a cowardly fashion."

I stood staring at her, unable to speak. I wanted to say I was devastated, but I think the only thing wounded was my pride. I hated the idea of standing in front of our guests and telling them that there would be no wedding. That seemed worse to me than Travis not showing up. What did that say about me—us. It said that I was in love with the idea of marriage, not the man I was supposed to commit my life to that day. I knew at that moment Jules was right, but I still couldn't find the words to tell her.

"Nigel and I will take care of this. Will!" she shouted. Her husband poked his head around the corner and looked down the hall at us. "Take Rush home. I'll have Nigel drop me off when I'm done dealing with this mess."

"Should I stop at the ATM?" he asked.

"What in the hell for?" Jules asked.

"Bail money," Will replied in a *duh* tone of voice.

"I love you," Jules said to her husband then looked at me. "Go home and process this in private. I'll be there as soon as I can."

There's this notion that to be strong you must stand alone and bravely weather the storms life throws at you, but that's not true. Strong people accept help when it's needed and lean on shoulders when offered.

"Don't you and Nigel do anything stupid," I warned.

"Define stupid."

"Gutting Travis like a fish," I replied. I dropped a kiss on her forehead then said, "Thank you, Jules."

Neither Will nor Racheal said anything on the drive back to my house. Once inside, I removed my tuxedo and tossed it negligently on the floor then put on comfy sweats and a T-shirt. I stared down at the pile of expensive clothes in disbelief. The parts of my tuxedo were supposed to be mixed with Travis's as we took turns undressing each other before we made love as husbands for the first time. We were supposed to stay at the Hilton and fly to the Caribbean first thing in the morning to begin a ten-day honeymoon.

Now what? Was I supposed to wait around here for Travis to show up and explain himself? I went into the bathroom and splashed cold water on my heated face; that's when I noticed that a lot of his things were missing, and not just stuff we packed in advance for our flight. His full-sized bottles of shampoo and conditioner that were there that morning were gone, as were several other things, like his extra razors, toothbrush, and aftershave. We had purchased trial sizes of most things and new toothbrushes for our trip.

I walked to the closet and threw open the doors. Travis's expensive suits were missing as were the garment bags he packed them in, and his shoes no longer lined the closet floor. I opened his dresser drawers and noticed they were practically empty, which meant that he came home and packed up most of his shit while I was pacing and worrying at the Crystal Gardens. This didn't seem like the act of a man who made a spur-of-the-moment decision; this felt deliberate.

When did he know? After I brought up kids again last night before we ended our call? Was it this morning when he saw the rain falling from the sky like a warning of impending doom? What made a man propose to another then leave him high and dry on their wedding day?

I knew Travis would give me the answers I needed eventually, and I would just have to wait until then. In the meantime, I would pick myself up by my bootstraps as my dad taught me and move forward with my life. I had major decisions to make, but I didn't have to make them right then.

Jules, Nigel, and Kent showed up not long after I changed. They brought Chinese takeout, several bottles of champagne, the top tier from my wedding cake, and the gifts that our guests left behind.

"You should've seen some of them snatching their gifts back off the table," Nigel said, between bites of kung pao chicken. "Kent was one of them," he said, jabbing his elbow into his husband's side.

"I thought they were looters," Kent said. "We put a lot of thought into our gift, and I wanted to make sure Rush got it."

Had Racheal not been there, the adults in the group would've made lewd suggestions about what was in the box. I smiled when I saw how much it cost my sister to behave herself.

"This isn't the steak and lobster I had planned to eat," Will sighed, poking his chopsticks around in a carton.

"Steak and Lobster," Jules scoffed. "What a pretentious bastard."

"Hey," I said, pretending to be offended.

"I know damn well that you didn't choose the menu," my sister fired back, pointing a chopstick at me. "Don't you even start with me."

"Yes, ma'am."

We stuffed ourselves with Chinese food, decadent cake, and drank copious amounts of champagne. Jules made me open the festively wrapped packages she referred to as the new-life-without-the-asshole gifts while they oohed and aahed. No, it wasn't the night I had envisioned when I woke up that morning, but we made the absolute best of it. I remained angry that Travis had so little regard for my feelings and sad over the way things ended between us, but I was very grateful for the amazing people in my life who made me smile on the rainiest of days.

8—I Want to Break Free

LINCOLN

"WHAT DO YOU THINK HIS STORY IS?" PHEE ASKED, tilting her head toward the bar in the cozy Chicago restaurant we'd chosen to break our children's hearts in.

It was a game that we often played over the years, and it felt good to embrace something familiar in a world that was suddenly strange and a little scary. Phee and I coexisted the best we could inside our home and at the office, but the strain had gotten to us by the end of September. We planned an impromptu trip to Chicago without telling our kids until we landed. I was a ball of nerves waiting for them to arrive at the restaurant, so Phee's attempt to break the tension was a welcome intrusion into my thoughts.

I looked over at the dark-haired, handsome man in a gray suit

66

slumped over a glass of liquor. He alternated between spinning his wedding ring on the gleaming mahogany bar and knocking back a drink of scotch or bourbon.

"Hmmm, judging by his attire I'd say he's an out-of-town businessman," I told Phee. "The way he's downing the liquor straight without ice tells me it's not going well."

"I think he's planning an affair," Phee suggested.

I watched as the bartender approached the man and gestured to his empty glass silently asking if he wanted another drink. The distraught man in the suit shook his head and said something, but we were too far away to hear his response. The bartender leaned forward suggestively to continue the conversation. When he pulled back, their gaze held and locked for several moments until a patron interrupted them by calling the bartender's name. It seemed like they communicated a lot during the pregnant pause; I couldn't help but wonder about their past. Or ponder if they had a future.

"Well, it doesn't look like the man will be lonely much longer," Phee said casually. There was no scorn or derision in her voice like the thought of two men together was offensive to her, but then again, those men were strangers. She hadn't shared her life with either of them for two decades. "And I want the same for you too."

I turned my head and looked at my wife across the candlelight. During the last few weeks, we had lived like strangers in the house that had seen so much love. It felt like the first week of college and getting used to a roommate all over again. I hated every single second of it. We each went our own direction in the house, mainly our separate bedrooms, and barely spoke outside of the office. Phee felt guilty for breaking my heart, which added to my misery. I was the one who shouldered the blame.

I grinned wryly at her over the table, and she knew what I was about to say. She shook her head no and blushed a pretty shade of pink like when she'd snuck home at two in the morning the previous week. Her hair had been a mess, her clothes twisted, and I'd never seen that euphoric look on her face. My heart seized in my chest, and I'd become nauseous—not because she'd obviously been in the arms of another man, but that she had waited so long to feel that good. She was well and truly loved physically, and the sappy smile on her face before she realized I was in the kitchen told me she was on her way to emotional love if she wasn't already there. I'd had that once in my life; I wouldn't begrudge her for experiencing it too.

"Check you out," I said, then whistled dramatically.

"We're not doing this," Phee said, shaking her head.

"Of course not, you're walking a little crooked, so I think you've had your fill tonight."

"Oh my God!" Phee covered her face in embarrassment before her laughter echoed around the kitchen.

"Here, you want some ice cream?" I asked, holding the carton toward her. "You could probably use some about now."

Phee stopped laughing and studied me like she was trying to peer into my brain. I understood her dilemma. What man offered to share his ice cream with his almost ex-wife after she returned home from having sex with another man? One who wanted to see his wife break free and find the happiness she deserved.

"Grab a spoon," I told her.

Phee grabbed a spoon from the silverware drawer and approached me as cautiously as she might a cornered animal. I smiled easily, hoping to erase her wariness. I saw the twinkle return to her blue eyes the moment she truly believed we would be okay. Phee scooped a large spoonful of cookies and cream and moaned around the spoon as it melted in her mouth. "So good," she said.

"That's what he said."

Phee's eyes widened, and she nearly choked, but that didn't stop her from wanting more of the sweet concoction I held in my hand. I jerked the pint of ice cream away just before her spoon reached its destination.

"Where's your mouth been?" I asked. "I don't want your dude's spunk mixed with my ice cream." A little sweet and salty never

hurt anyone; I just didn't want her guy's spunk to count as the salty component.

"Oh my God!" Phee said for the second time that night. Well, I suspected she'd said it plenty of times before she returned home, but it was the second time in a matter of minutes with me. "I can't do this with you, Linc."

"What? Share your man?" I asked. "I wouldn't ask that of you."

Phee threw her arms around my neck. "I love you so much, Linc. Thank you for not hating me."

"Never."

It was exactly the kick in the ass we needed to start focusing on our new futures which included new roles in one another's lives. I would be whatever Phee needed, and I hoped she would do the same for me when I felt brave enough to tell her the truth.

"Don't you start with me," Phee warned from across the table then glanced at her watch. "Where are our children?"

"I think a little patience is needed. It's not like we gave them much notice, and they probably had more exciting plans for a Saturday night. Besides, this rain is miserable."

"Yeah, okay," Phee agreed with a sigh.

Kennedy and Holden showed up a few minutes later looking apprehensive as fuck. Kennedy looked at us and burst into tears. "Is one of you sick? Is it cancer?"

Holden looked at his sister as if the thought hadn't occurred to him. "Oh my God!" He sounded so much like his mother that I couldn't stop the smile that spread across my face. Nothing about the situation was funny, but I hoped that the kids would feel better once they learned the reason we were there. "Are you dying?" he asked dramatically.

"Neither of us is dying," Phee said, hugging both of them to her.

I joined the group hug, and for reasons still unknown to me, said, "Just our marriage is."

"*What?*" Kennedy asked pulling out of the circle of arms to look up at her mother then me. "Is this some sick joke?"

"That's a far cry better than cancer," Holden said calmly.

"You're not funny, Holden," Kennedy said. "Our parents are having a midlife crisis, and you're cracking jokes." A fresh wave of tears started flowing down her face.

I glanced around and caught many sympathetic glances from the diners around us. Maybe a private venue would've been better. We had planned to have dinner then go back to either our hotel or the apartment the kids shared for the serious chat portion of the evening, but it didn't go according to plan.

I pulled Kennedy against my chest and held her tight. She hesitated to return the embrace at first, but then wrapped her arms around me and cried softly into my dress shirt. "Nothing changes, kitten. Do you hear me? Mom and I are still partners in business, friendship, and parenting. We love you and your brother so much. We just need to make some changes."

"But you're so happy together," she mumbled into my shirt.

"No, we're really not." It was the first time I admitted it out loud and tears of relief pooled in Ophelia's eyes. "We've grown apart as couples do sometimes and stayed together out of our love for you and respect for each other."

"You've found another woman," Holden said, sounding suspicious and angry.

"No," I said, looking into his eyes. I could tell by his expression that he was blaming me for the failed marriage. "I haven't met anyone else."

"Can we postpone this conversation until after dinner?" Phee asked softly. "We're making a scene."

Kennedy pulled her head off my chest and looked at her mother. "You think we have an appetite after this little bombshell?"

"I could eat," Holden said wryly.

"When don't you think about your stomach?" Kennedy asked her younger brother in disdain.

"When I'm thinking about my—"

"That's enough," I said before he could finish. "Let's just head back to our hotel down the street and have a chat. We can order room service later if we feel like eating."

"Sounds like a good plan," Phee agreed.

"Will you settle the bill with the waiter while I use the restroom?" I asked her. I reached for my wallet, but she stopped me with her hand.

"I got it."

I headed down the hallway to the bathrooms and heard masculine moans coming from a closed, unmarked door. I had noticed that the distraught man from the bar was gone and a new bartender was manning the bar, and I was pretty sure I knew where they went. A smooth voice said, "I'm going to make you feel so good that you'll forget all about your troubles." *If only it were so easy.*

The atmosphere was calmer once we were alone in my hotel room. I expected the kids to pepper us with a bunch of questions the minute we were alone, but they didn't. Kennedy and Holden sat close on the couch like they were trying to protect each other from the grimness of the situation. I hated like hell that I was the cause of Kennedy's tears and Holden's quiet speculation. It was all on my shoulders, even though Ophelia was the one asking for the divorce. Our family would've remained whole if I could've given my wife what she needed all these years.

The questions came one after the other once the kids felt more settled.

"Are you going to sell the house?" Kennedy asked.

"Yes, we're going to sell the house and split the profits equally so we can each have a fresh start someplace new." I knew how much she loved that house, and I could see how much my answer hurt her.

"Will you stay in the same area?" Holden followed. "All our friends are there."

"That's the goal," Phee replied, not pointing out that they both lived thousands of miles away and had made new friends.

"What's going to happen with Forever Home?" Kennedy asked.

"Nothing," was my quick reply. "Our divorce doesn't change a single thing about our real estate company."

"Do our grandparents know yet?" Holden asked.

"I told my parents," Phee said then looked at me sympathetically.

"I haven't," I told the kids. I wasn't close to my parents and avoided going back to eastern Tennessee like the plague. They would be deeply disappointed in me, and that was something I had managed to avoid in my adult life. I'd given them plenty of parental bragging rights, but that would end as soon as I told them about the divorce. To be honest, I wasn't sure what to expect from them going forward. It wasn't like they made a huge attempt to be part of our world either. My father railed about California being overrun by hippies and Democrats, and my mom was too afraid to speak up.

The kids lobbed one question after the other at us. Phee and I took turns fielding them until they asked the one question we had hoped to avoid.

"Whose idea was the divorce?" Kennedy asked. Her eyes darted between us looking for any clues.

I could tell Phee was going to let me answer that one on my own. She was prepared to accept whatever answer I gave, but there was no way in hell I was throwing the mother of my children under the bus. "That doesn't matter," I told our daughter.

"Of course, it matters," Kennedy argued.

"Why?" Phee asked. "Your father and I have both said that we grew apart and needed changes. Why can't that be enough?"

"She wants a bad guy," Holden said dryly. "Someone needs to take the blame for fucking up our lives. We come from a broken home now. We need to blame one of you when we become raging alcoholics or something."

"I do not need a bad guy," Kennedy argued.

"Then why ask whose idea it was? How does that even matter?"

"It just does," Kennedy told her brother. "I need to understand why and how it happened."

"It's not our business, K," Holden countered. "Mom and Dad are entitled to privacy."

"How can you be so blasé about it?" she asked. "You act like you don't care."

"I do care, and that's why I'm trying to support them, as they've always done for us."

I looked at my son, shocked by how much he'd matured in such a short time. It wasn't that long ago that his only concerns were his video games and whatever girl he was dating. Kennedy had always been mature beyond her years, so her emotional outburst was a testament to how hurt and surprised she was.

Holden ended up ordering Chinese food from his favorite restaurant through GrubHub, and we did our best to put thoughts of the uncertain future aside to focus on what we had right then. Phee and I did our best to assure our children that we would always be there for them, no matter what our living arrangements were going forward. I thought we'd gotten our point across by the time they left for their apartment.

Phee hugged me tightly before she left to go to her room. I relished the comfort and safety I'd always felt in her arms. "We're going to be okay," she whispered before she left.

I walked to the wall of windows and looked at the lights from the Centennial Wheel at the Navy Pier. It reminded me of the boy I once loved with all my heart and how brave he was, not because he got on the Ferris wheel at our county fair, but because he broke free and lived openly. I wanted to break free too, even though I wasn't sure how.

9—Better Things

Rush

"OH, WHAT ABOUT HIM?" NIGEL ASKED. HE'D TALKED me into downloading a dating app for gay men and was actively trying to find my next big mistake, my future ex. Nigel made a growling noise in his throat that I took as interest in whatever profile popped up on my phone.

"Give me that," Kent said, snatching the phone from his husband.

I glanced up from the salad I'd pushed from one side of my plate to the other without really taking a bite. Fuck, I was tired of eating like a damn rabbit. I might've volunteered my left nut to taste my aunt Gretchen's fried chicken and mashed potatoes and gravy.

Kent hummed appreciatively in his throat drawing a scowl from Nigel. "He does look very flexible."

"Give that back to Rush, dear. He doesn't need our help," Nigel told his husband. "You've got this under control, right?" Funny how Nigel didn't like it when the shoe was on the other foot. He could make growly noises at hot men, but Kent wasn't allowed to notice or comment.

"You betcha," I said confidently although I didn't feel it.

Three months had passed since Travis officially moved out after a tearful plea for me to forgive his cowardly behavior. He told me that he wanted so much to be what I needed but he couldn't. Marriage wasn't what he wanted for himself, and he didn't see kids in his future. He also said that he always felt like he was never enough for me. He gave me everything he could, but I always wanted more. He gave his heart; I wanted to live together. He moved in; I wanted to get married. He proposed marriage; I wanted kids. I realized we were never well suited and laziness had kept us together for ten years.

I couldn't say that I missed *him*, it was more like I missed not being... alone. I took on extra assignments which kept me away from home for longer periods of time, but I always returned to a house that was empty, cold, and devoid of my personality. I bought the brownstone before I met Travis and allowed him to redecorate when he moved in. The vast majority of the furnishings and decorations were things he picked out and paid for, so I ended up with the beat-up recliner that Travis hated, the large television that I had insisted on buying, and an antique clock hanging on the kitchen wall. Travis took everything else, including our giant bed.

That meant I'd needed to do a lot of shopping to make my home feel like mine again, but I hadn't found the energy. The only thing I'd felt in a hurry to replace was the bed. My new huge bed with the pillow top cushion gave me plenty of ideas on what I'd like to do in it, but the finding someone to do them with, or to, had proven harder. There was no shortage of interested candidates, and I'd even gone on a few dates with men that my *friends* had suggested. At the end of each night, I ended up adding another name to the friend column but hadn't found anyone to share a life with. Was it me? Had I gotten too picky? Why did the thought of taking these hot guys back to my place leave me feeling cold?

When I returned from my last trip, I decided to put energy into making the brownstone feel like mine again. I painted and bought new furniture and decorations. I hit up some flea markets to find pieces that spoke to me rather than hit a glitzy showroom filled with soulless art. I even bought a new Christmas tree and ornaments that were more my style. I still felt unsettled, but at least I wouldn't be ashamed to take the right guy home. I appreciated my efforts when the cute new guy from the gym made it really obvious that he wanted me to do more than spot him at the bench press.

I wanted to test out the new bed, but he didn't seem interested in getting that far into the house. We went at it like randy teenagers as soon as the door closed. I tried to break free to retrieve condoms and lube but the guy—we'll call him The Boy Scout for his prepared-ness—pulled the stuff out of his duffle bag.

"Gotcha covered," he said, slapping them in my hand before turning around to face the foyer wall. He pushed his sweats to his ankles and presented his bare ass, pushing the rounded cheeks out seductively. I was too turned on and too horny to realize just how cold and calculated his moves were.

All I thought about was sinking my dick between those perky ass cheeks, so I did. Afterward, the guy cleaned up in my bathroom and left without telling me his name. My body was sated, but the brief en-counter only made me feel lonelier. I saw him a few times at the gym, but he was too busy picking up the other dudes to notice me.

"He's sure mowing his way through the gym members," Nigel had said one afternoon when we were on the treadmills. "Comb your hair and look pretty when he comes this way."

"Been there and done that already," I had replied.

"When?" Nigel said, looking at me with big eyes. He nearly fell on his face from the shock. "Oh my God! I need the details."

"Not much to tell," I said. "We tumbled through the door, he dropped his pants and presented his ass to me."

"Huh." Nigel didn't sound all that impressed.

"I'm pretty sure I had a warmer encounter with my dentist during a root canal last year," I said dryly.

"Ouch," Nigel replied then looked over at the guy whose name I learned a week later was Adam. "Well, I guess it's better than your fist."

"That's debatable."

Since then, I'd stuck to my fist because it was less degrading. I gave in to Nigel's insistence that I try the latest app designed to help me find my forever gay—his words, not mine—instead of a quickie gay. Kent knew the developer, and I agreed to at least test it out and give feedback.

"So, you've found a solid candidate from the app?" Kent asked me.

"Are you asking as my friend or the app developer's friend?" I inquired with a raised brow.

"Yours, of course."

"I think the app has merit, and I will say that the guys who've joined thus far seem to be looking for more than a hand job or blow job."

"I'm sensing a *but* here, and not the kind you want to tap."

"Very perceptive," I told Kent. "It's just… boring." I realized how shallow it made me, but I was telling the truth. "It's kind of like he went to the extreme opposite of an app like Grindr when maybe he only had to scale it back just a little."

"You single gays are so damn picky," Kent said teasingly. "You say you want a site for quality dates with men who want relationships, but you're not satisfied when it's provided to you."

"Have you checked out the app?" I inquired.

Kent snorted and said, "No. I have a husband that I love. Why would I want to check out a dating site?"

"So that you don't sound like an idiot when you berate me for giving you honest feedback," I told him. "Would you like me to show you what I'm talking about?"

Kent looked at Nigel, who nodded his head. Nigel had looked harder at finding Mr. Right for me than I ever did. I knew he shared the same hang-ups with the site as me, but probably wanted to avoid telling Kent that his friend designed a lame dating app.

"Okay, but you're not allowed to be angry with me for telling the truth," I told Kent when he nodded for me to continue.

Kent blew out a long sigh and nodded his head. "You're right. I just want Thomas to succeed. He had a great concept, but I can't help him if I don't wear an objective hat while discussing it. Let me have it."

"Start by reading the reviews," Nigel offered. I cringed because the reviews were pretty brutal. "Like the one who said he found the IRS tax codes easier to understand, or the one that said the cheesy porn music was a turn-off. I mean, why does this thing have sound? Like anyone wants to alert people that they're trying to pick up men or possibly jerking it at work to porn."

Nigel rambled on for several minutes, saving me the hassle of having to talk about the reviews. I could tell that Kent was concerned about how much Nigel knew, and bothered by his lack of filter when discussing the app.

"You can read the reviews on your own time," I said gently. "Let me tell you *my* issues with it."

"Okay." Kent sounded so dejected that a person would've thought that he designed it.

"Here's my biggest issue: it shares too much information about a person. I agree that it's good to know more than if a guy wants to top or bottom, but discovering someone's hobbies and quirks is the fun part of dating. Knowing it in advance kind of takes the thrill out of getting to know someone. Grindr is one extreme, and Thomas's app is the other."

"He needs that data to help match you with candidates who would most likely appeal to you," Kent said.

"I didn't have an issue with the interview questions themselves; I just don't like that the answers are shared with your matches. Let it be enough that there are compatible matches for me without knowing the XYZs of it. Let me find out what makes us a good match. All of us signing up for the site answer the same questions about what we want in life as far as marriage, kids, pets, and so on. I would assume that the algorithm would avoid picking someone for me who doesn't want kids."

Kent perked up a little. "So, it's not that you don't like the questions, you just feel that the answers should only be used to match candidates, not made part of their dating profile."

"Right," I agreed. "Let me look across a candlelit table and find out who likes to knit or ski in their spare time. Allow me to fall in love with their smile while discovering what makes them tick. The getting-to-know-someone phase is the most fun. Your friend has already done that like it's a cyber speed date or something."

"I like your feedback more than his," Kent said, hooking his thumb in his husband's direction. "Stay off that site from now on, Nigel."

"I'm only on there to help Rush pick through the weeds so that he can find the daisies," Nigel said. "I've already found the man of my dreams."

"How sweet," I said in a syrupy voice. "Save that lovey-dovey shit for when it doesn't make me want to burst into tears."

"That jackass did you a favor," Nigel replied, sounding like everyone else who knew us as a couple. "So what if you haven't found Mr. Right already. That doesn't mean you won't. In the meantime, maybe you stop trying so hard with the dating apps and let fate happen on its own."

"Weren't you the one just picking out prospects for me on the app?" I asked Nigel.

"I was, and I was wrong. I'm not saying that there's anything wrong with dating sites," Nigel said to Kent before he could speak up. "I'm just saying that I want better things for you, not just different. I want you to have a love worthy of a romance novel, because by God, you deserve it. I want you to look into a stranger's eyes and see your future. I want you to glance across the laundromat—"

"The laundromat," Kent and I both said at the same time.

"What's wrong with his washer and dryer?" Kent asked.

"I hate the laundromat," I added.

"You guys," Nigel whined. "You're both being too literal." He puffed out a breath of frustration. "Okay, so you glance across the produce section as you firmly squeeze some kiwi in both hands—"

"Oh, he's demonstrating that he's good with his hands," Kent said, nodding as if he got it.

"I don't like kiwi fruit," I told Nigel. "I especially don't like hairy balls or the grocery store. I have my groceries delivered."

"Now we're talking," Kent said, cueing up the dating site so the cheesy music played. "Hello, Mr. Holden," he said breathily. "I've got your packages."

Watching the serious Kent Clark pretend to narrate porn was the funniest thing I ever saw. I glanced over at Nigel, but he wasn't laughing or smiling. He just blinked at his husband as if seeing him for the first time.

"Where would you like me to put it?" Kent asked with a pout.

"We're out of here," Nigel said. He rose to his feet and reached for his wallet.

"I got this," I said, waving him away. "You two go on home and play out the delivery guy porn scene."

They scrambled out of there without even saying goodbye. I waived my waitress over and asked for a juicy A-1 bacon and swiss burger with onion straws on top and a side of extra crispy fries. Extra crispy meant that they went two rounds in the fryer. Fuck that salad! At least one part of me was going to be satisfied that night.

On my way out of the pub, I saw an animal shelter adoption flyer hanging on the wall by the door. On the front was a gray pit bull who looked like he had seen the worst that life had to offer and just needed someone to love him. The flyer identified him as Brutus and stated he'd been at the facility the longest. I recognized the loneliness in Brutus's eyes and dialed the number on the flyer without thinking about the repercussions.

"I'm calling about Brutus," I said when a lady answered the phone. "I saw that the next adoption event is Saturday, but I was hoping you could make an exception."

"You want to adopt Brutus?" she asked hopefully.

"If he'll have me."

"Come on over," she said.

An hour later, I buckled Brutus in the rear passenger seat of my SUV. He looked over and gave me his best doggy grin, and I gave him my best smile in return. I went online and ordered the necessary items for him and had them delivered. I tried like hell not to laugh when the delivery guy showed up and said he had a package for me. I failed miserably, and he looked at me like I was a lunatic.

I took my new best friend for a walk in the park near our home. The cool, crisp air felt as invigorating as exercising with my handsome companion. Brutus walked proudly beside me, and I wondered how anyone could've passed him up for three years. Then I realized it was because he was meant to be my dog. We both had to endure less than pleasant environments before we could appreciate the good thing we found in each other. Brutus was the greatest Christmas present I ever gave myself.

Later that night, I thought about what Nigel had said. There *was* a difference between wanting better things and different things. I wanted better things for myself and Brutus.

10—The House That
Built Me

LINCOLN

I WOULD LIKE TO SAY THAT THE MONTHS THAT FOLLOWED THE
separation were filled with hot guys and even hotter sex, but I
was too fucking panicked to make a move beyond jacking off to
the gay porn I at least allowed myself to watch. The guilt that came
afterward made me wonder if it was worth it, but it became a pattern
I couldn't seem to break. It wasn't my attraction to men that made me
feel guilty; it was not owning up to it. By sneaking and hiding, I was
giving credence to every dumbass who implied that gay men were
perverts and deviants. I knew better, dammit. I just couldn't seem to
do something about it. Until I could admit I was gay, I would remain
in my self-enforced purgatory.

Phee sure as hell hadn't wasted any time moving on. She and her
new guy, Jackson, had flown to Chicago to meet the kids, but only

after formally introducing him to me first. I was very familiar with him on a professional level since he owned a construction company and used Forever Home to sell the houses. He was a good man, and Phee was obviously crazy about him. I wanted to be bitter that Phee could live so openly and be happy, but the smile on her face made it impossible. I had held her back from having the life and love she deserved for more than two decades, so I gave them my blessing for a happy future.

The hardest part about Phee moving on without me was feeling like I had lost my best friend. No matter what she said, our friendship would never be the same. She was the person I would tell my troubles to, but how could I tell Phee that our entire marriage had basically been a lie? A lie by omission is still a lie in anyone's book. My secret was the reason I couldn't be the husband she had needed. I picked up my phone to call her and even stopped by her office with the intention of unburdening my soul, but I could never find the right words to say to her. During the day, I wore my brightest smile into the office, and it stayed there until I went home. At night, I returned to my lonely condo and fantasized about a life I wished I was brave enough to claim and drank wine. So much wine. So much porn. So much masturbation. So much guilt.

There were several same-sex couples in my condo complex, which intensified all my emotions. I saw them greet each other after a long day at work or perform the simplest tasks like carry the groceries from the car or walk their dogs. As much as I wanted to feel a hot male body over, under, and in me, it was the little daily things I wanted to experience. I wanted the connection that rocked me to my fucking soul. I'd only had that once in my life, and I wanted it again.

With the rising longing and hunger came paralyzing fear—both fear of what would happen if I took a chance and if I didn't. The one person I needed the most was busy starting a new life, and I couldn't bring myself to intrude on her happiness a moment longer than I already had. I needed to accept my new role in Phee's life and be grateful for what I had.

The following March, Phee showed how much she loved me when my mom called to let me know my dad had died of a sudden heart attack. Thomas Huxley, my father and the toughest son of a bitch I ever knew, was no longer walking the earth. How was that even possible? I had always seen my old man as invincible. I would've been lost without Phee. She made the necessary travel arrangements for our kids and us, packed my bags, and made sure we got where we needed to on time. I remember telling her she didn't have to bother, but she waved me off.

"We'll always be a family, Linc. That hasn't changed." Her words warmed my frozen heart.

Returning to my childhood home in eastern Tennessee was bittersweet. It reminded me of both the happiest and worst times in my life, but it was the house that built me and molded the man I became. Phee stayed at a bed and breakfast nearby while the kids and I stayed with my mom. She sounded better than she had on the phone, but she still looked lost and exhausted. My parents didn't have a happy marriage, but it was the only life Lillian Huxley knew.

I sat across from her at the table in the tiny kitchen that hadn't changed since I left home. The walls were the same medium blue with white cabinets, and the same old goose wallpaper border lined the circumference of the room. In fact, my parents' entire house was like stepping back to a different decade through a time warp machine. My mom had been so excited to remodel the house back in the nineties, and it hadn't changed since. The living room still had the same couch that combined stripes and flowers in the ghastliest way, but she had seen it in a magazine and fell in love with it.

For the first time that I could remember, my dad had actually put effort into making my mom happy. He teased her about the expense, but I could tell he didn't mean it. The house was my mom's dream, and it was a source of pride for my dad that he could provide it for her. My mom had worked too, but only part time as a cashier once I went to junior high school. Sometimes she worked evenings, which left my dad and me to fend for ourselves. Thomas Huxley liked his meat-and-potato dinners hot and on the table when he walked through the door. He didn't like leftovers or frozen TV dinners.

I think the little bit of independence that my mom had found was the biggest source of their arguments, but for once, my mom was unwilling to give in to Dad's demands. I think my dad releasing his iron-fisted grip on the checkbook to redecorate was his sneaky attempt at manipulating my mom into quitting her job. Kind of like, "Look at your pretty house. How can you leave it?"

Mom got her pretty house *and* kept her job. The fighting intensified to the point that I spent every free moment at Rush's house. Of course, I wanted to be there for reasons besides the acrimony between my folks, but I could relive those memories when I had a few minutes to catch my breath. I was only in my old room long enough to drop my suitcase on my bed and return downstairs to comfort my mother.

"Why don't you come back to California with me for a while after the funeral, Mom?" I asked gently. "I have an extra bedroom in my new condo."

"I appreciate the offer, Linc. I might take you up on it after I sell the house and settle your dad's estate."

"Sell the house?" I was stunned.

"This house is just too much for me to take care of anymore. My knees hate that my bedroom is on the second floor and the laundry room is in the basement. This house needs laughter and little kids again. Your father and I talked about selling it this summer. We were going to hire someone to update it a little bit first. Then he…" Her voice broke off and she began to cry.

"I'm so sorry, Mom." I held her against my chest and let her cry as long as she wanted.

I was sad that my father died, of course, but what I truly mourned was the lost potential of growing closer to him. I guess I had never given up the hope that someday my father and I would click, but his sudden death ensured that it would never happen.

After several minutes, my mom pulled back and wiped her face with a handkerchief. "Anyway, you'll want to go through your room to see if there's anything you want to keep. I'm going to hire a company to clean this place out, paint it, and sell it as is."

"I doubt there's anything up there I want to keep," I said gently. Hell, I hadn't spent the night in that room but a few times after high school graduation. I rarely even came home for summer once I left for college. Spending time in that town without Rush was too damn painful. There wasn't a place I could go where memories of us didn't taunt me. Even though I was back in town for my father's funeral, my first thoughts were of Rush when we drove our rental into town.

Our innocent laughter echoed off the playground of our elementary school. I couldn't look at the ice cream parlor, Scoops, without seeing Rush's fevered delight over buying penny candy at the counter. God, he drove those ladies crazy by choosing five of one thing and ten of another then asking how much money he had left to spend. He'd repeat the process until he went home with a bag full of treasures he hid inside his treehouse so that his dad wouldn't find it. The familiar sounds of Friday night lights played through my mind as we drove past the high school. The marching band and cheering crowds were amazing times, but my heart pinched painfully in my chest when I recalled my favorite way of celebrating a victory. It involved two wild hearts that beat as one in the darkness of my dad's car, or anywhere we could be alone. It took everything I had to force those memories aside to focus on helping my mother the best I could.

"It's just some posters and trophies," I told her. The things I cherished most from my hometown were things that I couldn't display on a wall or shelf for people to see.

As the day wore on, my mother's exhaustion showed more and more. I convinced her to turn in early since my father's memorial service, burial, and gathering of friends and family was happening the next day. I tucked her into bed and kissed her forehead. "I love you, Mom. Rest well."

"I love you too, Lincoln."

Holden and Kennedy stayed downstairs to watch television while I went to my old room. I was hoping to enjoy some solitude, but I should've known that the ghosts of my past would join me. Deciding it would be best to stay busy, I unpacked my suitcase and toiletries. When I opened my closet to hang up my garment bag, my eyes latched onto my grandad's old metal WWII ammunition box my grandma gave me after he died. She'd told me that he kept his most precious treasures inside the box since it was responsible for getting him home from the war.

I just stood there staring at the green metal box because I knew what treasures I placed there for safekeeping. I was in no way ready to face them. Yet, I hung up the garment bag and pulled the box down from the shelf like I was under its spell.

I sat at the foot of my bed, trying so hard not to hear the remnants of laughter and love bouncing around in my head. It had captivated me so much that I almost expected the box to vibrate and pulse in my hand. It was my very own *Jumanji*, and I knew that only misery would follow if I opened that box and looked inside. I swiftly rose from my bed and set it on my dresser.

"Okay, maybe I'll take one thing back home," I whispered to myself, looking around the room. I had no desire to relive my gridiron glory days by taking home the trophies and awards. The movie and rock band posters made me smile though. Rush had the biggest crush on Jon Bon Jovi, and I used to get so fucking jealous.

A familiar ping of a rock bouncing off my window snapped me back to the present, or had it transported me back in time? Rush used to throw stones at my window to get my attention once my parents went to bed. Looking back now, it was amazing no one caught us sneaking around. My heart raced with the possibilities, even though I knew it was too ridiculous to believe. I pulled back the curtain and saw my ex-wife standing beneath my window in the early evening dusk instead of the boy who had looked at me with his heart in his eyes.

I raised the window and poked my head outside. "It's a little late for you to be out prowling the streets, young lady."

Phee steepled her hands in prayer beneath her chin. "Please don't tell my parents." Her shenanigans made me laugh and lessened the tension that had gripped my body.

"Why didn't you just knock on the door?"

"I didn't want to risk waking your mom," Phee answered. "Let me in. I want to see you and make sure you're okay."

"I'm fine."

"I need to see it for myself, so either come downstairs and let me in like a gentleman or I'm climbing that tree." She gestured to the big oak with branches that nearly reached my window. "What's it going to be?"

I placed my finger on my lip and tilted my head to the side as I pondered my choices. "Hmmmmm."

"I was excellent at climbing trees once upon a time," Phee said. To prove her determination, she kicked off one of her flats.

"Okay, you win," I told her before she took off the second shoe.

"What's going on?" Kennedy asked when I jogged down the steps.

"Your mom is silly," I replied.

Phee made a beeline for our kids as soon as I unlocked and opened the door, which made me suspicious of her true intentions of showing up at my mom's. Once she got her fix, she turned her attention back to me, and I saw that she really was worried about me.

"Let's go upstairs to my room," I told her, nodding my head toward the stairs.

"Uh oh," Holden said. "Better not let your boyfriend find out, Mom." He looked over the back of the couch at us. "Will it ever stop feeling weird when I talk about my mom having a boyfriend?"

"Yes," I told him. "This is still pretty new for us, but it won't be long before you can't remember a time without Jackson in your lives as long as you two give the guy a fair chance. He's a good man and really cares about your mom." Phee squeezed my hand in appreciation.

"We know, Daddy," Kennedy said. "We like him. It's just…"

"We know," Phee and I said at once.

"It's different," I added.

"Yes, but I was going to say that we want you to be happy too, Daddy."

"I'll get there, Kennedy. I just need to find the right person." I thought it was a huge step in the right direction that I hadn't said I needed to find the right woman. "Don't stay up too late," I told them. "It's going to be a long day tomorrow."

"Okay," they both said, even though they could've argued that I was treating them like little kids.

Phee followed me up to my room and sat on my bed. We chatted about my mom and the surprise she dropped about selling the house. "Mom asked me to go through my things to see if I wanted to take any of it home."

"There's so much to choose from," Phee said. She stood up and walked over to the shelves lining the wall, looking at each trophy. She stopped when she reached the dresser and her eyes landed on the ammo box sitting on top of it. "What a cool box. What's in here?"

"Phee, don't," I said, sounding like she was about to unleash cataclysmic chaos into the world. *Well, it would be for me anyway.*

"Ohhh, now you've got me curious." Phee lifted the box and clutched it to her chest. "Are there mementos from the girls who came before me? Evidence of your glory days?" She wiggled her brows suggestively, unaware of the acid churning inside my stomach.

"Ophelia," I said in a warning tone as I stood up. "Give me the box."

"No way. There must be something truly juicy inside this box for you to act this way."

She thought I was embarrassed, but what I felt was the terror of what would happen if she looked inside. It was truly Pandora's box, and she could never unsee the contents or undo the damage she would cause.

"Please," I begged, taking the few steps that separated us. I lunged for the box suddenly, but Phee turned at the last minute to avoid my hands. Instead of grabbing the box, I knocked it out of her hand. It felt like I was watching it fall in slow motion until it hit the hardwood floor with a loud clank. The noise was the least of my problems though, because the box had become unlatched as it fell, and my secrets spilled onto the floor.

"I'm sorry, Linc," Phee said, dropping to her knees. "Let me…"

"No," I said, falling to my knees beside her. I felt Phee stiffen beside me at my harsh tone, but worrying about her feelings was the last thing on my mind. Why couldn't she have left that box alone? My tenuous grip on my emotions was starting to unravel as I tried to scoop up the contents and put them back inside without really seeing them.

I realized the moment that Phee saw a hint of the secret that I had kept from her. She gasped softly and reached for a Polaroid picture before I could pick it up. I tried to take it from her, but she blocked me with her free hand then slid it down to link her fingers with mine. Phee looked at the photo in her hand showing two teenage boys who were obviously in love and the dozens of similar photos scattered on the floor. "What's his name?"

"Rush." Just whispering his name broke a dam inside me.

Ophelia released my hand so that she could get up and lock the door. When she returned, she helped me to my feet and guided me to the bed. I sobbed on the bed as she reverently placed each of my treasures back into the box and carried it to me.

"I'm sorry, Linc. I didn't mean to hurt you."

"I'm the one who's sorry, Phee. I promised you a life that I couldn't give you." I took the box from her but couldn't meet her eyes.

I was terrified of what I'd see. I expected her to leave the house and never want to speak to me again, but instead, she sat on the bed beside me and ran her hand through my hair to comfort me. I rested my head against her chest, and she looped her arms around me to hold me while I cried. "Please don't hate me, Phee. I tried so hard to be a good husband."

"Shhh, Linc," she said soothingly. "I'm going to need some time to process this because everything I knew about you—us—was wrong, but I could never hate you. Right now, I just want to take care of you. We can talk this out when we get back home. Okay?"

I nodded against her chest. Phee must've had a million thoughts and questions running through her mind, but she didn't voice any of them. She just rocked me back and forth as I released my misery. Once my tears turned to sniffles, she cupped my chin and raised my head to look into my eyes.

"Tell me about Rush."

And I did. I opened the box, and my heart, to relive those memories with my best friend by my side. I showed her the dried flower that Rush wore pinned to his tuxedo jacket. Fresh tears fell from my eyes when I told her about our private dance. Phee cried with me. We looked at the photos of Rush and me that told the story of our friendship to young love. I laughed when I told her about Rush getting the camera as a gift from his mom.

"I think Rush invented the selfie," I told Phee, pointing to a photo of us grinning at the camera that Rush had held above our heads. I thought he was crazy when he turned the camera around and aimed it at us, but the picture had turned out well.

"He was a brave boy who loved with all his heart and confronted his fears instead of cowering behind them. I wasn't as brave as him."

Phee listened to me talk about my first love until the early light of dawn crept through the windows. "This is a new day, Lincoln," she said from the pillow beside mine. "It's not too late for you to be brave too. This weekend might not be the right time to tell your mom but please tell her soon. Give her the chance to know the *real* you. She might get angry or feel hurt, but that's on her, not you."

"What about Kennedy and Holden?"

"Kennedy just told you that they wanted to see you happy. If she was telling the truth, she will love whoever you love." Phee ran the back of her hand over my jawbone. "Right now, you need to get a few hours of sleep. We'll form a plan later. Okay?"

I knew that long talks and revelations lay ahead of me, but I drifted to sleep with a glimmer of hope in my heart.

11—Begin Again

Rush

IT SEEMED LIKE EVERYONE I KNEW TRIED TO FIX ME UP WITH A guy who was "perfect for me." I understood that they wanted to see me happy, but it only added to my loneliness when it failed to work out. Sure, I had some great meals with some wonderful men, but the evenings lacked the spark of awareness that said something truly special lay ahead for us. I wouldn't exactly say I lived like a monk over the next few months because some of the dates did carry over into the bedroom. While the sex was physically satisfying in the moment, the missing emotional connection left me feeling empty and cold when I was by myself afterward.

I started to believe that I was the problem. The common denominator in every failed relationship, or potential one, was me. What was it about me that drove men away? I didn't learn my lesson after my Lincoln heartache and proceeded to get my heart smashed by several closet cases until I reached my mid-twenties. By then, I had found guys who were open with their sexuality but didn't want the same things I did. I thought that had changed with Travis, but I was so fucking wrong. Hell, I sent him running from the altar on the day of our wedding. Was I doomed to spend the rest of my life alone?

Brutus nudged my knee beneath my desk as if he sensed my loneliness and wanted to remind me that he was there. I reached down and stroked his silky ears, marveling at how quickly my mood improved.

"You're such a handsome boy," I said to my faithful companion just as Nigel walked into my office.

He gasped and turned around to face the door he'd just walked through. "Please tell me that you're petting and talking to your dog, not stroking your cock and ego."

"Hang on, Ni. I'm almost there," I grunted out like I was about to come. I removed my hand from Brutus's ear, and he stealthily crawled out from under my desk and crept over to Nigel.

"Gross," he said. "I need a raise. You don't pay me enough to—" His words cut off when Brutus shoved his nose against his right butt cheek. "Well, Mr. Holden, that wasn't the kind of raise I had in mind, but…"

Brutus nudged Nigel again and let out a *woof*.

My assistant turned and squatted until he was eye level with my dog. "I knew it was you all along. I'm just glad your master hasn't become so desperate that he'd literally take matters into his own hand during business hours. Who knows who could walk through the door."

"First of all, you're the only one who enters my office without knocking first," I told him dryly. "And second, have you ever caught me masturbating at my desk?"

"Not yet," Nigel admitted reluctantly, "but times are getting desperate around here."

He had no idea, but I refrained from admitting he was right. "What did you barge into my office for?"

"I need to rearrange your schedule for next week."

"What? Why?" My calendar was filled months in advance, and I didn't like last-minute changes. "People made those appointments months ago, Nigel. I'm not calling them the week before their appointment and telling them that I need to reschedule. No one is so important that they can't wait."

"Janessa Meriday." Nigel just chuckled when my mouth dropped open in surprise. Janessa was the modern-day Oprah Winfrey, in fact, people dubbed her Oprah 2.0.

"She wants me to come on her show?" I asked. Like her shero, she had a daytime talk show that was so popular she gave Ellen a run for her money. I figured the only advantages Ellen had over Janessa was the location, Los Angeles versus Chicago, and her connections to the celebrities in Hollywood. Even with those two things stacked against her, I figured it was only a year, two at most, before she became the number one daytime talk show queen. "It's great exposure, but—"

"Do you know what's better exposure than sitting in a chair on her set answering interview questions?" Nigel pondered out loud. He started humming game show music as I processed his question. He made a buzzer noise indicating that I'd taken too long to answer. "She wants to hire you to take her wedding photos this summer!"

"Really?" I asked. Of all the photographers she could hire, she chose me? I had made huge inroads in my career over the past few years with magazine contracts, connections to the best modeling agencies, and I was even a guest lecturer at the School of the Art Institute of Chicago. I was at the point that I could start cherry-picking the assignments I wanted and pass on the ones I didn't.

"Of course, she'd pick you. Who else?"

I opened my calendar to look at my appointments for the first week of April, even though I had it memorized. "When does Janessa want to meet?"

"She said she would work around your schedule since she knows you're probably booked solid." Nigel came bounding over. "Aren't you surprised that she's getting married so suddenly? Didn't Baxter just propose in January? Do you think they're eager to start a family of little Janxters?"

I looked up from my monitor to pin Nigel with an incredulous look. "Janxter?"

"You know, like Bennifer and Brangelina. Janxter is what they call Chicago's favorite couple since Barack and Michelle." Nigel couldn't contain his excitement. "Daytime television's darling and the hottest fucking quarter-something to ever live deserve a power-couple nickname."

"He's a *quarterback* for the Chicago Bears," I told Nigel, shaking my head in disbelief.

"He's fucking fine is what he is," my assistant said.

"He's all right. He's a little young for my taste."

Nigel squinted his eyes and scrutinized my face. "You may not look your age, but you're sure acting it." He started mimicking the use of a walker in front of my desk.

"I'm forty-three, not ninety-three," I reminded him.

"So start acting like a forty-three-year-old for fuck's sake. I half expect you to pull out your cardigan, pipe, and slippers when I come over to your house. Live a little, boss. Read a trashy book, watch reality television, and get caught up on your celebrity gossip."

Ignoring his cracks about my boringness, I said, "I just don't get into all that fuss about celebrities. They're people just like us. I would hate to have my relationships dissected publicly."

"You mean the one with your fist?" Nigel asked.

"Nigel," I said, not bothering to hide my exasperation. "Can we get back to the reason why you barged into my office and interrupted me?"

"Petting your pooch?" he suggested.

"Editing photos for a magazine spread," I replied like I didn't hear his snide comment.

"We're having dinner with Janessa and Baxter next Wednesday at Del Rios."

I felt my right eyebrow arch high on my forehead. "We?"

"I'm your right-hand man who assists you with everything," Nigel said. "You need me."

"Everything?" I could think of a lot of things I did with my right hand that didn't require Nigel's assistance. His face turned an interesting shade of pink as if his mind might've wandered down that same path. Why did he look embarrassed? Wasn't he the one who had brought up masturbation.

"Okay, there are some *personal* things that you take care of on your own, but you need me to go to dinner and take serious notes. You're getting forgetful at your old age and no one, including you, can read your notes."

"I'll use a tablet," I countered.

"Stop being mean, Rush. I'll stop harassing you about your masturbation habit in the office." He batted his eyelashes coquettishly at me. When that failed to win a response, Nigel slammed his hand on my desk and said, "I will slit your throat while you sleep if you don't take me to dinner!"

"Am I interrupting?" asked a voice I recognized all too well. Brutus began to growl until I snapped my fingers. Brutus came to me immediately. Nigel's eyes widened before he stepped aside so I could see my newest visitor. "Maybe I should've called first. I hate to break up the happy couple's discussion about masturbation and slitting-throats afterward. I hadn't heard that's what the kids are into these days."

"Travis," I said, impressed that my voice sounded much calmer than I felt.

"*We're* not a couple, but you always did think something was going on between us," Nigel said defensively. "It's called friendship and respect, jackass. You should give it a try sometime."

I felt the corner of my mouth tip up into a half smile. Nigel was nothing, if not loyal. "Nigel, will you give us a few minutes?" My assistant looked greatly disappointed, but I knew it had more to do with not hearing what Travis came to say. He was the nosiest little shit I'd ever met. I leaned forward and lowered my voice so only he could hear. "I'll tell you everything after he leaves."

"Fine," Nigel replied haughtily. "Every. Single. Word." He pivoted on his heels and exited my office, but not without calling Travis an asshole when he walked by him.

"It's good to see that Nigel hasn't lost any of his spark," Travis said as he slowly made his way toward my desk, his pensive eyes watching the large dog by my side who began to growl again until I placed my hand on the top of his broad head. "I see you've also made a new friend."

"Brutus."

"Perfect name for him."

"What brings you by today, Travis?"

"Um, are you free for lunch? If not today, could we possibly meet later this week?"

"I have about an hour I could spare for you before I need to be at SAIC at one o'clock," I replied.

"Will you?"

My brow furrowed in confusion. "Will I what?"

"You said you 'could spare' an hour and I'm asking if you will," Travis responded.

I had to admit that I didn't miss this part of our relationship. I was sure Travis's clients loved his attention to the tiniest of details, but it wasn't much fun when he analyzed my every word. Still, he had a point. I wanted to tell him to go to hell, but my morbid curiosity wouldn't allow me. "You're buying. I'm in the mood for Italian."

"Of course." He looked at my faithful sidekick who was throwing serious shade his way. "What about him?"

"He loves spaghetti and meatballs as much as I do."

"You want to bring him with us?" Travis sounded truly horrified.

"I do, but I won't. I'll leave Brutus here with Nigel until Gretchen picks him up."

"Who's Gretchen?"

"She's his dog sitter slash walker."

"You have a dog sitter?" Travis asked in utter disbelief.

I didn't care what Travis thought about my arrangement, so I just shrugged. "Are we doing this or not?" I looked at my watch and added, "You're down to fifty-five minutes now."

"Sure, let's go."

The shocked look on Nigel's face when I told him I was going to lunch with Travis was comical. "I'll call you later," I assured him.

"Every. Single. Word," he reminded me.

"You want to ride with me?" Travis asked when we exited my basement office. One of the things I loved most about my brownstone was the basement with a walkout door. I could enter my office from a private entrance from my house while clients and former fiancés used a separate entrance from the street.

"We'll drive separately since I'm heading to class."

"Sure thing," he replied, sounding disappointed.

Once alone in my car, I had to question just what the fuck I was doing. There could only be one reason for Travis reaching out to me again, and I wasn't interested in what he was going to offer. I wasn't so pathetic, hard up, or lonely that I'd set myself up for that kind of humiliation again. *Was I?* Fuck no!

The hostess, Tiffany, must not have received the memo that Travis and I were no longer a couple because she sat us at our favorite table near the back of the restaurant. She didn't bother to leave menus at our table since we were very familiar with everything they offered.

"How are two of my favorite customers?" Roberto asked when he approached our table. "Would you like to hear the lunch specials?"

"No," Travis and I said at the same time.

Roberto chuckled, but I noticed his usual gregarious smile was missing as his eyes stayed locked on Travis. "I didn't realize the two of you got back together." A person had to be blind to miss the tightness around Roberto's mouth. I knew he had always been attracted to Travis, but there seemed to be more going on here, because the waiter acted like he was owed an explanation.

"We're not," I told the waiter, drawing his attention to me. "Just two acquaintances having lunch."

Roberto quirked a brow but didn't vocalize his doubts. "Are you guys having the usual?"

"Yes," Travis said.

"No," I answered at the same time. "I'm just going to have a Caesar salad, Roberto."

"Breadsticks?" he asked me.

"Not today." I felt Travis's eyes on me during my exchange with the waiter.

"On second thought, I'll have the same thing," Travis said.

"Okay, two salads, no breadsticks, and two Diet Cokes," Roberto said. "I'll have your food out to you soon."

I noticed that Travis's eyes lingered on Roberto's ass when he walked away for several seconds before he shifted his gaze to mine. His cheeks turned an interesting shade of pink once he realized I caught him.

"There's no need to look guilty, Travis. You're free to ogle anyone you want."

"Ogling sounds creepy," Travis said sheepishly.

"Okay, you're free to *admire* anyone you want."

"Yeah, I guess so." Travis raised his hand and rubbed the back of his neck like he did when he was unsure of what to say. Then he dropped his hand and drew circles with his index finger on the checkered tablecloth. He stared at his hand for a long time while he worked out what he wanted to say. I only saw these nervous gestures a handful of times in all the years that I knew him. His unease triggered dread in the pit of my stomach. "Watching your figure?" He still hadn't looked up from the table.

"No," I said casually. I too watched Travis's finger circle around and around. It was oddly hypnotic.

Travis finally rested his hand on top of the table and raised his eyes to meet my stare. "Hot date?" What was the emotion that caused his breath to hitch? Regret? Jealousy? Couldn't be. Travis didn't waste energy on pointless emotions. He was a doer, not a feeler.

"No, I'm having dinner with Jules, Will, and Racheal. She's making herb-crusted chicken breasts and fettuccine. I figured I might as well eat a light lunch to balance it out." I leaned forward and gestured my hand back and forth between Travis and me. "What's going on here?"

"I've been doing a lot of thinking…"

"Oh fuck." I rubbed both hands over my face. "No, Travis." There was no point in wasting his time by allowing him to tell me he regretted what happened between us. There could never be an *us* again, especially not after the cowardly way he handled our wedding day.

"You don't even know what I was going to say."

"I can tell by your expression that you didn't bring me here to have closure. You're having second thoughts about breaking up with me."

"You're right. I am. I fucking miss you, Rush. I miss us."

I lowered my hands to the table and just stared at him in shock. I mean, I suspected that was the case, but it was still a shock to hear. A salad plate landed with a loud *thud* in front of me. I jerked my head up and saw Robert staring at Travis through narrowed eyes as he dropped his salad onto the table hard enough that some of the lettuce and croutons bounced off the plate.

"Would either of you like grated Parmesan?" he asked stiffly.

"Uh, no, thanks," I told him, offering a smile when he turned his angry countenance to me.

"That'll be all, Roberto," Travis said angrily.

"What's going on here?" I asked once we were alone again. "Do you have something going on with Roberto?"

"It was just once, and I'm afraid he hoped for more than a casual fling."

"After we broke up?" I asked.

"Of course," Travis seethed. "I was never unfaithful to you, Rush."

"Okay," I said, holding my hands up in surrender. "I saw the way you looked at the guy. I don't think he's the only one still interested."

"He's too young for me," Travis said as he stabbed pieces of salad with a fork.

"He wasn't too young to fuck, but he's too young to date?" I asked incredulously.

"Lower your voice," Travis whisper-yelled across the table.

"It was a really big dick move for you to bring me here knowing he has feelings for you."

Travis rolled his eyes in annoyance as he chewed. "You're the one who insisted on Italian," he said after he swallowed.

"You could've chosen a different restaurant," I pointed out.

"This is our favorite."

"It was, but now I can't come back here again since you pissed off the waitstaff. I don't want Roberto spitting in my food because he thinks we're getting back together again. We're not, you know."

"You haven't even heard what I had to say," Travis said. His calm veneer was cracking and allowing his frustration to show.

"It would be a complete waste of your time."

"Let me decide what's a waste of *my* time," Travis countered.

"Okay," I agreed and tucked back into my salad while Travis talked.

"As I said earlier, I miss you, Rush. Leaving you was the biggest mistake I've ever made. If I could turn back the clock and change things, I would."

"But you can't."

"No, but we could begin again." Travis stretched his hands out across the table, but I didn't meet them halfway. "All I'm asking is for you to give me a second chance." *All?* He was asking for a hell of a lot.

I won't pretend his asking for another chance wasn't a huge boost to my bruised ego, but I wasn't foolish enough to think that we wouldn't find ourselves right back where we were a few months ago. No, it was better this way, even if I was lonely.

"I am sorry," I said, repeating the same three words he used to destroy my hopes for a happy future.

12—Second Wind

LINCOLN

IT TOOK ME THREE MONTHS TO WORK UP MY COURAGE TO COME out to my mom. I knew that doing it over the phone was wrong; I owed her the chance to look into my eyes and tell me what she felt. I hated the thought of losing my only parent, but I just couldn't live under the strain any longer.

Phee, bless her heart, not only kept my secret but discreetly tried to set me up on dates. She quickly learned that out and proud men in their forties weren't interested in dating closeted men unless it was just for sex. They especially didn't know how to react to the closeted man's ex-wife playing matchmaker. There were many places in Southern California that I could go if I just wanted sex, but I wanted something meaningful that touched my soul. I'd experienced that once, and I had to believe I could find it again. I knew I'd never find the happiness I sought if I continued to lie—even by omission—to the people I loved. I wasn't as close to my mom as I wanted to be, but maybe it was because she didn't know the real me. I had to give it a shot.

I waited until after my childhood home sold then flew to Tennessee on a Friday morning in June to help my mom move into her new condo at the retirement community. There was a lightness to her that I'd never seen before once she was inside her new space. Although I regretted my father's passing, it warmed my heart to see her smile easier than she had the last time I saw her. Mom focused her attention on unpacking boxes to set up her new kitchen. I arranged her furniture and hung pictures and art on the walls wherever she wanted them, never once complaining when she wanted me to move them a little to the right or a little to the left.

My easy acquiescence wasn't just from my guilt that I might ruin her newfound happiness either. It was the first time that I felt like I was seeing Lillian Huxley and not Thomas's wife or Lincoln's mother. I loved how excited she was about the activities at the clubhouse and the new neighbors she had met. I wanted to tease her about eligible bachelors, but it was too soon.

My mom, on the other hand, didn't have a problem prying into my personal life. "Are you seeing anyone?" she asked over dinner.

"Not right now," I answered as I speared the piece of steak I'd just cut. "I've been too busy at work." It was the same excuse I used to avoid anything I didn't want to do.

"You need to make time," she said. "Ophelia sure does."

"Mom," I said in a warning tone. "All I want is for Phee to be happy."

"That's all I want for you too." She smiled sweetly at me across the table. "I'd love for you to meet a nice girl and…" Her voice trailed off. I figured my facial expression mirrored the emotional upheaval occurring inside of me. "Lincoln, what is it?"

"What if I want to meet a nice guy instead?"

Mom didn't say anything, didn't even move except to blink. She just sat there with her fork suspended in the air. When she closed her eyes briefly, I wondered if it was because she couldn't look at me any longer. Tears seeped from the corners of her eyes and ran down her cheeks.

"Mom, I…" My voice broke; I couldn't say anything else.

My mom slowly opened her eyes and set her fork down. I was relieved that I didn't see disgust in her eyes, but she couldn't hide her sadness.

"I think I always knew," she finally said. "How could I not see how crazy you were about Rush? The two of you were inseparable in ways that extended beyond friendship. I knew it then but was afraid for you. I prayed every night that I was wrong and that your father would never find out. God seemed to answer my prayers when you met Ophelia the first week of college." She paused and swallowed hard. "It wasn't real though, was it? You were trying to live a life not meant for you. That was so wrong of me, Lincoln." Mom reached for my hands across the table; I met her halfway. "I should've never prayed for something so cruel, but I can't regret my beautiful grand-babies. You're a remarkable father, Lincoln. I'm so proud of you."

"I'll never regret them either. Kennedy and Holden are my heart and soul, Mom," I said in a raspy voice as tears streamed down my face. "Or Ophelia. She's my best friend, and I can't imagine a world without her. So, instead of us wasting time on regrets, let's just say that things worked out the way they were intended to all along. We can't turn back the clock, but we can make sure we never repeat past mistakes. How does that sound?"

"I think a hug is in order," Mom said. I rounded the table and held her tight as silent, grateful tears continued to fall. I wasn't foolish enough to believe that my news would've received the same amount of acceptance when I was younger, but I meant what I said about not wasting precious time on regrets. "So, have you met any nice guys?" she asked against my chest.

I pulled back and looked into her smiling eyes. "Not yet. I decided that I needed to come clean to you and the kids first."

"Ophelia knows?"

"Yeah, she found out the weekend we came home for the funeral." Then I told my mom about Granddad's ammo box and the keepsakes it held. "Phee took one look at the photos and knew my secret."

"She took it well, I assume."

"Yeah, but I think it helped that she was already smitten with Jackson," I teased. "She just wants to see me happy."

"That's all anyone will want for you, including Kennedy and Holden." My mom tipped her head to the side. "Does Phee know that you named your son after your first love?"

"She does now," I said sheepishly. "I'm glad she wasn't upset. I tried to be a good husband to her, I really did."

"No regrets," my mom said before patting my face. "Remember that."

After dinner, I decided to tackle all my demons by visiting my favorite haunts as a kid. Scoops was packed, so I drove on out to the high school. Not much had changed since I moved away, except that the football field was turf instead of the natural grass I played on. I climbed the old concrete stadium steps and sat down at the fifty-yard line. I closed my eyes and was transported back in time to when I was the king of the gridiron, leading my team to two consecutive state championships. I heard the roar of the crowd, the marching band playing our fight song, and felt the eyes of the town on me as I took my position on the field. There was only one pair of eyes that I cared about though. I knew that Rush was standing somewhere on the sidelines taking pictures for the school paper and the yearbook. I felt his focus, and it made me strut a little bit more after each touchdown.

Thoughts of the victories reminded me of the way we celebrated—hot kisses, even hotter touches, and one of us buried deep inside the other. Nothing in my life had ever felt so right, and I realized I still hadn't been truthful with my mom. I had one regret: Rush. I regretted letting him get away from me and never knowing what became of him. I regretted that I never let him know how much he meant to me. Even years later, he was the one person I could never forget, no matter how much time had passed or how hard I tried. Lord knows I gave it my best, but Rush would come to me in the quietest or scariest moments. I would remember to be brave like him. I could've easily tracked him down with modern technology, but I didn't feel that I had the right. I also knew that I couldn't stomach seeing him happy with someone else. How fucking unfair was that? I went on to have a life without him; I couldn't expect him to wait twenty-six fucking years for me to get my head out of my ass.

I stopped by Scoops and picked up two strawberry milkshakes to take back to my mom's condo. I planned to crash on her couch for the night and begin the drive to Chicago early the next morning in the rental I picked up at the airport. I could've flown into O'Hare, but I thought the road trip might do me some good, not to mention, delay the awkward conversation I planned to have with my kids.

Even though Scoops was still busy, it was a younger crowd and no one there seemed to recognize me. I was relieved because I wasn't in the mood for small talk and catching up since I wanted to get an early start. I had just about made it back to my car when I heard someone calling my name. It was a voice I'd never forget. I turned and looked into the eyes of the man I owed my success to, in one way or another.

"Coach Holden," I said, plastering a fake smile on my face. He was the last person I wanted to see. "How are you, sir?"

"Fit as a fiddle," he said then his face sobered. "I was truly sorry to hear about your daddy. Alice and I were away on a ten-day anniversary cruise and didn't return until after his funeral. He was a good man, Lincoln."

"Thank you, Coach." I wasn't sure what else to say to the man. I hadn't talked to him since I graduated college and the silence between us felt awkward. I held up my hands to show the milkshakes.

"A little treat for my mom. I helped her move into her new condo today."

"You're such a good son. Too bad they're not all like you." His voice dripped with bitterness and disgust.

My heart sank because I knew he was talking about Rush. I'd heard the scuttlebutt the first time I came home from college. Rush and Jules left town and never looked back. My parents refrained from commenting out of respect for my friendship with Rush, but a few of my old high school teammates had no problem flapping their gums. The man who stood in front of me supposedly told Rush that he'd rather his son die than be gay. I had no way of knowing if it was true, but I wouldn't put it past the man.

I stood up straighter, towering over the older man. "Some parents don't deserve the kids God blessed them with either. Some kids are better off to leave town and never look back. Goodnight, Coach." I left him standing there staring at me with a shocked expression on his face. No one ever dared to talk back to the mean son of a bitch. I fumed all the way back to my mom's house, thinking of all the other things I should've said to him.

My mom was waiting for me when I walked through the door. "Oh, a milkshake. Please tell me it's strawberry."

"I haven't forgotten," I told her.

"What's wrong?" Mom's brow furrowed into a deep V as she looked at me. "I've seen thunderstorms that were tamer than the expression you're wearing on your face right now."

I recalled my encounter with the coach for my mom and repeated what I'd heard all those years ago about Rush and Jules.

"It's true," my mom said softly. "Alice told me herself. I don't think she ever got over it."

"She must not be too torn up about it if she's taking cruises," I tossed out there.

"I think she's doing the best she can to cope, Linc. You saw how domineering your father could be at times, and Butch Holden was a thousand times worse. I can't imagine what it must've been like for Rush to live under his roof."

"Who does he think he is discarding his kids then daring to bitch about them?"

"He's not a good man, but I don't think your father would've been much different. I want to say that I would've stood up for you and told your father to go to hell, but I just don't know. God, I can't stand the thought of losing you like that."

I pulled my mom tight against me and rested my chin on her head, uncaring that our milkshakes were rapidly melting. "Shhh, Mom. Let's not waste precious time on what might've been. We're okay now, and that's what matters."

"Okay," she said tearfully. "I know that you're right."

We ended up eating popcorn and watching reruns of *Magnum PI* for a few hours before we both got too tired to keep our eyes open after the long day.

"I had such a crush on Magnum," my mom said.

"So did I."

We burst into a fit of giggles at my confession. "Well, at least you have good taste in men."

"We'll see if that still holds true," I said.

"Have faith, my son."

I left my mom's house at five the next morning to get a jump on my nearly five-hundred-and-forty-mile journey. I didn't want to wake her, so I left her a long, heartfelt note about how much I loved her and appreciated her support, ending the letter with *no regrets*. The drive was supposed to take just over eight hours, but it ended up taking closer to ten due to car accidents and traffic jams.

I hadn't bothered calling the kids ahead of time because I didn't want them to freak out. The last time I showed up unannounced was when Phee and I told them we were getting a divorce. My news would be equally as big, but there was no need to stress them out before I even arrived.

I booked a room at the Ritz Carlton and planned to order room service and crash early. Once in my room, I couldn't tear my eyes off the Centennial Wheel on the pier. I couldn't look at any Ferris wheel without thinking about Rush and remembering the moment I knew what love and bravery were all about.

I suddenly felt an invisible pull to go to the pier and ride the damn thing. No, Rush wouldn't be with me in person, but the memory of him would be. I walked the short distance and bought tickets for the Centennial Wheel. The pier was packed with families and friends just looking to have a good time and enjoy the beautiful June weather before the serious humidity hit later in the month.

I felt a little silly as I approached the long line by myself, but I passed the time by texting Phee and checking my email. The line had suddenly stopped advancing, and I wondered if the ride broke down or something. Then I heard the chatter about newlyweds posing for photos with the grand Ferris wheel in the background.

"Look how handsome the grooms look," someone said.

"It so good that people don't have to hide any longer," another person added.

I stepped out of line to see for myself, and my heart thudded to a stop in my chest before it raced with recognition. It wasn't the grooms that held me spellbound; it was the photographer. I'd know that stance anywhere because I sure as hell had seen it enough times growing up. The camera he held in his hand was a lot different and more expensive than the ones he used to own, but the way he stood and cradled it like a rare treasure was all the same. *Rush!* But how was this possible? My mind had to be playing tricks on me. This moment was nothing but a fantasy brought on by all the trips down memory lane I'd made the past twenty-four hours. I would wake up to find that I fell asleep in the hotel room instead of walking to the pier.

There was no way in hell that Rush, *my Rush,* was a few hundred feet away from me. It had to be someone who resembled him. The photographer turned around and smiled at something his assistant said to him. I started walking toward him without stopping to think if I should. For the first time in more than twenty-six years, my world felt right. *My Rush.*

It felt like I'd caught my second wind.

13—In Your Eyes

Rush

"U M, DON'T LOOK NOW, BUT SOME HOTTIE IS HEADING toward us with a determined look in his eyes," Nigel said.

"He's not packing a weapon, is he?"

"What's your definition of a weapon?" Nigel asked suggestively.

"The lethal kind." The intrigue I heard in my assistant's voice made me curious, so I glanced up to check out the situation. My breath caught in my throat when I looked into familiar dark eyes. "I don't fucking believe it." I had to be dreaming, but my racing heart told me it was real. Fate wouldn't be that cruel to me. I handed my camera to Nigel before I dropped it.

My obligations were temporarily forgotten as I walked to Lincoln with joyful laughter spilling out of me. He opened his arms wide, and I landed hard against his broad chest. I circled my arms around his waist at the same time those strong arms wrapped around my shoulders.

"I can't believe it," we said at the same time then laughed like we did when we were kids. And if that wasn't enough, we both said, "Jinx."

"Okay, now it's getting ridiculous," I teased.

"What's ridiculous is that it's taken me more than two decades to see you again," Lincoln countered.

I pulled back enough to look into Lincoln's warm gaze and welcoming smile. I closed my eyes against the swiftly rising emotions that threatened to consume me and rob me of the ability to speak. I pressed my forehead against his and said, "It has been too many years, but my heart would recognize you anywhere, Linc."

"As would mine," Lincoln said huskily. He chuckled then pulled back from me slightly. "Perhaps I should've asked permission to hug you instead of mauling you."

"I pretty much launched myself into your arms, so I obviously welcomed your robust greeting."

The rest of the world was all but forgotten as we stood there staring into each other's eyes and smiling like goons. Nothing had felt so right since the last time Linc held me in his arms and slowly spun me around that empty classroom. Jesus, I hoped our parting was so much sweeter than it was the last time.

"Um, excuse me," Nigel said from behind me. "I hate to break this up, but the grooms have a reception to get to."

Lincoln reluctantly lowered his arms. I turned to face my assistant without putting too much space between us. I wanted to feel his body heat radiating off him even though it was eighty-five degrees. I found it comforting and familiar, not stifling. I just found Lincoln again and couldn't stand the thought of parting from him already.

"Hey, you take care of what you need to, and we'll meet up later. That's if you want to, I mean," Lincoln added, sounding uncertain.

"He does," Nigel said.

"I do," I confirmed. Nigel stood looking expectantly between the two of us. I could tell he wanted an introduction, but I decided to torture him a little longer. "I'll be tied up for the next hour or so, but I can meet you for dinner afterward."

"Sounds great. Where do you want to meet?"

"There's a diner called Jenn's just down the way," I pointed down the pier. "She makes the most incredible lasagna with sliced home-made meatballs in between the layers." I looked at my watch and saw that it was almost four thirty. "I'm thinking no later than six thirty, but I can text or call if I finish earlier."

"Sounds perfect," Lincoln said.

We exchanged phone numbers and hugged once more. Neither of us wanted to let go, so we held tight to each other until Nigel cleared his throat impatiently. Without thinking, I pressed my lips to Lincoln's for a brief kiss. For all I knew, he could've been married or in a relationship. His eyes darkened with desire just like always, and I had to leave while I still could.

"See you soon, Linc."

"You can count on it," he said as I walked away.

"He's not wearing a ring," Nigel said out of the blue. "In case you were worried that you publicly mauled someone else's man." There was no censure in his voice, only joy. "Are you going to tell me who he is?"

"Nope," I teased. Nigel knew almost everything about my life, both past and present, but I'd never told him about Linc.

"Okay," he said calmly, which should've worried me. Nigel was the kind of person that had to know everything about everyone. Seconds later, I heard him ask, "Who was this Lincoln guy your brother was sucking face with at the pier when he was supposed to be taking wedding photos?"

I turned my head fast enough to get a crick in my neck. *That little shit!*

"Whaaaat?" I heard Jules yell through the phone. "Lincoln?"

"Give me that." I yanked the phone from Nigel's hand.

"What did he look like?" Jules asked, thinking she was still talking to Nigel.

"Tall, dark, and very handsome," I said. "He has a little gray at his temples and in his beard. Just fucking delicious."

"Oh, Rush. Is it really him?" I heard the happy tears in her voice.

"It is, Jules. I couldn't believe it when I looked up and saw Lincoln walking toward me."

"Sucking face? You don't waste any time, little bro."

"Jules, it was one chaste peck on the lips."

"What's Linc doing here?"

"I don't know," I replied. "I didn't have time to ask."

"You were too busy hugging and making moony eyes at each other," Nigel said loud enough for Jules to hear too.

"Moony eyes?" Jules and I both asked.

"I'm meeting Linc after I finish this job." I didn't tell my sister where because I knew she'd hightail it downtown and crash our dinner… plans. I wasn't sure the word date would apply since I knew nothing about Lincoln's situation. I glared at Nigel and dared him to rat me out. He looked at me with wide-eyed innocence, but I wasn't falling for his crap.

"Honey, I'm so happy for you."

"It's dinner, Jules."

"It's so much more, and you know it. Grab hold of Linc with both hands and don't let go this time."

"Um, I think that's a felony in all fifty states," I said casually although my heart and mind raced with the possibilities. It was a huge moment and no amount of downplaying it would change the way I felt. "I'll call you in the morning."

"After *he* leaves," Nigel added. *From Nigel's mouth to the universe's ears!*

I disconnected the call and handed the phone back to Nigel. "So,

Lincoln is an old flame?"

"I need to focus right now, Nigel. I promise I'll tell you all about him later."

"Fine," Nigel said dramatically, "but I expect you to call me as soon as you finish talking to Jules."

"Deal."

I passionately loved capturing all the wonderful moments of my clients' special day for them to cherish for the rest of their lives. I had never felt impatient or irritated by the sometimes-demanding wedding party, or their families, until I knew Lincoln was waiting on me. What should've lasted for an hour to ninety minutes pushed well past two, which made me late meeting Lincoln. I nervously texted him a few times to let him know I was running behind, and he gave me the same reply each time.

Take your time. I'm not going anywhere.

Regardless of his assurance, I half expected him not to be there when I finally announced that I was on my way. I stowed my equipment in my SUV and headed to meet him at Jenn's. I stood at the door, closed my eyes, and sucked air into my lungs to calm my freaking nerves and racing heart.

Inside that diner is the one guy you never got over. Like I needed a reminder. *Just breathe.*

When I opened my eyes, Lincoln stood looking at me through the glass. He gave me that crooked smile that I loved so much. It showed me that he was nervous too, which gave me the courage to finally open the door.

"I worried you were going to bolt," Lincoln said huskily, reaching for my hand.

"I thought I dreamt you here."

I went into his arms again, not giving a fuck about anyone

around us. God, he smelled and felt so fucking good—both familiar and different at the same time. I felt tears burning behind my closed eyelids and knew I had to rein myself in. I'd save that for a private meeting if we had one.

"I feel it too, Rush," he whispered before he pulled back. "You must be starving."

"Oh, I am." I hungered for more than just food. I'd been starving for him since we parted. I don't think I realized just how much I had missed him until that moment.

"Let's get a bite to eat and catch up a little." *And see where this goes.*

I followed Lincoln to a booth in the far corner of the diner, as-suring us a little bit of privacy. "I don't quite know where to begin," I told him honestly. "Let's start with what brought you to town."

There was a pregnant pause before he said, "I'm making a sur-prise visit to my kids."

He knocked the air out of me just like the time that I crashed Jules's bike. "Kids?" I croaked out.

"I'm not married," Lincoln assured me. "Well, not anymore. Phee and I got divorced earlier this year. Both of our children attend colleges here, so I dropped by to tell them something important." He ran his finger along his collar nervously, but never took his eyes from mine. Damn, I wanted to stare into those eyes for-fucking-ever.

"What will it be, fellas?" the waitress asked when she ap-proached the table.

What I wanted couldn't be found on any menu, but my growl-ing stomach reminded me that I hadn't eaten since early that morn-ing. Still, my hunger for the man staring into my eyes rivaled that of my stomach, and I wasn't sure which appetite to feed first. It didn't matter that decades and God knew how many miles separated us; my need for him was still there. "Could you give us a few minutes?"

"Sure, honey."

"Maybe we should've had this reunion in a more private

setting," I said sheepishly.

"That can still be arranged."

It would've been easy to fall into bed with this man, but I couldn't survive him breaking my heart again. Jumping into sex with Linc too fast could be a recipe for self-destruction.

"Or not," Lincoln said when he saw my hesitation.

"Let's just have some dinner and see what happens."

Lincoln nodded his head. "Fair enough."

When the waitress returned, we placed our order and resumed talking. "So, I see that Southern fried foods are still your favorites." I ordered Jenn's famous lasagna that made my mouth water.

"I doubt very much that this fried chicken and gravy can hold a candle to my mama's," Linc said.

"You might be surprised," I told him. "How is Lillian?"

"She's doing better." When I quirked my brow, he went on to explain that his father had passed away earlier in the year, and he'd just helped her move into her new condo.

"I'm so sorry to hear about your dad, Linc."

"Thank you, it was a huge shock." He took a big gulp of his soda, running his finger up and down the glass. I watched the trail he made through the condensation and wanted to feel that same finger bump along my spine again. "We talked about you a lot yesterday. Were your ears burning?"

"Me?"

"Mmm-hmmm." One corner of his mouth tipped up in a sly grin. "It turns out that my mom was onto us all those years ago. She hadn't been prepared to hear the truth back then, and I doubt my father ever would've been ready, but it felt so good to be honest with her now."

"You just came out to your mom? This weekend?"

"Yeah," he said softly. "Ophelia, my ex-wife, has known for a few months, but I just now told my mom." Lincoln swallowed hard and said, "That's why I'm here in Chicago. I need my kids to know the real me."

"They do know the real you," I told him. "Maybe just not this one part of you. Your sexuality doesn't define who you are, Linc."

"I'm not sure how they're going to take it, but…"

I reached across the table and laid my hands on top of Lincoln's when his words trailed off. "Kids are more open now," I told him. "Of course, they're going to be surprised, but give them time. I know they'll come around."

Lincoln laughed and asked, "How could you possibly know that?"

"Because they're *your* kids, and I bet they're amazing young adults." I gave his hands an extra squeeze before I pulled away. The situation with Lincoln was pretty complicated. I wasn't sure how much I wanted to get involved with him, beyond friendship, until he had it all sorted out. Then he turned his full, megawatt smile on me and my resistance melted. It might be the dumbest thing I ever did, but I wasn't about to let Lincoln leave town without lying naked in his arms once more. Unless… "Does that mean you're seeing someone? Is that why you're taking the big leap?"

"I wouldn't be looking at you like this if I was seeing someone, Rush."

"How are you looking at me?" I teased, feeling more lighthearted than I had in years.

"Like I would prefer to make a meal out of you instead of fried chicken."

"We call that dessert, sweetheart," the waitress said as she returned to our table. "You sure you don't want me to box these to go?"

It was on the tip of my tongue to say yes, but I wanted more assurance from Lincoln that I wasn't about to figuratively slit my wrists and bleed for him all over again.

"We're good," Lincoln told her with an easy smile. She set our plates in front of us and left. "I'm coming out to my family because it's the right thing to do. I won't regret my children, because I love them more than anything, but for the first time in my life, I want to live for me."

"I'm proud of you," I said, earning a scoff. "What? I am."

"You're the brave one," Lincoln said. "My mom told me how your parents reacted when you came out to them. I'm sorry, Rush."

"First of all, staying in the closet isn't a cowardly act, Linc. It's great that some people have supportive families, open-minded employers, and live in welcoming communities, but that's not the reality for most. For some, coming out can even be a life-or-death decision. That should never be taken lightly, and you should be proud that you're able to step out now. Don't let anyone make you feel ashamed." I took a steadying breath. "As for my family, it's all water under the bridge. It was hard at first, but Jules and I got by. We shared an apartment and worked odd jobs while attending community college. We made ends meet the best we could. We had each other, and that's what mattered the most."

"How is Jules?"

"She hasn't changed much," I replied. "She looks at least ten years younger than her true age."

"It must run in the family," Linc said, his eyes roaming all over my face. "Your body is obviously more filled out than the last time I saw you, but you don't have a single gray hair and you look like you're twenty-eight instead of almost forty-four. I'd like to know your secret."

"I try to eat right and take care of myself, but that's it. I didn't find a miracle drug or drink." I let my eyes roam freely over his face. I loved the crow's feet by his eyes and lines around his mouth, it meant that he laughed a lot. Lincoln's happiness was always important to me. My fingers itched to run over his facial hair to see if it was as soft as it looked. I wanted to feel it against other parts of my body too.

"I look old and gray in comparison," he said softly, sounding insecure.

"You look sexy as fuck." That got his attention and made him sit straighter in the chair. "That touch of gray looks good on you, Linc. You're bigger and stronger than you were the last time I saw you. How often do you work out?"

"Six days a week," he replied. "It helps me manage stress."

"How long are you in town for?"

"That depends on you," Linc replied.

I arched a brow in surprise. "You can just take off as much time as you need?"

"I'm my own boss for the most part. I had planned to take a few more days off, but I could stretch that out for longer. If you were interested in having me hang around the city that is."

"I'm interested." Life was about taking risks, and taking Linc home was a big one. He could destroy me, or we could finally have the life we dreamed about when we were teenagers. There really wasn't much to decide. I signaled for the waitress to bring those boxes after all. We had barely touched our food, and I had a feeling we might be a lot hungrier later.

"I still see the boy I loved so much when I look in your eyes. I really want to learn about the man you've become, Linc."

"I want that too."

"Your place or mine?" I asked him.

"I want to be in your space, Rush." *Oh lord, that could be taken so many ways, all of them really fucking good.*

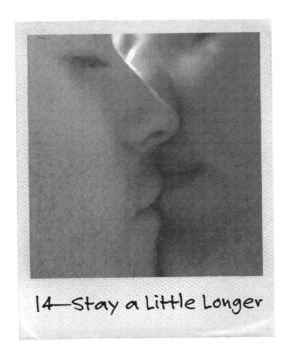

14—Stay a Little Longer

Lincoln

"I s there anything you need from your hotel?" Rush asked after we left the diner. It sounded like he didn't expect me to return to my room anytime soon.

I looked at him with a quirked brow.

"That sounded pretty bold, didn't it?" He tilted his head back and laughed, but it didn't disguise his nervousness. "Jules told me to grab hold of you with both hands and not let go." *Damn, that sounded good to me.* "But I want you in my home because *you* want to be there and for no other reason."

"Jules knows I'm here?"

"Thanks to Nigel." Rush proceeded to tell me about Nigel calling Jules for the skinny when he refused to divulge anything about our past. "I have to remind him at least three times a day that I'm the boss and not the other way around."

"He must really care about you." I only saw curiosity in Nigel's eyes when he looked at me on the pier, not the jealousy of a lover, or someone who wanted that role in Rush's life.

"He does," Rush agreed. "Some might say he cares about me too much." Then he realized how that sounded and shook his head. "Not like in a sexual or relationship way," he clarified quickly. "More like he thinks I need mothered, as if my sister doesn't do enough of that. Then there's Kent."

"Who's he?" *Wow, I sounded all growly.*

Rush stopped at a sleek, charcoal-gray SUV and turned to face me. "I kind of like this knuckle-dragging thing you got going on."

"Sorry, I have no right to act like a possessive beast." I wanted the right though.

"Kent is Nigel's husband," Rush explained as he hit a button on a key fob to unlock the doors for us. "He has this friend who created a dating app for gay men who are interested in real relationships and not just hookups."

"They sound like Phee," I joked. It was Rush's turn to raise a brow. "She's been trying to set me up on dates too."

Rush started the car and said, "You guys must have a really special relationship. I'm not sure I could try to fix an ex up with someone else." He tipped his head to the side for a minute. "On second thought, I did try that recently."

"Ophelia is my best friend and the mother of my children. I love her dearly. I just couldn't love her like she deserved. No matter how hard I tried, I felt like a fraud. She's met someone who really makes her happy, and she wants the same for me."

"That's great, Linc," he said, backing out of his parking space.

"So what about this app? I don't think I've heard of it."

"It's in the testing phase of development. There are about a thousand guinea pigs in or around Chicago who're trying this damn thing out," I explained.

"You're one of them?" I had no right to be disappointed. It wasn't like I had saved myself for him all these years. "How's that working out for you?"

"Horribly," Rush admitted. I should not have been so happy about his misery. "I told them that I wasn't doing it anymore. Good God." He proceeded to tell me about the conversations he's had with Kent Clark—what were his parents thinking—and the developers. "I swear to God, I'd rather die a lonely man than rely on that app to find Mr. Right for me."

I wanted to say that I was his Mr. Right. But that was ridiculous, we hadn't seen each other in a very long time and both of us had most likely changed a lot. Sure, the attraction was just as hot as it ever was, but I wasn't some randy kid looking to get off. Even if our emotional connection was as strong as ever, I lived and worked nearly two thousand miles away. The reality of the situation creeped in and burst my euphoric bubble. Were we just setting ourselves up for more heartache?

Rush reached over and patted my leg just beneath the hem of my khaki shorts. I wondered if he noticed that I'd changed clothes since we parted. I felt gross after traveling all day and a hot shower awakened me. *All of me.* "Nothing has to happen, Linc. We can just use tonight to talk and be together. I'm so fucking happy to see you again. That's enough for me." I prepared my body for more than just talk, not that I had any expectations.

My skin burned and tingled from the skin-on-skin contact. Instead of removing his hand, Rush squeezed the muscle. I bit my lip to keep from moaning as my dick hardened. It had always been like that with him. One simple touch and I was ready to fuck, but we both deserved better.

Before I could respond, my cell phone rang. I leaned over to the left, so I could pull it from my right, rear pocket. Rush used that opportunity to slide his hand beneath the fabric of my shorts a few inches. No matter what either of us said, we both knew exactly where we were heading that night.

Seeing my mom's name on the caller ID screen cooled my ardor some, but didn't extinguish it fully. "Hey, Mom."

"I assume you've made it to Chicago by now," she said dryly.

"Oh shit! I'm sorry I didn't call you. I ran into an old friend as soon as I arrived, and I just lost track of time."

"Old friend?"

"Hello, Mrs. Huxley," Rush said.

"Lincoln, is that Rush?" she asked in disbelief.

"Sure is."

"Oh my! I think fate is trying to tell you something, love." Although it seemed silly to wish it were so, I couldn't stop myself from hoping she was right.

"I'm sorry for worrying you, Mom. I'll call you tomorrow."

"I love you, Lincoln."

"Love you too."

I was quiet for several moments after I disconnected the call. Rush must've taken my silence as having second thoughts because he removed his hand and placed it back on the steering wheel. I missed his touch immediately.

"I am having second thoughts, Rush, but not about us." I swallowed hard and looked over at him. He kept his eyes on the road, but his body visibly relaxed as tension faded from him. "Never about us."

Rush looked over at me once we reached a traffic light. Not only did I have his eyes on me, his hand returned to my leg. When he turned back to watch the light, his hand remained. I felt branded by him, and I loved it so fucking much.

"Linc, I want to tell you that the world has changed and it will be much easier for you now. It's true that we live in a more open time, but it's still hard as hell."

"Especially when you've pretended to be straight for forty-four years," I said dryly.

"You don't just come out once, Linc. You come out every single time you meet someone new, or when a person tries to set you up with a woman. There will always be a time when a colleague or business associate mentions bringing a girlfriend to an event. People haven't stopped making assumptions about us based on our gender yet. They see a male and think he needs a woman. In every instance, you relive that fear of rejection. It does get easier with time, and you do start to care less about people's opinion, but it never completely goes away. You ask yourself if you'll lose business or friends over it. Sadly, the answer is yes. If you can accept that, then you're going to be okay."

I thought of all the acquaintances that Phee and I made over the years. They were never my friends because I made no attempt to let them know the real me. There wasn't a single out and proud gay man or woman in our inner circle. I had Phee in my corner, but it would be nice to have a confidant who understood the struggles I faced.

My eyes roamed over Rush's profile. I didn't realize how much I truly missed our connection until the moment I held him in my arms again. It was so much more than the desire that raged through my body too. I felt whole again. "I don't need easy, Rush; I need real. My entire life feels like a fraud."

"You haven't been living a lie and you're not a fraud, but only time will prove that to you." His grip tightened on my leg once more then he pulled it back to parallel park in front of a stately-looking brownstone. "This is home sweet home for me," he said when he put the car in park.

"It's truly lovely." The realtor in me couldn't help but admire the architectural beauty of the ornate home. Phee specialized in modern homes, while I passionately loved older ones. Of course, Chicago was known for its brownstones and deep-dish pizza. I was a huge fan of both. "Damn, those corbels are stunning."

"What's a corbel?" Rush asked.

"Those beautiful stone structures supporting the porch over the front door," I said in awe. "I don't see them like that in California."

"Is that where you live?"

I nodded and said, "San Diego." Then we exchanged grins. "We have a lot to learn about each other, don't we?"

"I plan to enjoy every second of it," Rush said breathlessly. "I had planned to do this once we were inside, but I can't wait any longer." I recognized that look; he was going to kiss me. We released our seatbelts and met each other halfway. Instead of kissing me, Rush traced my lips with his index finger. "Regardless of what happens tonight, I definitely want you to stay in town a little longer. You might find that we don't connect the way—"

His words died in his throat when I nipped his finger, but he gasped in delight when I sucked the digit into my mouth to soothe it. "Our chemistry is off the charts, and you know it. Hell, everyone on the pier could see and feel it too."

"That didn't bother you?" Rush asked softly.

"You know, I never thought about it. I just acted on instinct." I cupped his jaw with my hand. "I saw you, and it was like these past twenty-six years without you didn't exist. There was just you and me like it used to be. Never in my life have I met anyone who makes me feel the way you did, and still do, Rush."

"Linc, we need to get inside my house now before we're arrested for public indecency or some shit."

"Okay," I said, unable to look away from his mouth.

Rush wrapped his hand around my wrist then turned his face and kissed my palm before he pulled free. I felt that brief touch in every part of my body. His green eyes darkened with heat and promise. "Come inside with me, Linc." Rush got out of his SUV without another word because he saw the answer in my eyes. If that wasn't enough, I eagerly met him on the sidewalk in front of his brownstone. Somehow, I remembered to grab our carryout bags from the floorboard.

I admired Rush's taut ass as I followed him up the steps, imagining all the things I wanted to do to it. Squeeze it, bite it, and bury my dick inside it were the top three contenders, and I even imagined them in the proper order. My mouth was salivating by the time Rush unlocked his front door, but that cooled a bit when I heard the ferocious barking coming from inside the house. I gulped as the sound of clicking toenails on the hardwood floors got louder as the beast that shared a home with Rush got closer.

"Where's my boy?" Rush called out.

Right here. Right here.

The dark-gray pit bull rounded the corner at the end of the hallway and ran full throttle to his master. Rush dropped to his knees to hug his dog, and I tried my best not to get jealous. "I missed you too, Brutus. Have you been a good boy for Gretchen today?"

Brutus focused solely on his master, other than a brief look in my direction. He responded to Rush's question with a short bark.

"I knew it," he said to his dog. "You're the best boy in the world." Brutus finally looked away from his master's adoration to give me his best doggie smile.

"Hey there, big guy." I'd always wanted a dog, but my dad was highly allergic and Phee always felt we weren't home enough to own one, which limited my pets as a child and an adult. I extended my hand and approached slowly. "You sure are a handsome boy."

"Thank you," Rush said jokingly as he rose to his feet. "This is my best boy, Brutus. He was a gift to myself after a bad breakup."

"That guy was a fool."

Rush grinned up at me. "You don't even know the circumstances. How do you know I wasn't the asshole that caused the misery?"

"I know you," I said, cupping his face once more while Brutus sniffed the plastic bag of goodies I held in my hand. "It doesn't matter how much time has passed, I know one thing that has remained constant: you are all that is right and good in the world." Rush blushed prettily, and I longed to see him flushed everywhere. "I haven't forgotten about the way your body blushes either."

"Food," Rush said abruptly, "then I need to shower." He narrowed his eyes at me when my grin stretched across my face. "Pretty sure of yourself aren't you."

I glanced down to where his dick pressed against his jeans and grinned broadly. "I've been just as hard since we climbed into the car." Hell, I'd even rubbed one out in the shower at my hotel to take the edge off so I didn't embarrass myself if I was given the opportunity to get naked with him again. I was pretty sure that Rush would expect me to have better staying power than I did when I was a randy kid loving him for the first time.

I dropped the bag on the hardwood floor and pushed Rush against a set of ornate doors that most likely led to a study or living room. I no longer cared about putting anything in my mouth except his cock and balls.

"Linc," Rush practically purred, rubbing himself against me and sending flames of lust down my spine to zap my balls. "Is this fucking real?"

I nipped his bottom lip hard enough to make him gasp. "Fuck yes, it's real. I'm not going to second guess my good fortune or overthink the situation. I'm going to react." If I wasn't careful, I'd *react* too fucking soon.

Rush groaned as I continued to rub our erections together through our clothes. "Upstairs. Now."

He slid out from under me and raced up the steps two at a time. Running fast had been his specialty, but he was better at long distances. I was the one with explosive starting speed. I caught him before he reached the top of the stairs, but I didn't tackle him to the ground. I wrapped both my arms around him and lowered one hand to cup his bulge while I pressed my dick against his ass.

"I want to feel this inside me, Rush," I growled in his ear as I stroked his cock. Shouldn't there have been some kind of hesitation on my part? I hadn't been with another guy since him, but all I felt was a need strong enough to drive me to my knees to beg.

Rush pushed his ass against my hard-on, and I thought I was going to blow. Perhaps waiting for him to take a shower was a good idea so I could get myself under control. "I want to feel you too." We'd always taken turns topping, so it didn't surprise me that he was just as eager to have my dick stretch and fill him.

Rush pulled from my embrace and led me down the hallway to a set of elegant double doors made from a luxurious, dark wood. I wanted to explore his gorgeous home after I could think about something other than getting him naked. Once inside his room, I couldn't help but stop and stare at the setup. Rush's bed was a glorious four-poster bed that took up a significant portion of the room, but it wasn't the bed itself that took my breath away. It was the view I'd have if he left the double doors to the bathroom open while he prepared his body for mine.

"Oh fuck," I uttered in a stunned voice. "That's a large, glass shower."

"I spent a lot of money modernizing this house," he said proudly. "I tried to stay within the traditional architecture and design, but I got carried away with the bathroom." Rush turned to me and tugged the hem of my polo shirt loose from the waistband of my shorts. "I want you naked and on the center of my bed where I can see you."

A shiver worked its way down my spine at hearing the raspy desire in his voice. "Afraid I'll run off?"

"Something like that," he said, as he slid his hands beneath my shirt to touch my bare skin. Rush had tried to keep his tone light, but I heard the hint of doubt that nagged him. "Jesus, your body is a work of art."

I grabbed my shirt and pulled it over my head, baring my chest to his lustful gaze. As I told him before, I spent a lot of time in the gym working through stress and frustration and it showed. I wasn't one to preen about, but Rush's delight in what he saw made me want to strut my shit. If Rush wanted to look out the glass shower walls and see me naked and waiting for him, then that's what I'd give him.

Rush ran his hands all over my muscular chest while I undid my belt and shorts. The breath left his lungs in a whoosh when I shoved my shorts and briefs to my ankles. I toed out of my shoes and stood completely naked in front of him.

"Fuck me," Rush said hoarsely, as he looked at my body. "There's so much of you to touch and taste."

My dick twitched with anticipation. "Get in that fucking shower right now."

It took every ounce of control that I possessed to turn from him and walk to the bed. He was still standing in the exact same spot, his eyes fixed on my ass then my dick when I turned to face him again. God, his desire made me feel bolder than I ever had in my life. I stroked my cock a few times, but turned loose before I jizzed all over his fancy fucking floor rug. I situated myself in the middle of the bed and tucked my hands behind my head on the pillow to keep from jacking off while he put on a show in the shower.

Rush stared at me while he undressed, adding his discarded clothes to the same pile as mine. It was my turn to stare at his bubble butt while he padded to the shower. He looked over his shoulder a few times while waiting for the water to warm up, as if to reassure himself that I was still there. I smiled and winked at Rush each time to let him know I wasn't going anywhere. Watching Rush wash his hair and body was the sexiest fucking thing I'd ever seen. My dick was the hardest it had ever been, and a trail of pre-cum dripped to my stomach. I fisted my hands in my hair to keep them still, because one pump and I'd blow. The smirk on Rush's face told me he knew how badly I wanted him. It was my turn to grin when I noticed he didn't linger on his cock and balls any longer than it took to clean them. I suspected he was just as turned on as me.

All the saliva dried in my mouth when he stood on the rug outside the shower and towel-dried his blond hair because it made his erection bounce like it was greeting me. I planned to reintroduce him to my ass at the earliest convenience. I loved the ripple of muscle beneath Rush's tanned skin as he dried his body. I felt his eyes on my body as surely as he felt mine on his. God, the only thing as beautiful as grown Rush was the younger version that I had loved with all my youthful heart. I couldn't stop the flood of memories when he dropped the towel and approached the bed with a wicked gleam in his eye.

Rush stood beside the bed as if he still couldn't believe that I was truly there. I reached for his hand and brought it to my leaking cock.

"I'm real, baby."

Rush purred low in his throat as he stroked me up and down. "So fucking hard for me." If he kept that up, I wouldn't be hard for long.

"Always for you." I wasn't sure if, or when, I should tell him that he was the only man to know my body. I stilled his hand because I felt my orgasm coming on. I crooked my finger, and he climbed onto the bed as if under my spell.

I pulled him into my arms, our legs tangling together as we truly kissed for the first time in twenty-six years. Rush placed quick, teasing kisses on my lips until I couldn't take it anymore. I placed my hand on the back of his head and held him still so I could lick into his mouth. He parted his lips, and we both groaned at the first contact of our tongues. Then it became a dance of seduction as we took the time to relearn one another's mouths. Fuck, kissing had never felt this good with anyone else. It was so much more than a meeting of tongues; it was a connection of souls. It felt like a giant rift in the atmosphere aligned to form a perfect universe where only we existed.

Every gasp we made was captured by the other, every slick slide of his tongue against mine made my balls draw tighter against my body. I must've been a glutton for punishment, because I rolled and pulled him on top of me. I felt his dick twitch against mine and knew he was just as close to the edge as I was.

"Fuck, I'd hoped not to embarrass myself," I said honestly. "Just let me hold you a minute."

Rush ground his erection against mine, but I slapped his ass to still him. "What?" he asked. "I'm just settling in to get comfortable."

"I hope I don't come twice before we even have sex like I did our first time together in that cabin."

"You were so hot for me," Rush said, his nostrils flaring with the memory. "It drove me wild to see how I affected my big, strong Lincoln."

"I am still so fucking hot for you." I closed my eyes and gritted my teeth as I felt the sticky gathering of our combined pre-cum dribbling on my cock and stomach. "So much for relieving some of the pressure earlier."

Rush pushed against my chest to raise his upper body so he could look down at me. "Did you jerk off when you changed clothes?"

I opened my eyes slowly and smiled sheepishly. "Yeah. I'm still going to blow like a virgin as soon as you slide your gorgeous dick in my ass." I looked between our bodies and saw our cocks pressed together. "Or sooner."

Rush smiled wickedly as he started to slide his body lower. My dick cried out at the loss of his, but then wept for joy when the ridges of Rush's stomach rippled over it. I shook my head no. Rush had always loved sucking cock, and I loved having his mouth on me, but I didn't want to come in his mouth right then. I wanted to wait until his dick was back where it belonged, buried inside me.

His long bangs fell forward to cover his eyes as he looked at my needy cock. I fisted my hands in the silky blond strands and raised his head before he could press that talented tongue to my cock. "I want your dick in my ass."

Rush rose to his knees between my parted thighs and pushed my legs up higher to better expose my hole. "Right here?" he asked, teasing my pucker with a finger. "I want to eat your ass, Lincoln."

I inhaled so sharply that I choked on my own breath. That was something that I'd only seen in porn before, but I imagined it felt amazing. "Later," I rasped out. "Fuck me now, Rush. Please."

He only hesitated for a second before he left me long enough to pull the condoms and lube from the drawer. My body shook with nervous anticipation as he rubbed lube on his fingers and slowly reached between my legs. Instead of going straight for my ass, he massaged my balls and taint, pulling a strangled hiss from my lungs.

"Rush," I growled.

"It's part of the prep," he said, as he slowly dragged his finger over my taint until he reached my needy pucker. He pressed just the tip inside then retracted to circle my opening again. "So tight, Linc. How long has it been?"

I swallowed hard, unsure of what he would think about my confession. I didn't want him to think I was using him to get my jollies off. "I've only used toys recently for anal play, but prior to that, there's only been you."

"That's a long time, Linc." I saw how much my words pleased him. I'd given him a part of me that no one else could claim.

"An eternity," I confessed.

"Are your toys as big as me?" Rush stroked his cock with his free hand.

"No, and they didn't feel as good as you."

"It's been a long time, so how can you be so sure?" His teasing finger stilled, and he sounded a little unsure.

"Rush, there are things my body will never forget, and the feel of you inside of me is at the top of the list. In fact, all but a few involve you and the things we did together."

My words must've appeased him, because he resumed teasing my hole with the slightest pressure. "I'm going to take my time and prep you right," he said before he leaned over my body to kiss me. His luscious lips and skillful tongue helped relax me so that I wouldn't tense up against his penetration. Soon, that long, slender finger wasn't enough, and I started rocking my hips, fucking myself to get more friction.

"So good," I whispered against his lips.

"Just the beginning, baby." I loved the cockiness in his voice and the little endearment he used for me. "I'm going to make you feel so good soon." He punctuated his promise by adding another finger to stretch me out even more. The bite of pain didn't dim my excitement in the slightest; it ratcheted up my need a dozen notches.

"Fuck me now."

Rush shook his head. "You're not ready."

"Dammit, I'm ready," I practically snarled.

"Then you do it," Rush said, raising himself back up to sit on his heels. He held up a condom wrapper in front of him. "Put this condom on my cock, lube it up, and guide it inside your body."

The picture he painted made me growl in need and lust. I jack-knifed into a sitting position and snatched the condom from his hands. When I reached for his cock, I stroked it a few extra times before I slid the latex down the length of his hard-on.

"Lots of lube the first time," Rush suggested as I squirted a small amount on his covered dick.

"No," I said between gritted teeth. "I remember how I liked it." I preferred just enough lube to ease his entrance, but I wanted to feel the sting of penetration. I craved it, in fact.

"I remember too, Linc." Rush closed his eyes and swallowed hard as I coated his cock evenly. "Wait," he said when I lay back down and reached down to guide his cock. Rush grabbed a fluffy pillow and propped it beneath my ass to angle my hips higher. "That way you can see me sliding in and out of you."

"Oh fuck," I growled hungrily. "Someone has learned some new tricks." I should've been jealous, but I decided that I would benefit from everything he learned over the years apart.

Rush positioned himself between my legs, his cock jutting proudly from the neatly trimmed hair at its base. "Now."

I reached between our bodies and guided the head of his slick dick to my hole, pressing against it until the burn of penetration made me cry out. "Rush!" Maybe I'd been a little hasty with my demands to fuck without more prep.

"Breathe, baby. You can take me," Rush said tenderly. "Push out against me." I did as he instructed and felt my body relax enough to take the head of his cock past the tight ring of muscles. "That's right, just like… Ohhhh fuck, you're so goddamned tight." Rush's body shook with restraint and his chest heaved. I knew he wanted to bottom out inside me. I wanted that too, but fuck me, his control was a thing of beauty.

I panted through the discomfort then guided him the rest of the way inside me. "So sexy," I groaned, loving the erotic slide and fullness from having Rush's dick inside me. I felt my passage tightening around the intrusion, and Rush's needy whimper let me know he felt it too. I started to pull my hand out of the way so that he could fuck me long and deep but stopped on his command.

"Leave your fingers down there so you can feel that it's me claiming your ass, not some plastic toy." Rush tilted my hips a little higher. I could see his penetration even more. I formed a V with my index and middle fingers and squeezed against his cock as he worked in and out of me. It must've felt as good as it looked, because his hips lost rhythm and snapped forward hard. "Fuck, yes."

Rush started rocking in and out of me a little faster, the fat head of his cock tagged my prostate every thrust home. Between the sexy position and the pleasure rippling through my body, I knew I wouldn't last long. My eyes rolled back in my head as my balls retracted further inside my body.

"Let's see if I can make you come without touching your big cock," Rush said between pants. I'd always been so fucking responsive with him. It turned me on even more to know that he remembered it too. Instead of stroking my cock with my free hand, I reached up and played with one of my hard nipples. "You're a sexy bastard, Lincoln."

Rush nailed my prostate once more and I shot all over my stomach and chest with a roar. I expected him to knock my hand out of the way so he could go at me hard, but Rush pulled out of me instead and lowered my hips. I stared at him, dazed and confused, as he quickly yanked the condom off and tossed it aside before he straddled my hips and began stroking his cock.

I ran my hands all over his upper body as the hair on his ass teased my sensitive cock while he fucked his fist.

"Yes!" he roared when he released all over my abs and chest, mixing his cum with mine.

Rush didn't collapse on my chest like I expected, he lowered his body so that his head hovered over my stomach. He stared into my eyes as his tongue slid out of his sinful mouth and licked a path through our combined spunk. Rush pushing his dripping tongue inside my mouth was the sexiest thing I'd ever experienced. I pulled him onto my chest and tasted the perfection of us together as we kissed long and hard. By the time he pulled back to smile down at me, the cum in our body hair had started to glue us together.

"It's going to hurt like hell when we pull apart," Rush whispered against my swollen lips.

"You better stay right here then," I said, tightening my arms around him. I wasn't sure I could ever let him go again. I had no fucking clue what the hell would happen between us, but I knew I had to stay a little longer to find out.

15—Pillow Talk

Rush

"HOW DO YOU FEEL ABOUT CHINESE DELIVERY?" I ASKED Linc, looking down into his drowsy eyes. He'd come so fucking hard, and I could tell that all he really wanted to do was hold me while he slept. I wasn't opposed to that, but fucking had made me even hungrier.

"We brought home food," he said, his mouth curved into a sated, half smile. "Oh, Brutus."

"Yeah, Brutus." I smiled back. "There's no way he didn't tear into those Styrofoam containers and devour our meals. So, Chinese? Mexican? Pizza? Chicago has it all."

"This is so different from when we were kids," Linc said then laughed. "What was our after-sex snack back in the day?"

"Fruit rollups," I suggested, and we both laughed. "I seem to remember you mowing your way through those Tyson chicken pat-ties that my mom bought. She would get grouchy, and my dad would tell her to knock it off. If his prize tight end wanted chicken patties then he ate chicken patties."

"There was no way my mom would've let me eat processed chicken products, and I drove Phee nuts with them when we were first married. I snuck them to the kids along with Kraft macaroni and cheese when she wasn't home." Lincoln stiffened when he realized what he said. "I'm sorry."

"For having a good life? Don't be, Linc. I've always hoped that you were happy and well-loved wherever life took you." I ran my thumb over his beard. "I never wanted you to be unhappy."

"I tried my best," he said softly. "I was never going to be truly happy until I was honest with myself and everyone around me."

The conversation had turned serious quicker than I expected, and I knew food was required if he wanted more out of me than grunts. "I'm going to separate us now," I warned. "Then we're getting something to eat so we can talk."

"Can we be naked at the same time?" Linc asked hopefully.

"While we eat? I'm not keen on sweet and sour in my pubes, and I don't think it would feel much better than the dried spunk we got rocking right now."

"I meant during the talking afterward. I'll tell you anything you want to know, as long as I can feel your skin against mine while doing it."

"Mmmm. Pillow talk sounds pretty damn sexy," I replied.

"On the count of three, let's try to pull apart," Lincoln suggested.

"Like the time you said we should jump off the bridge into the river," I told him.

"We were going to hold hands," Linc reminded me.

"Like that would've made a difference. Had Sheriff Barkley not drove up just as we were about to jump, we probably would've broken our legs, necks, or both."

"And what was the good sheriff worried about? 'Son, you'll end your promising football career before it's truly had a chance to start.' Not a word about broken necks or legs," Lincoln said shaking his head.

"Your gridiron exploits were the only thing good happening in that town, Linc. I'm sure he was concerned about your overall health too," I offered. "Start the countdown and let's get cleaned up."

It didn't happen fast, or pain free, but we finally unglued our not-so-happy trails and got in the shower to wash off. I saw the heat in his eyes and felt the answering twitch in my dick, but I shook my head and handed him a washcloth and bar of soap.

"Save it for after the food and pillow talk," I told Lincoln. "I need you to fuck me like you mean it."

"Oh, I'm going to mean it, Rush."

Just as I suspected, Brutus had himself a damn good meal with our dinners and was snoring his ass off on the sofa. "I'm going to place our order on GrubHub then I'll clean this up."

"I'll get started cleaning. Where do you keep the supplies?"

I told Linc where he could find the trash can, broom, and mop. "I won't be long. Wait, you didn't tell me what you wanted to eat."

"Your ass, but that can wait," Linc tossed over his shoulder.

I dropped my phone on the hardwood floor and was grateful I didn't bust the screen out on it. I had myself back under control by the time Linc returned.

"I've watched a fuck ton of gay porn since my divorce," he told me. "I made a mental list of all the things I wanted to try. Rimming wouldn't be something I'd do with just anyone." Lincoln cupped my chin and kissed me hard and fast. "There's not a part of you that I won't lick, suck, or kiss."

"Or fuck," I added. "I'm starting not to worry about food."

"We're eating," Linc said firmly. "I remember how you get with low blood sugar. I promise you that I'll make it worth your while."

"If you're going to eat my ass, then we better stay away from anything spicy," I teased then looked up to see if that grossed Linc out.

"Good call."

We got enough Chinese food to feed an army, but I steered away from the spicier selections. Brutus barely looked up at us when we walked past him to eat in the dining room.

"Damn, your house is an architectural wonder."

I took immense pride in my home and loved it even more once Travis's crap was gone. "What is it that you do?" I asked Linc then laughed because I usually knew at least the basic information about a man before I took him to bed.

"Phee and I own a real estate company called Forever Home in San Diego. We started it with the money I made from my brief NFL career. I might've busted my knee in my first season with the Raiders, but I made a lot of contacts. I'm really proud of the company we built from scratch." He looked up from his sweet and sour chicken and smiled. "This is so much better than any after-sex snack we had in the past."

"God, remember the trail mix you took to the cabin with us?" I asked.

Linc snorted then dryly said, "I was such a romantic."

"You were so damn thoughtful, Linc. I wasn't making fun of your resourcefulness." Then it was my turn to snort. "However, I was happy we learned to use something other than hand lotion for lubricant. These gay guys have it so much better now than we did back then."

"Lube is a vast improvement over Vaseline petroleum jelly."

"Oh man, I forgot about that one," I said then laughed until tears ran down my face. "We got that stuff every-fucking-where."

"In our hair…"

"I think I even found it in my armpits a few times," I said.

"No doubt," Linc replied with a wicked grin. "I probably had one hand on your shoulder and the other just beneath your pit. I was always looking to find the best leverage to fuck you."

I'd just taken a bite of broccoli and chicken and nearly choked. Linc slid my second egg roll toward me. I had scarfed down the first one in two fucking bites. I reached for the spicy mustard, but Linc blocked me.

"Rim job," he reminded me. It wasn't that I forgot, I just wasn't sure he was serious. I saw in his eyes just how much he meant his words. "Eat your damn dinner."

"Eager to do some pillow talking?" I teased.

"Eager to get you naked and relearn your body so I can compare all the places you've changed and adore the ones that are the same."

"I'm full now," I said, standing up.

"Sit back down and eat your dinner. You didn't eat half of what you ordered."

"There's more food than I could eat in a week," I told Linc. "A few more bites then we can come down here later for more after-sex snacks." I ended up eating the rest of my meal, my second egg roll, and one of his while he watched in shock.

"How the fuck can you eat like that and stay in such great shape?" Linc asked dumbfounded. "I bet I have to fuel an extra forty pounds than you, and I couldn't eat like that."

"Metabolism," I said with a shrug. "I don't eat like this often, and I do work out a lot too. Jules and I both seem to be able to eat what we want without gaining weight."

"I gotta see Jules before I leave."

"She'd love that, Linc. You'll love my niece. She's just like her mama and the light of my life."

"I'm surprised you never had kids," Linc probed softly.

"It wasn't from lack of desire to be a father. I just never met the right guy. Looking back now, I should've adopted a child on my own. Single men and women raise kids all the time. I guess certain traditional ideals still remain inside me." Linc raised his brow and I hurried to clarify. "Not that a kid needs a mom and a dad, per say. I was thinking more along the lines that two parents are better than one, but I know that's a bunch of bullshit."

"It's not too late, you know."

"You must've been really young when your kids were born," I said then dug a forkful of his fried rice out of his container.

"Yep," he replied. "I met Ophelia the second day of college. I literally almost ran her over. She ripped me a new one, not at all caring that I was the school's new shiny penny. We got married before we graduated college and had our first child when we were only twenty-two."

"I think I would like her."

"You would love her, and she would feel the same about you. Actually, she kind of already does."

"What? How?"

I listened to the story of how Ophelia found out that Linc was gay. I couldn't keep the sappy smile off my face as he told me about the night he was outed by his ammo box of treasures and the way his ex-wife supported him. Then I led him back to my bedroom, but not for the reason he thought. Well, yes, I wanted more sex, but I wanted to show him something first.

Lincoln sat on my bed while I retrieved something from my closet. "This old cardboard box might not be as cool as yours but check this out. There might be some things you remember." I set it down and watched his expression as he slowly reached for it. "Nothing in there will jump out and grab you."

"If it's anything like mine, everything inside will jump out and grab me," Linc replied ruefully, rubbing his hand over his heart. "It was bittersweet to relive all those moments again."

"At least I'm here with you now, and we can relive them together. I can promise you only sweet things will follow." I had specifically meant that night, but it sounded more like a prediction for our future. *Our future.* I couldn't let my brain go there because it wouldn't take long for my heart to get its hopes up. What would happen if Linc decided that being out was harder than he thought? What if he decided I wasn't worth it? My heart wouldn't survive his rejection again. I'd grow into a bitter old man like Arthur who lived in the brownstone next door.

"Where'd you go just now?" Linc asked, jerking my attention back to him. I could tell by the dimmed merriment in his expression that he had an idea of where I went. Instead of opening the box, Linc picked it up and carried it to my dresser. "We can open this later. Right now, I just need to touch you. Your body is a treasure map of memories that I want to relive up close and personal."

It didn't take us long to lose the sweatpants we had put on before going downstairs. Of course, the pair that Linc borrowed from me didn't quite reach his ankles, but it gave me a lovely view of his long, elegant feet. Linc wasted no time reaching for my dick which was already at half-mast just from seeing his naked body. I hardened instantly in his hands, my heart turning to putty like it always did. Linc pushed back the extra skin at the head of my dick to tease that sensitive spot beneath the crown. Fuck me, I wanted his tongue there. It was all I could do to keep from suggesting what he could do with my cock, preferably from his knees. Instead, I reached for him and repeated his actions except for the extra skin part. Linc had a gorgeous, cut cock.

"Do you remember the first time I saw your cock?" Linc asked. Humor and desire glittered in his dark eyes when he smiled at me.

I threw my head back and laughed, but I never stopped stroking him. Linc's laughter joined mine, bouncing off the walls of my bedroom. The high ceilings had never before heard such passion, dirty talk, and laughter as I shared with Lincoln that day.

"You thought there was something wrong with it," I replied. "You were still too turned on to say something and risk me not jerking you off."

"Well, duh. Come first, ask questions later. Isn't that the standard motto for a horny teenage boy?" Linc asked me. "I seem to recall that you didn't mind my obsession with that extra skin and all the ways I could make you crazy." Linc dropped to his knees, and I groaned. I knew what was coming and began to tremble.

"You would come hard and explosive then torture me until you got hard again," I said breathlessly, running my hands through Linc's hair as he licked his lips like he couldn't wait to taste me again.

A strangled cry erupted from me when Lincoln took my cock straight to the back of his throat, only making a slight gagging sound. Linc locked his dark eyes on mine and eased off until the tip slid out of his mouth with a wet pop. "It's like riding a bicycle."

"I hope I don't break my arm this time," I teased.

Linc's answer was to ease my foreskin back and lick the pre-cum that had pooled inside the folds. He licked his lips like it was the best thing he'd ever had before he whispered huskily, "I'll catch you this time if you fall." Were we still talking about riding bikes or...

"How about I ride your cock?" I suggested.

"Later," Linc said between licks. Then he sucked the foreskin between his lips and tugged, gently stretching it. "Maybe I want to make you come fast and hard then tease you back to arousal first." When we first started having sex, it bothered Linc how responsive he was to me, but I fucking loved it. He thought he should be able to last longer, but his exuberance made me feel strong and powerful, like maybe the playing field had become level when we were naked and alone.

"I adored the way you loved me with so much passion and excitement," I told him. "I lived for those stolen minutes, Lincoln. Without them, I don't know if I would've survived that house." Linc stopped exploring my dick with his lips and tongue and looked up at me. I hated that my words had caused the mood to take such a drastic, unexpected shift.

Lincoln rose to his feet and cupped my face. "Let's get one thing straight." His lips quirked up a little, because there was nothing straight about us. "You were always the strong one, Rush. Yes, you had fears, but you overcame them. You faced them headfirst and came out stronger after each battle. I had size and I had physical strength, but inside where it counted, I was weak."

"You weren't weak," I refuted. "God, someday I hope you can stop berating yourself."

"You would've gotten through without me, but I'm so glad that you didn't." Linc lowered his head until his mouth nearly touched mine.

"Me too," I whispered against his lips then closed the gap.

I tangled my hands in his hair and kissed him with every ounce of passion I possessed. I released the heartache, the loneliness of time spent apart, and reveled in the joy of our reunion. I ignored the nagging little voice in my head that questioned how long it would last. Linc had a life somewhere else, and Chicago would always be my home. But then he ran his hands slowly over my bare skin as if touching it for the first time, and I forgot to be afraid.

The second time we made love, it was slower, and we both catalogued the changes in each other using our hands, teeth, lips, and tongues. I trailed my lips over Linc's strong pecs and down the line that bisected his cut abs. Linc nibbled and bit along the hard muscles I developed in my legs from years of running. I placed my nose in the juncture of Linc's thighs where his natural, masculine smell was the strongest and breathed him in. His tongue got up close and personal with my ass like he said it would. I fucking loved every minute of it.

"I have so much to learn and do," Linc whispered gravelly after I came hard with his tongue in my ass. I could hear just how close he was to coming too. "Right now, I want one of my favorite things," he said, flopping to his back on the bed beside where I was still on my hands and knees. I suspected he wanted me to blow him, and I was all for it. "I'm going to get you hard again, and then you're going to ride me, Rush." That sounded even better.

He pulled me on top of his chest and ran his hands all over my back, gripping my ass while he made love to my mouth. I was sure that I couldn't get it up again so soon, but I was wrong. The feel of his hard-on pressed against my stomach and the thorough way he continued to finger my ass had me rebounding quicker than I dreamed possible. I sheathed his cock in latex, smeared on the lube, and mounted Lincoln in the center of my bed. I had one thought in mind when I began to move: I was going to give him the ride of his life.

It took more control and restraint than I knew I had, but it was worth it to draw out his pleasure like he'd done for me all those years ago. We came together, loud and long, then lay in a tangle of sweaty limbs for quite some time.

Linc went to the bathroom to discard the condom and brought back a warm washcloth for me. I was too spent to move, so he lovingly cared for me. I was fast asleep before he climbed back between the sheets. My brain returned to reality a few hours later, but I was too tired to open my eyes or even move. I was convinced I'd dreamt the whole thing, and that I'd come down with some strange virus as an explanation for my fatigue until my leg bumped into his hairier one. I opened my eyes to find Linc sitting up in bed beside me as he looked through my treasure box in the dim light cast by the bedside table lamp.

He wore a sappy smile on his face as a few sentimental tears tracked down his handsome face to disappear in his beard. As if he felt my stare, Linc turned and looked at me. He reached into the box and pulled out the boutonniere we had exchanged at the end of our one and only prom dance.

"I have yours too," he said, voice thick with emotion. "I've absolutely hated dancing since then."

"Me too."

"Life is too short to hate dancing," Linc told me.

"We were just waiting to dance with the right person again," I said sitting up. I pulled my music up on my phone and hit shuffle. The song that popped up made me laugh. "Pillowtalk."

"Can I have this dance, Rush?"

"As many as you want."

The dance was totally different than the one we shared on prom night, and not just because we were both naked. Twenty-six years ago, we thought we were saying goodbye, and the look in our eyes was one of misery and heartbreak. As we spun around in my bedroom, our expressions showed our delight in our rediscovery. We didn't say goodbye all those years ago, we said until I see you again. My heart pinched in my chest knowing that soon Linc would return to California. I couldn't help but wonder how long I'd have to wait before he held me in his arms again and turned me in awkward circles in the middle of my bedroom wearing nothing but a look of adoration.

16—So You're Saying

LINCOLN

THE NEXT MORNING, I WOKE UP ALONE IN RUSH'S BED. I HAD reached for him before my eyes were fully open, but my hands found cool sheets where I expected to find a warm body. I groaned as I sat up, feeling the results of last night in every muscle in my body. I might've vigorously fucked like a teenager, but my body reminded me that those years were long past gone. I didn't panic that Rush wasn't in bed with me because I could sense his presence. A quick glance at his bedside clock showed that it was almost ten o'clock. I hadn't slept that late in… I couldn't tell you.

I grabbed my borrowed sweats off the floor and pulled them up to my hips. I felt a sexy little smile tug at my lips when I recalled how much Rush liked it when his sweats rode low on my hips, showing off the V-shaped cut of my pelvic muscles. He especially loved to trace it with his tongue. I told my brain to knock it off because it was going to be impossible to piss with a hard-on. The longer it took me to piss, the longer it would take me to find my guy. My nose detected bacon, and not that turkey shit that Phee forced me to eat for the last two decades.

Rush had set out a new, unopened toothbrush on the counter for me to use. I appreciated his thoughtfulness, but couldn't stop myself from wondering how often he did this? Was there a drawer full of spare toothbrushes for his overnight guests? I was beyond curious, but I didn't want to get caught rifling through his vanity drawers. Besides, some things a person didn't need to know. It didn't matter anyway, because I was back and there would be no revolving door of men. *Whoa! Slow it down there, Linc. It was just one night.*

It didn't matter that I wanted it to be so much more, because I didn't get to unilaterally decide our future. Hell, I'd already done that once when I ran off to Columbus. *Maybe this time we take a breath and take things one day at a time.* All I knew for certain was that I was staying for the rest of the week. I would work remotely if I needed to, but I wasn't going anywhere until I had more time with Rush.

I found him in the kitchen, cooking bacon at the stove. Music played softly from a Bose speaker on the counter, and it wasn't until I got closer that I realized it was one of his favorite Madonna songs from our younger days. I let my eyes roam over his lean, sexy body and mourned that he wasn't naked. I couldn't blame the guy for putting a layer of clothes between him and sizzling grease. Unaware that I had entered, he started to dance at the stove as he turned the bacon while Brutus watched from a safe distance.

It was the dog who noticed me first and greeted me with a welcoming woof before he ran to me for an ear scratching. Rush looked over his shoulder and smiled at me.

"Good morning," Rush said cheerfully.

"Good morning. Have you been up long?"

Rush ran his eyes down the length of my body, lingering at my

V playing peekaboo with him. "Which part of me specifically are you inquiring about, Linc?"

"Um, all of you," I suggested.

"Well, my cock was wide awake before my brain or the rest of my body because it knew you were in the same bed."

Rush turned back around and shut off the stove before he slid the pan over to a cool burner. My long legs ate up the gap between us. I wrapped my arms around his waist and pulled him tight against my chest while he transferred crisp bacon strips to a paper towel-lined plate to drain.

"What did you do with your morning wood, Rush?" I didn't recognize my own voice. I'd never heard it so deep and gravelly.

"Well, I wanted to rub it all over you. Maybe paint your torso with cum to mark my territory, but I let you sleep while I tried to tame my eager cock with a long run with Brutus followed by a cool shower. Neither helped much."

I palmed his erection through his sweats, and he pushed his ass into my groin. Jesus, I couldn't think about anything but coming all over his tight ass. I pulled him away from the stove and guided him to the kitchen island.

"Hands on the counter and don't move them."

"Officer, am I under arrest?"

"Fuck yes," I growled in his ear as I continued to tease him through the cotton, loving the damp spot spreading on the front of his sweats that matched the one on mine. "You're too fucking sexy to be walking the streets. It's surely a crime."

Rush snorted and opened his mouth to speak, but his words died in his throat when I yanked his sweats to his knees. I stepped back and pulled his hips toward me to pop his ass out even more. I lowered my sweats to my thighs, slicked my cock with spit, and pushed my erection between his plump ass cheeks. I gripped both cheeks and squeezed them around my cock as I slid it up and down his crack.

I couldn't look away from the sexy fucking picture we made.

"Christ. I can't wait to be inside this sweet ass again." I almost growled that he and his ass were mine, but I caught myself just in time. "Want you so goddamned much, Rush." I rutted against his fine ass, feeling the telltale signs of a pending orgasm. "Stroke your cock, baby. Come with me."

Rush cried out as he wrapped his hand around his dick and began stroking it in fast, jerky motions. He was right there with me, I could hear it in the way his breath hitched in his throat and feel it in the way his body tightened.

I painted his ass with my spunk at the same time he sprayed his island cabinet. Rush collapsed against the counter, and I leaned against his back, careful not to put my full weight on him.

"I haven't been this horny since ninety-three," Rush said between pants. I snickered because we had found a way to fuck like rabbits our senior year of high school. "Fuck! Charlie horse," he cried out, stretching his calf. "This sure used to be easier when we were kids."

"I know what you mean," I said, massaging my lower back. "I thought I was in great shape, but my body is feeling our marathon sex everywhere today."

"Let me put the bacon in the microwave so that Brutus doesn't eat the B in our BLTs while we get cleaned up."

As I ran soapy hands all over Rush's body, I mentally calculated if I could stay longer than a week. I hardly ever took time off from work and felt I was overdue for some personal time. I just didn't want to leave Phee shorthanded.

"What are you thinking about, Lincoln?" Rush asked after I'd gone silent for several minutes. He turned to face me, and I saw worry etched in the lines around his eyes and mouth.

I ran my thumb over the deep V in his brow to smooth the lines. "I'm wondering how long I can manage to stay in Chicago without upsetting everyone's lives."

His relieved smile melted my heart, and I wondered how long before Rush would stop bracing himself for me to deliver bad news.

"So, you're saying that you want to hang around here a little longer?"

"Is that okay with you?" It was my turn to brace myself for rejection.

"Better than okay," he said with a smile. "Best news I've had in... twenty-six years."

Later that afternoon, my knees bounced anxiously while I waited for my kids to arrive at my hotel room. They were stunned to hear that I'd made another surprise visit, but accepted that I decided to swing by to see them since I was in the general region. I had no intention of misleading them, but I also didn't want them imagining the worst-case scenarios like they had when Phee and I dropped by to tell them we were getting a divorce.

It worked too because neither of them assumed I was dying from cancer, but they both looked at me in silent speculation after I greeted them with hearty hugs. I kind of held on like I might not get another chance.

Kennedy finally broke the silence when she tipped her head to the side and said, "You look different."

"Different how?" I asked, hoping they couldn't tell I'd spent the night having the best sex of my life.

"You look like Mom after she met Jackson," Holden said.

Kennedy gasped then gave her brother an incredulous look. "Wow, you're a rude little dumbass."

"I just meant he looks happy," Holden said defensively.

"You implied that Daddy couldn't get the job done for mom," Kennedy informed him.

Holden grimaced and looked at me with apology in his eyes. "I guess that did sound really bad. I'm sorry, Dad."

"Don't be," I told him. I thought about what Rush had said about coming out and how you didn't just do it once. I knew he was right, because I'd already done it twice, but this time was the scariest. The thought of my kids rejecting me made my stomach churn and my pulse race. I looked into the eyes of my most precious gifts and prayed that they would be open-minded. "You're right, son. Like Mom, I've finally found my happiness."

"That's great," Kennedy said with a warm smile. "You deserve to be happy, Daddy. Have we met her?"

"This is the part where you need to sit down," I told them. I kept my voice teasing and light, instead of dark and mysterious. I couldn't expect them to accept me as a gay man if I led with a tone that indicated it was something bad. I blew out a nervous breath once they sat beside each other on the sofa and said, "This isn't about a specific person that I'm seeing; it's about me being honest about who I am and what I want out of life." The silence in the room was deafening as they just looked at me through unblinking eyes. "There's only a few people who know what I'm about to tell you, Mom and Grandma are two of them." I opened my mouth to say more, but my breath seized in my throat. *Fuck, this was harder than I thought it would be.*

Kennedy reached across the coffee table to hold my hand. "Do you remember that time I had a meltdown over getting a C on a midterm exam? Hell, it was so insignificant that I can't remember what class it was."

"Algebra II," Holden supplied. "That tantrum was fucking epic, K."

"Zip it, dweeb," Kennedy said, but she grinned from ear to ear as she playfully elbowed her brother. "Anyway, once you talked me off the ledge, you sat me down and told me that you were going to love me no matter what my grades were, the occupation I chose, or who I loved. Do you remember that?" She sounded so fucking mature, and I had never been prouder of her.

"I do."

"Alright, so it's my turn because I can see that you're really struggling with something. If I'm honest, I've seen it for a while now. There is nothing you can say or do that will make me love you less, Daddy."

"What she said," Holden contributed, hooking a thumb in his sister's direction. He wasn't one to get overly mushy, but I saw moments of sensitivity and vulnerability in him. I knew he was going to be an amazing partner when he found the right person to bring those traits out in him.

They smiled reassuringly at me, and I knew, it was now or never. "When I was ten years old, even younger if I'm honest, I fell in love with a boy." They sat up a little straighter but didn't say anything. I took that as a good sign and continued. "But being gay wasn't accepted in eastern Tennessee during the height of the HIV and Aids epidemic in the eighties. I heard things like gay people deserved to get sick and die because they were going against God's word. People called them perverts and pedophiles, and preachers liked to use them as evidence that the end of the world was looming. I was surrounded by a repressive religion that didn't support anyone who didn't look, believe, or love like the parishioners in our church did."

"Did Grandma and Grandpa say those hideous things?" Kennedy wondered. Holden had remained silent, but I saw the same curiousness in his eyes.

"No, but they didn't refute it, so I thought they believed the same things. Maybe I wasn't being fair to them by keeping a secret this big," I told my kids. "Now I'll never know if your grandfather loved me or just the idea of me." My dad wasn't a demonstrative guy, other than to bitch, so I didn't know if he was even capable of love. I felt his loss strongly in that moment, as I tried to reconcile my past with my present, and hopefully my future. Rush's smiling face from that morning appeared in my mind and the ache dissipated. "Anyway, I walked away from the boy I loved and started a brand-new life when I left for college. I convinced myself that, if I tried hard enough, I could bury that part of myself and live a "normal" life." I even used air quotes to highlight the ridiculousness of that word.

"It's a bullshit word," Kennedy added, "unless it's used to reference the results of medical tests."

I was relieved that my daughter seemed okay with the news, but I really wished Holden would say something. He just looked at me with an unreadable expression on his face. "Son, are you angry?"

"No, I'm just surprised is all," Holden said. "Dad, normal is overrated."

I smiled and took my first easy breath since they arrived. "You both make excellent points, but I wasn't brave enough, nor did I have enough faith in myself, to go against the norms I knew. So, I chose denial. I met your mom right away, and I was immediately smitten with her."

"So, you're saying that you're bisexual?" Holden asked. Was he hopeful? Perhaps he thought this was just a phase or part of a midlife crisis.

"It doesn't matter," Kennedy snidely said. "Let the man talk."

"To answer your question, Holden, no, I don't consider myself bisexual even though I obviously had sex with a woman for more than two decades." I prayed they wouldn't ask me how I accomplished that because it wasn't a conversation I wanted to have with my kids. Instead, I went with, "I loved your mother to the best of my ability, but I couldn't give her what she truly needed because I'm gay." There, I said it. Again. I'd keep repeating it until it was no longer necessary. God, I felt so relieved that I slumped back in the club chair I'd chosen.

"Wow, you look ten years younger," Kennedy said.

"Nah, that's a stretch. That gray in his beard gives his age away," Holden said, his mouth tipped up into a crooked smile, and I knew we were going to be okay. "Does Mom know already?"

"She was the first person to find out." I told them about the weekend at Grandma's house. "At first, she just wanted to comfort me because I was really upset and emotional. When we got back home, we had a long conversation. She told me that it made sense in a way because we just never clicked the way other couples did. We had so much love between us, but it wasn't the physical kind." I grimaced when I thought that I told them too much, but neither of them commented or made faces like they were going to vomit.

"Is that really why you got a divorce?" Kennedy inquired. There was no judgement in her voice, just basic curiosity.

"Kennedy, picture how your mom smiled when she was married to me and compare it to the smile she beams at Jackson." I saw the moment she understood what I was saying. "Your mother is my best friend, and that will never change. I loved her with everything I had, but it wasn't enough. I was never unfaithful to her, nor was she to me, but we didn't complete each other. We got a divorce because we don't belong together. It makes me so happy to see the way she lights up when Jackson enters the room. Mom deserves to be loved like that every single day for the rest of her life."

"Have you started dating too?" Holden asked.

"Your mom tried to fix me up with a few guys, but they weren't interested in dating a closet case in their forties." The kids grinned when they heard their mom was trying to find the perfect man for me. "I just came out to Grandma on Saturday night and drove here yesterday."

"Why didn't you call us when you arrived?" Kennedy inquired.

"Well, um… I ran into an old friend." I stopped and shook my head. "Damn, that's such an understatement."

"Was it him, the boy you loved?" Holden asked. "He's here in Chicago?"

"Yes," I said, choking up. I cleared my throat a few times and said, "I couldn't come out to Grandma without stirring up so many memories of Rush. I couldn't look at a Ferris wheel without thinking about him. He loved and feared them as a kid, and I convinced him to ride one with me. It was the moment that I realized I loved him. As tired as I was when I arrived after the long drive, I decided to walk to the pier and ride the Centennial Wheel. And there he was."

"Wow," Kennedy sighed sappily. "That sounds like a beautiful ending you'd find in a romance novel."

"They don't write romance novels about two dudes," Holden said.

"Of course they do," Kennedy countered then looked at me. "You remember the Wrights that I interned for two summers ago, right?" I nodded. "Chase's grandmother is Agnes Simmons, the famous romance writer."

"Hell, even I recognize that name. My mom and her friends used to read her books all the time," I told Kennedy. "Grandma will freak out when she hears."

"Agnes turned to writing gay romance full time after her grandson, Chase, came out. She decided that every heart deserves a happily ever after and every type of love should be represented in literature. It was a slow transition at first, but eventually her gay romance books took off. She is the neatest, feistiest woman I have ever met."

"You working for the Wrights really triggered the need for me to be truthful about myself. When I researched the company, I saw the life that the two men built together. I knew that I could have that too, if only I were brave enough."

"You're the bravest man I know, Daddy," Kennedy said. And just like when she was a little girl, she climbed onto my lap and threw her arms around my neck. Holden joined us but sat on the arm of the chair and looped his arms around us both. I couldn't have stopped the grateful tears from falling if someone offered me a trillion dollars. My children's love was priceless.

"Now we know why you didn't call us when you arrived yesterday," Holden teased. "Does that mean you're moving to Chicago?"

"I have no idea what any of this means right now, son. I'm just playing it by ear this week."

Kennedy lifted her head from my shoulder and looked up at me. "Can we meet him?"

"I'd love that, and I think he would too." No matter what happened between Rush and me going forward, I wanted my children to meet the man who had such a massive impact on my life.

17—No Place That Far

Rush

"DO I LOOK OKAY?" I ASKED STRAIGHTENING MY TIE FOR at least the tenth time as we waited for Linc's kids to arrive at Mario's. I cringed when I saw my panicked expression in the mirror behind the bar. "Fuck, I should've at least gotten my hair cut. I look a mess."

Sexy laughter rumbled up from Linc's chest and our eyes connected in the mirror. Just like that, all the air was sucked out of the room and everyone around us faded into oblivion. There was only him and me; the way it was meant to be. We turned our heads to look at each other, and I knew exactly what he was thinking when he ran his hand over my hair. He was recalling the way he liked to fist it in his hands when I knelt at his feet. Or maybe he was remembering the ideas he had about what we could do with our ties once we got back to my place.

A masculine cough and a feminine giggle interrupted my thoughts that were best suited for when we were alone. Lincoln didn't immediately pull back to greet his children, which surprised me. Instead, he ghosted his thumb over my cheekbone and jaw. I expected him to be a little more reticent about showing affection in public, but he surprised me all the time. That doubting voice in my head said it was because he felt safer here in a city where people didn't know him. He had nothing invested here, nothing to lose.

"Hello, children," Linc said without looking away from me.

"Oh, great. Another one bites the dust," Holden said, then hummed the famous Queen song. "Mom hasn't called me in over a week."

That got Linc's attention, and he broke eye contact to address his son. I also turned in their direction and couldn't get over how much they both resembled the man I loved. Yes, loved. I knew it was stupid to let myself fall so hard and fast for him again, but if I was being honest, I'd admit that I never stopped loving him. It was like I'd gone into remission for the past two decades, and everything I felt for him roared to the surface when our eyes met on the pier.

I could tell from photos on Linc's phone that Kennedy had Phee's coloring, but the shape of her eyes, nose, mouth, and even chin were all Lincoln. Holden looked so much like his dad that it was uncanny.

"Try calling her occasionally, jackass. The lines run both ways," Kennedy told her brother then turned her attention to me. "Excuse us for being rude." She extended her hand and said, "I'm Kennedy and this is my idiot brother, Holden."

"It's nice to meet you, Kennedy," I said shaking her hand before I extended mine to Linc's son. "And you as well, Holden."

"Kennedy, be nice," Lincoln said.

"Okay," she grumbled.

"Don't I know you from somewhere?" Holden asked me. "You look familiar to me."

"Um, I…"

Holden snapped his fingers then pointed his index finger at me. "I've seen you around the SAIC campus. Are you a professor?"

"No, but I act as a guest lecturer for photography classes on occasion," I said. "You must be a talented artist to attend SAIC."

Even though the kid exuded confidence, he just shrugged casually.

"He is," Linc and Kennedy said at the same time, making his cheeks turn a little pink.

I wanted to ask about the various mediums that he studied, but decided to wait until later since he was obviously uncomfortable. "Our table won't be ready for fifteen minutes, so why don't you join us at the bar?" I suggested. I moved down to make room for the Huxley siblings to sit between us. Kennedy chose the stool next to me while Holden settled in next to his dad.

"Loyola, huh?" I asked Kennedy. "That's an impressive school."

"I love it so much. I love everything about Chicago," she said emphatically. "I really thought I'd miss California, but I don't."

"Not even the mild winters?" I asked her.

"She loves the snow," Holden said, shivering dramatically beside his sister. Linc laughed and patted his son's shoulder.

"Holden isn't a fan of snow."

"Lake effect snow, Dad. Feet of snow, not inches," Holden offered in rebuttal. "I suppose you'll soon learn that for yourself when you move here."

You could've knocked me over with a feather. Lincoln and I hadn't discussed anything beyond the current week. Did his kids know something I didn't, or was Holden just making assumptions?

Linc saw the surprise in my eyes and offered a warm smile before he looked at his son. "Holden, no decisions like that have been made."

"Uh-huh," he said in a disbelieving tone. "I bet you already looked in to getting a real estate broker license here."

"I, uh…"

"That means he has," Kennedy said. "He probably already has an exit plan. I don't see what you have to lose, Daddy. You'll still be a partner in Forever Home, and maybe you can open another branch here in Chicago. The real estate market here must be insane."

"Well, if it's that easy…" Linc teased them. "You guys, let's not scare Rush off so soon."

"Dad, you named me after him. If that didn't freak him out, then nothing will."

I had to close my eyes to fight against the tears that threatened to spill when I remembered the sound of Linc's voice when he talked about holding his son in his arms for the first time. He said they'd had a different name picked out, but he took one look at his little miracle and told Ophelia that he wanted to name him Holden. She agreed without question. "It was the best way I knew how to honor you," he'd whispered against my lips.

"I don't scare easily," I quipped. Truth be told, I was fucking terrified of the way that Linc made me feel. Over the years, I had convinced myself that I totally exaggerated the love we shared, but I had grossly underestimated it. Everything felt both familiar and new, scary and exhilarating. It was everything I'd experienced with him as a teen but magnified by a thousand times.

"Hello, Rush," a breathy voice said from behind me. Holden's mouth dropped open and his eyes bugged out of his head like a cartoon character.

I turned and faced the young model whose face put me on the map. It was the photos I took of her that graced the covers of fashion magazines all over the world. I swore up and down that she was the reincarnation of Marilyn Monroe. "Hello, honey. How are you?" I kissed the cheek she presented to me, fully aware of our audience. "This is…"

"Mystic Rose," Holden said as breathlessly as Mystic sounded a few moments ago. "Wow, you're even more stunning in person. I thought for sure that a lot of your allure was from photoshopping."

"Hey," I said in mock horror. Of course, I used Photoshop to edit my images, but I had a strict contract with magazines that my images were not to be altered after we agreed on a final image. The amount of photoshopping that most magazines did was horrifying. They took images of beautiful, healthy women and edited them until they looked plastic, fake, and sometimes unhealthy.

"I like you," she said as she approached Linc's son. "What's your name, handsome?"

"Uh…" It was fucking adorable how Holden practically swallowed his tongue when Mystic turned her full attention on him.

"His name is Holden," Kennedy said. "I'm Kennedy. Our father, Lincoln," she gestured to her dad with a flourish, "is Rush's boyfriend."

"It's lovely to meet you, Mystic," Lincoln said without refuting the title Kennedy gave him.

Mystic smiled briefly at Kennedy and Lincoln before she turned her attention back to Holden. "Can I please have your phone?" Mystic held her hand out, palm up.

"Sure," Holden said and eagerly placed it in her hand.

"I'm going to program my number in your phone, and I'd like you to call me, Holden."

"Oh God." The kid sounded like he was about to rupture something. I suspected I knew just what. His dad had the same effect on me.

"Jesus," Kennedy muttered under her breath.

Mystic programmed her number in Holden's phone and handed it back to him, but she didn't stop there. She leaned forward and kissed him softly on the cheek. "I just sent a text to my phone so that I can add you in mine as well. Goodbye, Holden."

"Uh, b-b-bye," he stuttered, earning a giggle out of Kennedy while Linc and I exchanged knowing smiles. "I'll call you tonight."

"I'll answer." She wiggled her fingers in a goodbye wave and rejoined her friends at the hostess station.

"We've lost him for the night," Linc said as Holden continued to stare as the alluring model and her group of friends were shown to their table. He still looked for her after she was gone until Kennedy snapped her fingers in front of his face.

"Come back to us, Holden," she said dramatically, as if he were on the verge of dying instead of falling in lust.

"Huh?" he asked. "What the hell just happened?" He shook his head.

"The most popular supermodel in the world just gave you her phone number and commanded you to call her. Dude, I hope you're trimmed up down there. A girl like that will expect things to be nice and tight below the belt. No wild bush and hairy man berries."

Holden looked down at his crotch like he was trying to remember if he'd manscaped or not.

"Come on, Kennedy," Linc said. "I don't want to hear about Holden's bush and berries."

I threw my head back and laughed like I hadn't in years. Holden snapped out of his fog, looking like he could strangle his sister. The teasing and laughing continued all through dinner and spilled over onto the sidewalk when we left. We waited with the kids until their Lyft driver arrived, then they hugged us both before they got in the car.

"Don't forget to call Mystic," I told Holden.

"She was serious about that?" he asked, sounding unsure.

"Very," I told him. "I've known her since she was sixteen years old. She doesn't say things she doesn't mean, and she goes after what she wants."

"Me?" he asked.

"You. Don't let her fame intimidate you, buddy. She's fun, vibrant, and down to earth. You'll kick yourself in the ass if you don't try."

"Okay, Rush," Holden said. "It was good to meet you. Thanks for making my dad so happy. I've never seen him like this."

"Thank you," I replied, unsure of what else to say. "Have a good night," I told them before Linc shut the door.

I had no fucking clue going into the evening how it would turn out, but it couldn't have gone any better. Linc's kids were as amazing as I thought they would be, and I loved seeing the mutual adoration between them. He and Ophelia raised remarkable young adults. It made me even sadder that I'd never experienced fatherhood for myself.

It was impossible to remain sad with Lincoln looking at me with so much desire in his eyes. There was another emotion present, but I was too afraid to believe it just yet. "Can we swing by my hotel so I can grab a few more things?"

"Why don't we just check you out? There's no sense in paying for a room you're not using."

"Are you sure? I don't want to be in your way, especially since you work from home."

"Linc, I love having you near me. It will make my workday go by faster and give me something to look forward to each night. Brutus loves having you there, and I think you're enjoying your daily walk as much as he does."

"He's a damn good dog."

"Let's check you out of the hotel so we don't lose any more precious time for the remainder of your visit."

Linc pressed his forehead to mine. "Deal."

When we got to his hotel though, we were greatly distracted by the enormous bed he hadn't slept in yet. Linc hadn't come to Chicago for a hookup and I was sorely unprepared. I ended up making a mad dash to the little store in the lobby with my shirt partially unbuttoned, swollen lips, and messy hair from Lincoln running his hands through it.

"Have a good night," the store clerk said with a crooked grin.

"Plan on it," I said, glancing over my shoulder to give him a grin of my own. When I turned back around, I saw that Travis was standing just outside the door. I hoped he wouldn't see me since I had a naked man sprawled and waiting in a bed four floors up, but luck wasn't on my side.

"Rush?" Travis asked, his eyes taking in my current state of disarray.

"This is exactly what it looks like," I told him as I hurried by. "Have a good night."

"What are you doing here?" Travis demanded. I could tell from the proximity of his voice that he was following me. "The Ritz is a little pricey for an escort service."

I turned to face him when I reached the elevator. "I'm not here with a goddamned escort." The elevator doors opened, and Travis moved to follow me. I held out my hand to stop him. "Stop following me, Travis. There's nothing left for us to discuss, and I don't fucking share."

He looked stunned by the possessive growl that rumbled out of my throat. I held on to that energy until I reached Lincoln's room and let myself in. My God, that man was so fucking beautiful that he took my breath away. All those muscles, that smooth skin, and his urgent erection was nothing compared to the adoring look in his eyes when I returned.

"Took you long enough," he said, patting the bed.

I tossed the items on the bed and peeled out of my clothes as fast as I could. Linc lunged and reached for me as soon as I put my knee on the bed. He pulled me against his chest then rolled me to my back.

"You were too far away." Linc nuzzled his nose along the shell of my ear then nibbled it. "Jesus, I need to touch you all the fucking time. It feels like you're slipping away from me, and I'm going to lose you all over again."

"Linc, there's no place that far. I will find you this time." It was a grand declaration, but I wasn't just blowing words up his ass. I meant every single one of them.

18—Sweetest Goodbye

LINCOLN

"**Y**OU BETTER GO TO SLEEP," RUSH WHISPERED, HIS HOT breath stirring my chest hair.

"I can't," I whispered back then pressed my lips to the top of his head. My eyes burned with exhaustion, but my heart raced from more than the last round of sex that carried us into the early morning hours. It was panic—plain and simple.

God, my brain was just as spastic as my heart. What would happen once I returned to San Diego? Were we really going to attempt a long-distance relationship? Was that what either of us wanted? My kids were right, I had considered getting a real estate broker license in Illinois, but wasn't it too soon to even think that way?

"Linc, it's going to be okay. We're going to find a way."

"It feels like the first time we said goodbye, maybe even worse,"

I confessed. "I had this glimpse at what my future could look like and..."

"Just breathe, baby. We're not saying goodbye. We're not even saying so long for now."

"What will we say when you drop me off at the airport tomorrow?" I asked.

"Five hours," Rush corrected sleepily. "And I'm not just dropping you off. I'm going to walk with you as far as I can, I'm going to kiss your gorgeous mouth, and then I'll say see you soon. I *will* see you soon, Linc. I'll fly out to San Diego as soon as I can."

I closed my eyes and held on to the words he spoke because he sounded so damn certain. I didn't mean to fall asleep, but I did. We woke two hours later when my alarm went off. I pulled Rush on top of my chest and he nestled between my parted thighs. Both of our cocks were eagerly seeking pleasure, as if we hadn't blown through a record number of condoms that week. Jesus, I'd never get sick of the look on Rush's face when he slid balls deep inside me or the sound he made when he filled the condom after loving me so thoroughly.

Afterward, Rush struggled to stay awake, so I gently rolled him to his back and looked into the green eyes that had haunted me my entire adult life. "I'll call a car service so you can get some rest."

"No fucking way." Rush threw back the covers and headed to his bathroom to piss and start the shower. I joined him at the double sink and reached for the toothbrush I had used all week long. I ran my fingers over the bristles and attempted to push the encroaching blues away, because sadness would ruin the moments we had left together.

I wanted to tell Rush that I was afraid I'd make an ass of myself at the airport when we said "see you soon," but I held my breath. It seemed wrong to rob him of the moments he wanted with me at the airport just because I was afraid of losing it. I could do this. I would do this. For him. For us. As I watched Rush perform the simplest tasks, like brush his teeth and wash his hair, I realized just how badly I wanted there to be an us.

It was too soon to swear my undying love to him. Hell, we'd only had a week together. Some would say that it wasn't too quick, or that it wasn't even love at first sight since we were high school sweethearts once upon a time, but we lived in reality and not some fairy tale. I had loved the boy with my whole heart, but I wanted to love the man with my entire being. That would take time and commitment. I had both in spades if he wanted them.

The mood between us was pretty somber, even though we touched and kissed until it was time to leave. I checked in for my flight, and we grabbed a small bite to eat at a café in the airport. I tasted nothing, but I gave it my best. We lingered as long as we could, but the lines to go through security kept getting longer.

We held hands as we stood in line, not really speaking because what could we say that we wouldn't doubt later was a product of the high emotion racing through us. When I reached the front of the line, Rush pressed his lips to mine for a lingering kiss. I swallowed hard to dislodge the lump that had formed in my throat. It was the sweetest goodbye.

"This isn't goodbye. I *will* see you soon, Linc."

I nodded and kissed him briefly once more. "See you soon."

I slept the entire flight home and was groggy and grouchy when I got off the plane and tracked down my luggage until I saw Phee waving excitedly at the passenger pick-up.

"I've missed you so much," she said, throwing her arms around my neck. "Our children haven't stopped talking about Rush. Okay, Kennedy talks about Rush while Holden talks about the model. How are you, honey?" she asked once she noticed my silence.

"Um, grouchy and hungry."

"I can take care of one of those things, but maybe Rush can lend a hand with the other. You call him while I toss this suitcase in the back seat. This is all you have?" Her disdain made me smile for the first time that day.

"I didn't plan on staying for a week," I reminded her.

"Oh yeah. Did you do laundry every day?"

"I wore Rush's gym shorts and T-shirts mostly." I might've stolen a few things just to bring pieces of him home with me.

"Aww, that's so cute," she said, her voice rising with each word until she reached a squeaky pitch. "You're sharing clothes."

I didn't respond because Rush answered his phone. "Hi, babe," he said, his warm voice sending waves of joy through my body. "Did you have a good flight?"

"I don't know. I slept through the entire thing."

"I bet you were exhausted after last night and again this morning," Rush said huskily.

"I'd say it was a culmination of the week's activities."

"That too."

"Hi, Rush," Phee said loud enough for him to hear when she got behind the wheel. The two had talked a few times on the phone when Phee had called to discuss business. They'd hit if off right away, just as I knew they would. It made my heart happy that all my favorite people got along so well.

"Hi, Phee," Rush said.

"He sends his regards," I told Phee.

"Listen, why don't you call me after you've had a chance to eat real food and rest."

"Sounds good, babe. I miss you already."

"I missed you before you left," Rush replied. His voice sounded a little strangled, and my heart squeezed painfully in my chest. "Talk to you soon."

"Soon," I said into the phone and disconnected.

Phee didn't say much until we were seated at our favorite Mexican restaurant with a large basket of chips, a bowl of salsa, and two huge margaritas. "You're going to miss this place after you move. I'm sure you can get a lot of amazing food in Chicago, but nothing beats the authentic Mexican food in Southern California."

"You're assuming that I'm moving too, huh?"

"You're an idiot if you don't," she hummed as she glanced over the menu, as if she wasn't going to order the same thing she ate every time we came here. She was stalling or waiting for the right time to tell me something. That's when I spotted the big diamond on her left ring finger.

"Congratulations, Phee. Have you picked a date yet?"

She set down her menu, and her bright smile made the sun look dim in comparison. I held up my hand like she was blinding me, but she just laughed and covered my hand with hers. "Soon," was all she said.

"Is there something else you want to tell me?" I asked. Was there a reason why she was hurrying into a marriage?

"I'm not pregnant," she said dryly, "but we do want to try for a child. I'm not getting any younger. Linc, am I crazy to want to start all over again?"

"You're the best mother I know and any child will be lucky to have you."

"If my eggs aren't viable then we'll adopt. Jackson really wants to raise a child with me."

I turned my hand over and linked our fingers. "I'm so fucking happy for you."

"What about you? Would you do it all over again for the right person?" she asked.

"In a heartbeat," I said without hesitation. Rush had confessed to me how sorry he was that he hadn't adopted a child. If things went the way I hoped, I could see us adopting a baby together. I'd had a vasectomy after Holden was born so fathering a child was beyond my capabilities. Rush was adamant that he wanted to adopt rather than find a surrogate. *So many kids need love.*

"Our lives sure took a completely different turn than the one we planned," Phee said. "Who would've thought that we would sit at a table at our favorite restaurant and talk about starting families with someone other than each other."

"We have new lives and new dreams, but we still have each other. Phee…" My voice broke off and I couldn't continue. How could I properly express my gratitude for all the roles she played in my life? I couldn't.

"I love you too," she said softly. "Usually it takes at least two of those huge drinks before you start getting teary-eyed."

"I'm running on fumes," I confessed.

"Let's get some food in your system so that you can get some rest."

I enjoyed the great food and company, but I was so relieved when I walked through my condo door. I went straight to my bedroom and crashed on my bed without bothering to undress. When I woke, the sun was still up but had lowered considerably in the sky. I glanced at the clock, calculating the time difference. Rush would still be up, so I dialed his phone number.

"Evening, sleepyhead." I heard what sounded like water moving on the other end of the line.

"Are you in the bathtub?" I asked.

"Yep," he admitted. "I'm soaking my sore body. Someone gave me a workout this week. Care to join me?"

I groaned as I imagined him sitting between my spread legs and reclining against my chest in that big tub. I would run my hands all over his beautiful body. "I wish," I said, feeling my dick lengthening.

"You can, baby. Draw a bath and call me on Skype."

"Fuck me," I whispered because that hadn't occurred to me. "Modern technology is amazing."

"Just don't drop your phone."

I ran a bath, grabbed a glass of wine, and called Rush on Skype. As soon as I saw his face, all my sadness faded away. "Hello, handsome. It's so good to see your face." I wanted to see other parts too, but I wouldn't cheapen the emotions he stirred inside me by focusing on my cock first.

"I looked at my schedule and I can fly out in six days," Rush said, stealing my breath. "I can only stay for three days, but…"

"I'll take it. I'll look at my schedule and see how quickly I can return to Chicago."

Rush's sweet smile melted my heart like it did when we were kids. "We're really going to do this, aren't we? This is real."

"We have to try, because I've lived more in the last week than I have the past twenty-six years. It feels like the first time all over again, Rush, but better. No more sneaking around, no more pretending that we're not dying to be in each other's arms."

"So much better," he agreed. "I was afraid to believe, and maybe a small part of me is still afraid."

"That's understandable, babe. There's only one way I can prove how committed I am to making a go of this with you."

"What's that?"

"Time," I told him. "Will you give it to me?"

"I'll give you anything you want." As you can imagine, that changed the direction of our conversation and bathtub activities quickly.

19—Lights Down Low

Rush

THE SIX DAYS WITHOUT SEEING LINCOLN FELT LIKE SIX YEARS, and the few hours I spent on the flight to Cali felt like months. I was so excited to see him, but also a little afraid of how he'd act in his own element. Would it be like high school all over again? No touching, holding hands, or kissing in public? I knew Lincoln hadn't changed his mind because we skyped every single night, but a private conversation with me wasn't the same as eating out in a restaurant. I wasn't sure how I'd react if the stilted, standoff-ish-in-public Linc from my youth returned.

I kept reminding myself that I needed to be patient with him. I had been out for multiple decades and he'd been out for a few weeks. My emotions were all over the fucking place, and I was tightly wound by the time my plane landed. All my concerns faded when I spotted

Linc in the crowd of people waiting to pick up passengers. It wasn't hard to do with his height and distinguished looks making him stand out from the rest. My eyes found him first, so I had a few moments to see his genuine emotions as he waited for me. The hopeful look in his eyes and nervous way he nibbled on his lip set my mind at ease. Then his eyes found mine, and I was enveloped in so much joy and love that it stole my breath. In all my life, only Lincoln looked at me as if I alone created the universe. It had been that way from the moment he stopped fighting his feelings for me when we were sixteen years old. The lost time and distance between us no longer mattered; we had found each other again.

The only thing wider than Linc's smile when I approached were his open arms, ready to embrace me. He held me tight against his body as a tremor of awareness rippled through both of us. Sex over Skype was fun and relieved our physical needs, but it couldn't replace the real thing. Then we took a collective breath and pulled back to look into one another's eyes. Linc stared down at my lips for a brief moment before he kissed me.

"Gross," someone mumbled as they walked by, but neither of us paid attention.

I must've looked as surprised as I felt because Linc chuckled richly before he reached for my hand and led me to his luxury sedan. I wasn't surprised by the sleek car because privilege and wealth oozed from his pores. Years ago, I might've been intimidated by his success and questioned if I belonged in his world but not any longer. Wealth hadn't changed the parts of Lincoln that I adored the most.

"I was serious when I said I wasn't hiding any longer," Linc said when he opened the passenger door for me. "Not saying I won't fuck up now and again, but please don't doubt me." As if to prove the point, he kissed me again and allowed his lips to linger long enough to make us both groan softly.

Once he got in the car, Linc said, "I wanted to wine and dine you, but…"

"They served a delicious dinner on the flight." First class has some amazing perks, and the salmon and wild rice dinner I ate was one of them. "Besides, food is the last thing on my mind right now." I reached across the console and placed my hand on his thigh, loving how the muscle bunched beneath my touch.

Linc laughed as he merged into traffic exiting the airport. "Phee wanted us to have a late dinner with them, but I told her it would need to wait until tomorrow."

"You think to gorge yourself on my body tonight so that we can play nice tomorrow?"

"Something like that," he replied.

I'd had to take a later flight than I wanted to, which meant the sun was starting to set when the plane landed, it made a beautiful back-drop for our reunion. Of course, I wanted to see Linc in every shade of light. That also meant it was well past his dinnertime, and knowing him, he'd been too excited to eat much.

"Do you want to stop and get something for yourself?"

"No," he said emphatically. "There's only one thing on my mind."

"Keep both hands on the steering wheel," I commanded when he started to reach over for me at a stoplight. I moved my hand up his leg to cup his crotch and found he was just as hard as I was. I continued to tease the rigid length of his erection during the entire drive to his condo, which took a surprisingly long time for the short distance. I changed the tempo and pressure to keep him on edge.

"California traffic," Linc growled as his body shook with the need to mate and come.

"Chicago can be pretty hateful too, but nothing like this," I said casually, like I wasn't leaking jizz in my pants like a randy teenager.

By the time we reached his condo, all traces of the sun were gone and stars twinkled in the dark sky. Linc turned off his car and looked at me. "I don't want you here just for sex."

"I know that, baby." I gave his cock one last teasing squeeze before I retracted my hand. "I think it's adorable that you're worried about my feelings, while I'm only worried about how much longer it'll be before you shove your big dick in my mouth or my ass."

"Jesus, Rush." Linc whipped off his seatbelt and was out of the car before I could unbuckle myself.

I met him at the trunk of the car where he pulled out the small suitcase I brought. Hell, I probably could've used a backpack for clean underwear, condoms, and lube. It was quite possible that I didn't even need the underwear, and I was sure that Linc was well-prepared for the marathon of sex we'd have over the next three days. So, really I had only needed to bring myself and a few outfits in case we actually left his condo.

"Seconds," Linc said when he grabbed the handle of my suitcase.

"Huh?"

"You're seconds away from having my big cock in your mouth or your ass. But first…" Linc slammed the trunk and pressed me against his car. "If this was a private garage, I'd fuck you right now." He ravaged my mouth with hungry kisses that somehow left me feeling boneless and brittle at the same fucking time. My legs felt limp, but my dick was hard enough to break. "Inside now," Linc said once he broke our kiss.

I followed him to his condo and waited patiently while he unlocked the front door and opened it. Beneath the ambient glow of his porch light, I saw the wicked promise in his eyes. Linc gestured for me to enter first then guided me inside with his hand at the small of my back.

"Lights down low," Linc said. The lights he'd left on in the living room dimmed at the same time a slow song began to play. Linc chuckled as he slid his hand down to the swell of my ass. "Well, that part is new."

"Which part?"

"The music," he said. "Apparently, that's the name of this song. I'm just getting used to these smart home features."

I released my suitcase handle and turned to face him. The hand that had been caressing my ass started to rub my erection. I returned the favor. "The song does seem kind of fitting for what I had in mind for you."

"Hand jobs in the foyer?" he inquired.

"Not exactly," I said, reaching for his zipper as I dropped to my knees. Linc opened his mouth to protest, but I stopped him by squeezing his cock, hard. "You promised me seconds."

Linc collapsed back against the door and made no additional moves to stop me when I released his cock from the confines of his jeans and briefs. He only panted heavily and ran his fingers through my hair when I licked his cock from root to tip.

"Did you picture me on my knees this week when you stroked yourself off?"

"Fuck yes," Linc whispered hoarsely.

I sucked his virile balls into my mouth one at a time, as I rubbed that sensitive spot behind them with my middle finger. Looking into his hungry eyes, I asked, "How does that compare to the fantasy?"

"No comparison."

"Did you miss my dick when you fucked yourself with the blue dildo?" I'd never forget the first Skype session where we introduced toys. The way Linc's eyes rolled back in his head and the sound of him moaning my name when he came was permanently etched into my brain. I had every intention of using those toys together while I was here.

"Missed it so much."

"How about this?" I asked before I sucked him to the back of my throat. I hummed happily and Linc shouted in pleasure as the vibrations bounced along his engorged flesh.

Lincoln's fingers lost all their gentleness as he fisted his hands in my hair and began to slide his cock in and out of my mouth. I could tell he was trying to maintain control and not hurt me, but I wanted him to lose every ounce of inhibition and take what he wanted from me, so I allowed my teeth to lightly graze the sensitive underside of his cock.

"Fuck!" he roared as his control shattered. Linc fucked my face relentlessly, giving me exactly what I wanted—needed—from him. I relaxed my throat and breathed through my nose so that I could take him deeper. My eyes stung and watered when I swallowed around the head of his cock, but my throat didn't reject him. "Is this what you wanted? Wanted me to fuck your sexy mouth? Come down your throat?" I hummed in response and Linc's thrusts became shorter and choppier the closer he got to blowing his load. "Maybe you want to wear my cum instead?"

Fuck yes, paint me. Mark me.

The first spurts of his salty release hit the back of my throat, but he pulled out toward the end to coat my tongue, lips, and chin. When he was completely spent, Linc used the head of his cock to spread his spunk all over my mouth. "I'm going to relive this memory when we're apart. Your lips all swollen and shiny with my cum."

Linc lifted my chin higher and bent to kiss me, tasting himself on my lips and tongue. I felt dizzy from the need to come too and reached between my legs to ease the ache. God, it wouldn't take much to get me off. The slightest touch would send me pulsing over the edge. I didn't want to use my hand though, not when the man I wanted more than anything was breathing the same air as me and within touching, sucking, and fucking range.

I pulled back from our sticky-cum kiss and got to my feet. "Suck me off, Linc. I need to feel your mouth on my cock."

Linc led me into the living room and hastily undressed me and removed his shirt before he sat down on a large, square ottoman. Hell, that thing was big enough for me to straddle his lap and ride him. I decided I would do just that before I boarded a different plane to take me back to Chicago.

It was my turn to fist Linc's hair and fuck his face. My legs quaked as I worked my cock in and out of his hot, wet mouth, driving for release. I wanted to pull out and spray his chest and face, but his mouth felt too fucking good. He swallowed every drop I gave him and pulled me down to straddle him when my legs threatened to give out.

"That took the edge off," Linc whispered against my lips. "Now, I'm famished."

"I could eat too," I said.

"Good! I'll fix my favorite meal for you."

"Babe, you don't have to go to any trouble. We can have something delivered," I suggested.

"Oh no, this is something really special," Linc protested. "It's no trouble at all."

"Okay, but let me help."

"No way," he said, shaking his head adamantly. He stood with me in his arms like I weighed nothing and settled me in the chair that matched the ottoman. He covered my naked body with a blanket that was placed on the back of the chair. "This is a surprise. You watch television or just rest while I fix us something to eat."

A long day of traveling followed by an amazing orgasm caught up to me, and my eyes started to feel heavy. "Maybe I'll just shut my eyes and rest," I said, nestling beneath the blanket.

The next thing I knew, Lincoln was waking me with kisses on my neck. "Wake up, sleepyhead, dinner is ready." I stretched and yawned while he continued to love on me.

"Mmmm, I'm waking up all right."

"Food first," Linc said. "Open your eyes and check out the feast I made you."

The pure joy in his voice penetrated my sleepy brain quicker than lust could. The coffee table was set with lit candles, fancy china, and real silverware. A bottle of wine was sitting in a silver bucket of ice and two crystal wine glasses were already filled and ready for consumption. "What the heck is going on here?"

"I made us dinner," Linc said, gesturing to the covered serving dishes in the center of the coffee table. "Let's eat."

My mouth watered at the familiar, nostalgic aromas wafting in the air. "I don't believe it," I said when I realized what I was smelling.

"Nothing but the best for you, baby," Linc said. He proudly crawled over to the serving dishes and lifted the covers to reveal the Tyson chicken patties and Kraft mac and cheese he'd made. "Just like old times."

"Except the china, silverware, and crystal," I said, gesturing to the serious upgrades from the paper plates and cheap silverware I grew up with.

"Well, I figured it resembled us in a way." He replaced the lids and returned to where I sat in the chair.

"Oldie but a goodie?" I asked.

"No." Linc smiled and shook his head.

"A cheesy classic?" I teased.

"Nope." He cupped my face and said, "Our surroundings may be different, but we're still the same where it matters."

I don't know if it was the thoughtfulness of making our favorite meal from our childhood or his sappy words that allowed me to shake off any lingering doubt that might've clung to me. I was going to tell him that I would be returning to Chicago without my heart because there was no way I would leave without giving it to him, but I realized that he'd had it all this time. I had never stopped loving him, and I never would.

"That's not all," he said excitedly, sounding like an infomercial. Linc pulled a gift box from the other side of the ottoman and handed it to me.

"You bought me a gift? I didn't bring you anything."

"You being here is my gift. This is just a little something extra." He nodded to the box. "Open it."

I lifted the lid and burst into laughter when I saw what was inside. "I know it's not the exact same one that you had, but it's close."

I lifted the old Polaroid camera up and saw several boxes of film inside. The weight of it felt so right in my hands. "This is amazing, Linc. Thank you so much."

"I already loaded some film inside it for you."

I held it up to my face. I saw Linc smiling at me through the viewfinder and snapped off a picture. The familiar sound of the camera discharging the picture made me smile. Linc grabbed it before I could and fanned it back and forth like I did back in the day to help it develop faster. Of course, it never worked.

Linc laughed so hard he couldn't breathe once the picture developed. I set my camera aside and grabbed for it but he held it just out of reach. I tackled him to his back and distracted him by rubbing my dick against him until I could wrestle the photo from his grasp.

"Oh my God!" It was my turn to laugh until there was no breath left in my body.

"You gonna frame it?" Linc asked, holding me against his chest while I stared at the picture I somehow took of his cock and balls instead of his smiling face.

"I think I'll keep it for my personal stash," I said, setting it aside. "So, I'm a little rusty with the outdated camera."

"We'll make sure you get plenty of practice these next few days."

"Practice makes perfect," I agreed, looking down into his smiling face. I couldn't recall a time where I saw him look happier or more relaxed as he lay beneath me. "Don't move a muscle," I instructed him, reaching for my camera. "I want to capture this moment."

"I have a better idea," he said, pulling me down beside him. "Let's reenact our first selfie."

It took a few tries before I got it right, then I took a second one so Linc could have one also. I snapped pictures until Linc said that I was starving him like a model. I relented and captured our feast on film instead. Later, I took the camera into the bedroom where the angles and subject matter took a playful turn. They were definitely photos of my trip that I had no intention of sharing with anyone back home.

20—Whatever it Takes

Lincoln

"I NEED TO TELL YOU SOMETHING, LINC," RUSH SAID WHEN I parked my car at the airport a few days later. "It might sound crazy, but it doesn't make it any less true." His smile faltered, and his mouth opened, but no words came out.

"I love you too," I said. "Always have, always will."

"Not too soon?"

"Hell no," I replied emphatically. "It's not like we care what people think anymore." The people who mattered most to me, Phee, my kids, and my mom, supported my relationship with Rush wholeheartedly.

"True."

"Rush, do you remember the last sleepover we had at your house before we started junior high?"

"How could I forget?" he asked. "It was the last time you

voluntarily spoke to me for years. I'm not sure you would've ever spoken to me again if not for my dad deciding I would make a great math tutor."

"Mmm, you were the absolute best math tutor," I said, recalling all the kisses we shared. "I never told you why I stopped talking to you though, did I?"

"No," Rush said softly. "I always wondered but was too afraid to mention it for fear it would happen again. Tell me now, babe." Rush reached over and ran his hand across my beard. I had contemplated shaving it because I thought the shot of gray mixed in with the darker strands made me look older, but Rush loved them. I loved the marks my beard left on his beautiful body.

"It all started that afternoon we rode the Ferris wheel," I told him. "You reached for my hand and I felt something stir inside me that I'd never felt before and it startled me. Then you leaned into me and giggled with glee."

"I didn't giggle," Rush scoffed.

I nipped the fleshy pad of Rush's thumb when it neared my mouth, making him gasp. "Oh yes, it was definitely a giggle, and it was so fucking adorable. I loved the feel of you tucked under my arm, and I was determined to earn your hugs as often as I could." I closed my eyes to fight the rising tide of emotions the bittersweet memories stirred within me. "Do you remember the last sleepover we had a few years later. It was right before we went to junior high." Rush nodded. "You beat me at a video game and I got even by tickling you until you *giggled*. I got aroused for the first time and it shocked me. There'd obviously been some changes going on down there, but I'd never had a full-blown boner until that night. I'd heard some of the football players say that looking at girls gave them boners, but I'd never had that. Of course, I bullshitted my way through it with lies."

"Hey, stop beating yourself up," Rush said gently.

"Anyway, there we were rolling around and BAM, I'm hard as a fucking rock. I rolled off of you really quick and tried to play it cool by challenging you to another game." I smiled at the memory. "I was equal parts thrilled that I sprung wood and terrified that it wasn't for a girl. I knew that my feelings for you were more than friends, but I never really had examples of what love looked or felt like. My parents could barely stand each other by that time, and we didn't live near any relatives. Your parents weren't much better, so I was walking through this maze of emotions by myself."

"You were never by yourself," Rush told me. "I was by your side and just as confused as you were."

"I know that now, but back then… I was an idiot."

"You weren't an idiot. Tell me the rest of what happened that night? Did you rub one out at my house while I slept?"

"No, I think my outright terror made it go down on its own." I leaned forward and kissed the lips I would miss so fucking much. "I watched you sleeping beside me and knew I had to pull away from you before it was too late. Even though it crushed me, I didn't think I had any other choice. There were so many things I would miss, but what I dreaded the most was how empty my arm would feel without you tucked beneath it. I had become addicted to feeling you against me, and after we parted, I had a phantom sensation of you there. Sometimes, when I walked down the hallway at school, it felt like you were there, tucked up close to my heart. I missed you so fucking much, but my body's reaction to you only confirmed what my heart knew all along: I was gay and in love with my best friend. I knew there was no fucking way I could have you the way I wanted, so I cut ties with you to try to be something, or someone, else. You know the rest."

"I do," Rush said.

"I'm not that scared kid anymore. I'll do whatever it takes to make this work between us, Rush."

"As will I."

That became our motto as we tried to forge a new life together. It would've been great if we could spend every weekend in each other's arms, but Rush worked a lot of weekends and I had deals that I just couldn't walk away from at the spur of the moment. We made the best of our situation with romantic gestures, such as sending flowers or small gifts to each other. Sometimes those gifts were of the naughty variety and we'd test them out during our Skype chats. Watching Rush get off on whatever toy I sent him was beyond thrilling, but my favorite sessions were our dinner dates. The time difference made it a little odd because his dinnertime felt more like lunch to me, but those nights were truly amazing. We had subscribed to the same fresh food service and prepared the food together while chatting, which often resembled more of a comedy routine when one, or both of us, didn't follow the instructions during a certain step. Sometimes we reverted back to our old favorite of chicken patties and macaroni and cheese.

Hearing his voice and seeing his face always made me feel better, but I ached to touch and smell his skin. I didn't just want to hear his moans of pleasure, I wanted to taste them. As the weeks and months went on, it became harder and harder to pretend I wasn't fucking miserable without him. I had zero doubt where I belonged, but I couldn't just move to Chicago and leave Phee high and dry either. We hired new sales associates that we felt best represented Forever Home as soon as I returned from Chicago after reconnecting with Rush. It might've seemed hasty, but I refused to waste a single minute on doubt when I could have the life I always wanted. It took a few months of training our newest recruits until I felt comfortable that Phee would be surrounded with the staff she needed.

Word trickled out that I was in a relationship with another man, not that I tried to keep it a secret. Hell, on my desk at work sat an eight-by-ten photograph of us cuddling together on my couch, enjoying a Sunday paper and coffee. Phee had taken it with her phone when she dropped in one morning, and it became my favorite picture ever, regardless of my hair sticking up in many directions. There was no denying how much I loved the man who was lounging against my bare chest.

For the most part, not much changed in my day-to-day business dealings. Some of the men looked at me speculatively, some of them refused to meet my gaze at all, and others acted like it was no big deal. One in particular, showed a whole lot of interest though.

"Are you free for *lunch*?" Maxim Detwiler asked when he approached me in the locker room at our gym. And by lunch, I knew he was offering himself for me to dine on. The thought turned my stomach.

"I have plans with Phee."

"Still using her as your beard?" he joked. "Everyone knows you like cock now."

I finished buttoning up my shirt and turned to face him. I didn't like how close he stood next to me, so I took a step back. Detwiler smiled wickedly like I was playing some kind of game with him. "Everyone needs to know that I'm in a *committed* relationship with a man."

"One who doesn't live around here," Detwiler added. "He'd never know."

"I would know, asshole." I closed the distance between us and lowered my voice. "It's never going to happen, Detwiler, so fucking move on."

I'd never met such an arrogant, despicable man in all my life. I told Rush about it during our phone call that night. I was having issues with Wi-Fi and couldn't Skype him. I raged about Detwiler's creepy behavior for a few minutes while Rush listened. He'd gotten so quiet that I thought he fell asleep.

"Rush?"

"I'm here," he said softly. Something in his voice made me regret my decision to tell him what happened that day. "Does he hit on you often?"

I hesitated long enough for Rush to think there was more to my story.

"Never mind," Rush said. "I don't want to know the answer."

"You do or you wouldn't have asked," I told him. "He started hitting on me a few months before I came out. He apparently suspected that I was into men, or was at least curious. I shut him down those times just like I did today."

"Is he sexy? Do you find him attractive?"

"I was insanely attracted to the man when we first met," I admitted. I hoped it didn't cause problems between us, but we wouldn't have a future together if we couldn't be honest with each other.

"But you're not now?" he asked, sounding unsure. "What changed?"

"I couldn't stand his personality once I got to know him. He's a guy who thought it was okay if I fucked around behind Phee's back, and now yours. His looks are not enough to make up for his lack of character. I would've hated myself if I slept with him."

"Linc, I sometimes worry that you're rushing into a relationship with me because it's convenient."

I closed my eyes and inhaled slowly. The last thing I should do was overreact and make things worse. "Being thousands of miles away from you isn't convenient, Rush. Not being able to hold you when you fall asleep isn't convenient. Not being able to make love to you whenever I want isn't convenient. Not being able to feel your laughter vibrating against my chest and taste your smile isn't convenient. Nothing about our relationship is convenient, baby, but I wouldn't trade it. You're where my heart belongs. You're my home, Rush."

"How do you know that? You've only had sex with two people your entire life. I'm the only guy you've known intimately. Maybe you need to date…"

"Is this too much for you, Rush? Have *you* met someone else?"

"What? No! I just don't want you to regret giving up your life there to be with me. I…"

"You what?"

"I don't want to be the safe bet, Linc. I don't want you to destroy my heart again when you find out that what we have isn't real. I don't want you to settle."

"Baby, settling is what I've been doing until you came back into my life. How could you believe differently?"

"Linc, do you remember how you talked about the example our parents set for us?"

"Sure."

"What if our family dynamics have impacted us more than we realized. You stayed in an unhappy marriage for two decades and I stayed in an unhappy relationship for ten years. We made the best of our circumstances, but we still settled for what we had instead of finding what we wanted. It would kill me if I woke up one day and realized that you were only with me because you were afraid to hurt me, or you thought it was the best you could do. I want all your passion, your heart, and everything, or I can't do this. I don't think you can truly know that I'm what you want if you don't date other men."

Jesus, I thought that I was going to puke. *Was he breaking up with me?* "I love you so fucking much, Rush, but that is complete and utter bullshit and you know it. This is the distance and loneliness talking," I said desperately. "We haven't breathed the same air in three weeks."

Rush let out a long, shaky sigh. "Maybe."

"I'm rearranging my schedule and getting on the first flight to O'Hare."

"You don't need to do that, Linc."

"I want you to look me in the eye and tell me you think I'm settling. I want you to feel the way my body responds to yours and tell me it's nothing more than nostalgia. I don't need to fuck my way through San Diego to know where I belong. I think you're the one who needs a reminder." I swallowed hard and said, "I'll call you once I know my flight schedule. And, Rush?"

"Yes?"

"Make sure that Nigel isn't lingering after hours to chat. We don't need an audience."

Less than twenty-four hours later, I held my naked, sated lover in my arms and listened to him practically purr in pleasure.

"Okay, maybe it was the loneliness talking, but I think it was mostly my insecurities taking over," Rush admitted. He raised up and propped his chin on my chest. "I'm sorry that I overreacted to that guy hitting on you. It must happen a lot."

"It really doesn't."

"Most likely you don't notice like back in school. You were oblivious to the girls' attempts to date you."

"That's because I was too busy trying to impress you."

"You only needed to breathe, babe."

I didn't get to stay in Chicago beyond a few days, because I needed to get back to close a deal. Phee could've covered, but I wanted to see it through to the end. In fact, I decided it would be my last California deal, because I needed to focus on establishing residency in Illinois so that I could obtain a broker license there also.

I immediately started going through my belongings to see what I wanted to keep, what I wanted to donate, and what I wanted to toss. I'd done a little of that when Phee and I separated, but I held onto things I would never use again. It was one thing to move them a short distance, but thousands of miles was a different story.

In November, I boarded a plane for Chicago for good. We would spend our first holidays together without having to stress about traveling and rearranging schedules. No more late-night Skype sessions, no more missing Rush like crazy, and no more fucking lonely nights. I would go to bed sleeping beside the man I loved and wake up beside him the next day. There wouldn't be any more guilt over last-minute canceled trips because of business, and by God, I could give my right hand a rest.

I hired a company to transport most of my stuff, including my car, and only packed what I immediately needed in my suitcase. I wanted to surprise Rush and only told Nigel my arrival time. They were going to be gone on location for the better part of the day, giving me plenty of time to hire a car to take me to his place and fix a surprise supper.

There was an amazing market in walking distance from Rush's brownstone, and I bought ingredients to make lobster bisque soup for our first course, along with filet mignon, roasted potatoes, and sautéed snow peas for our main course. I bought a cheesecake from the bakery inside the market for dessert because I couldn't bake worth a damn. My mother said it was psychological because following a recipe required the same skillset for savory foods that it did for baked goods.

When Rush arrived, he was so happy to see me standing in his kitchen and even happier that we weren't eating chicken patties again. "You didn't have to go to so much trouble," he said, looking at the table I set.

"Wait, those aren't my dishes. Isn't that your grandmother's china and silverware?"

"Yep."

"How and when did they get here?"

"I had a little help setting up your surprise. I had them shipped here a few days ago, and Nigel stashed them for me," I told Rush. "It's okay that I'm here, right?"

Rush's fevered kiss was my answer. "God, I love that you're here and some of your things are too. I have to admit, when I thought of you keeping things at my house, I thought it would be more along the line of clothes or lube."

"I brought those things too."

"Wait, are you saying what I think you're saying?"

"I promised you that I would do whatever it takes to make this work and moving to Illinois was a critical step. I can't begin the broker licensing process until I become a resident, so…"

"You're moving in with me." It was a statement, not a question.

"I don't have to move in with you, babe. I just need to find a place to live and get the appropriate documentation to show that I live in Chicago. If you're not ready…"

Once again Rush's mouth silenced me. "Of course, I want you here with me," he whispered against my lips. "I'd hoped it would happen soon, but I was afraid to get my hopes up too high."

My heart tightened painfully in my chest. "Because I've let you down before?"

"No, because in spite of our best intentions, life doesn't always work the way we want it to. I was prepared to wait as long as I needed, but I'm so damn glad you're here now."

"Here is where I'll remain, if you'll have me."

"How long before dinner?"

"The bisque is ready and simmering. I haven't started the steaks yet because I wasn't sure when you would be home. Nigel said around five thirty."

"Nigel helped set this up, huh?" Rush shook his head. "He can't keep a damn secret to save his life."

"He can when it's a surprise for someone he cares about, Rush. He was thrilled to help me."

"If the soup will keep, do you mind delaying dinner for just a bit so that I can give you a proper welcome home?"

I turned off the stove and set the covered pot on the back burner to keep Brutus out of it. Lobster was too expensive to be a dog treat, and I knew my man and I would be hungry. When we reached Rush's bedroom, we took our time undressing and kissing one another's bodies. Touching Rush felt different, more poignant, knowing that we weren't going to have to say goodbye in a few days. He tasted richer, like the finest chocolate or an expensive vintage wine. He held me tighter when I slid inside his body like he was afraid it was too good to be true.

"I'm finally fulfilling my promise to you," I said against his lips when I rocked in and out of his body. "You and me forever." I'd said those words to him once when we were teenagers, after I made love to him for the first time. I just never guessed it would take me so long to deliver on that promise.

Rush's eyes widened at the memory, and then he came apart beneath me. "You and me forever, Linc."

21—Believer

Rush

I WOKE UP TO FIND MYSELF ALONE IN BED, AND FOR A SPLIT SEC-
ond, I panicked thinking that I had dreamt that Lincoln had fall-
en asleep beside me. The disorienting fog from a hard sleep lifted
enough for me to sense his nearness, or perhaps it was the low rum-
ble of his voice as he talked to Brutus that made me smile and sit up
in bed.

"Isn't it the prettiest thing, Brutus?" Lincoln asked my—his—
dog. Brutus had made his choice of master pretty clear when he started following Linc everywhere he went. At first, I said it was because
Linc was home more, but I realized that Brutus was meant to belong
to him as much as I was. Apparently, it wasn't enough that he stole
my niece's affection, he had to steal my dog too. "It's so quiet and
pure as it blankets the earth."

"Until it turns gray from pollutants," I said wryly. I'd lived in Chicago for a long time but had never adapted to the winters. I wanted to hunker down until spring, but Brutus and Linc loved playing in the cold and snow. "Did you say you still haven't sold your condo in San Diego?"

Linc looked over his shoulder at me and the moonlight coming in through the window highlighted the wry smile stretched across his face. "Oh, so now you're not mad that I still have it?"

It was our only argument during the few weeks we'd lived together. I saw it as Linc's safety net in case things didn't work out between us. After he got past his shock over my lack of faith in us, he explained it was for business purposes only. I felt like a complete ass when he started explaining the laws regarding broker and managing broker licenses. He and Phee needed their attorney to advise them on how Linc permanently moving to Illinois would impact their corporation. I felt like a complete idiot when he offered to resign and sell his condo. Of course, I didn't want him to resign from the company he built with Phee. There was no amount of makeup sex that made me feel better about my pettiness, but his joking eased the tension that had crept into my shoulders at the memory of my foolishness.

I threw back the covers and padded over to the window. Wrapping his arms around me, Linc pulled me back against his chest and kissed the sensitive skin behind my ear while I watched the snow fall. Maybe it was a little pretty.

"Phee did say she wanted us to come for a visit during the holiday season. We missed Thanksgiving, so that leaves Christmas or New Year's Eve," I said. "I have the rest of the year off…"

Linc's hands began to move all over my bare chest as he pressed his growing erection against my ass. As far as distraction techniques went, it worked fucking well. Brutus, the smartest dog on the planet, returned to his bed on the floor beside ours. He probably sensed what was about to happen and was just happy we stopped locking him out of the bedroom. That would all change if I felt his cold nose pressed against my bare ass ever again.

"Put your hands against the windowpane," Linc whispered hoarsely against my ear. "I want to make love to you in the moonlight with the snow falling all around us like we're inside some magical snow globe."

I groaned and pushed my ass against him because his words and touch revved me up, fueled my soul, and created as vivid a picture in my mind as I would see looking through my camera. "What about the neighbors?" I asked, clinging to what was left of my lucidity. "I'm not an exhibitionist."

A possessive growl rumbled low and slow out of him. "I'd never let anyone watch us," Linc said softly. "I've been standing here for at least twenty minutes, and there's no movement or lights coming on in the brownstones across the street. The curtains are still drawn and haven't moved. It's two in the morning, they're all smart enough to be asleep."

"You sound like you've been thinking about this for a while," I told Linc. "Have you been standing here thinking dirty thoughts about me?"

"I want to do the filthiest things to your body while the light of the moon blesses us."

"That sounds almost spiritual."

"I'm not a religious man, but I have faith," Linc told me, his fingers dipping into the waistband of my underwear just enough to tease me. "Someone brought you into my life twice, Rush. I don't believe that's a coincidence; it's fate. Your pure heart is my religion and your body is my temple where I kneel and worship. No one will ever convince me that my love for you is wrong, or rob me of the delight from joining our bodies together." He finally slid his hand down to grip my aching cock while he covered my heart with his other. "Heaven on earth is right here in my arms." I melted against him, grinding my ass against his erection. "You make me a believer, Rush. I love you so damn much."

"I love you too, Linc. I love you more than I ever could as a naïve kid." I turned my head seeking his mouth. His lips touched mine, and like always, the only thing that existed for me was this man. Linc sipped from my lips, teasing them open before he claimed my mouth like only he could. Our tongues twisted and slid against each other until we both shook with need.

"You won't disappear if I retrieve the lube, will you?"

"Hurry back," I answered, shucking off my underwear and tossing them aside.

"It would be so much sweeter if you didn't sleep in underwear," Linc said when he returned, "but then again, unwrapping your sweet ass is like a never-ending gift." He nodded to the window and returned my hands to the cold glass.

"Sweet Jesus," I groaned when Linc slid an oiled finger inside me just enough to tease and torment, but not deep enough to nail the spot that drove me wild. "More, dammit."

"So needy and greedy," he teased, but he slid a second finger inside me.

"Yes!" I pushed my ass back, fucking myself on his fingers. I didn't want him to take his time opening me up. I wanted to impale myself on his cock and get as close to him as I could. If I could crawl inside his body and live in his heart, I would do it. I'd sacrifice every golden sunrise and pale-pink sunset if I could fuse myself to his soul. I could live out the rest of my days nestled in his warmth while the music of his heartbeat played like my own personal symphony. Since I couldn't, sex was as close as I could physically get to Lincoln.

Outside, it was cold and blustery as the winter storm intensified and raged on, but our bedroom was hot and sultry. My hands were cold from pressing against the chilled glass, but my body burned from his possession when Linc entered me. The contrasting physical sensations and the emotional stimulation swept me up in a powerful cyclone, spinning and twisting until the pleasure neared pain.

"Too much," I gasped as Linc began to fuck me in earnest, "but not enough." All signs of teasing tenderness faded from Linc as his hips snapped forward and backward, his pelvis slamming into my ass. I did that to him. Me! I turned Lincoln into a rutting, savage beast, and I loved every damn minute of it, craved it even. For in those moments, he made me feel powerful and alive, whole and blessed, both filthy and pure. He made me a believer too. "Gonna come, baby."

"Come hard for me, Rush. Don't hold back." The last was said through gritted teeth as he tried to stave off his own orgasm.

And I did. Loud and very messy as my hot cum splattered against the fogged-up windows. Linc tightened his fingers in a bruising grip on my hips as he came too. Fuck, I loved the throaty growls and grunts he made when he filled my ass. One of the first things we did when he moved in with me was get tested so we could lose the condoms. It was a freedom that I had only ever shared with him.

"That was definitely a communion," I said, resting against Linc while he kissed my sweaty neck and caressed my chest.

"You left one hell of an offering," he said, gesturing to the cum on the glass.

"We should probably stop before we get struck by lightning," I teased.

"Probably," Linc said, easing his softening penis out of me. "Besides, we have a lot of shopping to do tomorrow."

I groaned.

"Stop that," he said, slapping my ass hard enough to make the cheek bounce. "Mmmm, I like the way that looked." I liked the way it felt, but if I told him so, we wouldn't be getting much sleep. "We need to split up for a little bit of private shopping because I need to find you the perfect gift."

"I don't need things, baby. Just give me love."

Linc looked at me incredulously as we cleaned up in the bathroom. "I want to give you something tangible you can hold onto for the rest of your life."

I lightly squeezed his cock. "I've already got that."

"You can't carry that around with you," Linc teased. "I love you, but I'm not handing my dick over so you can carry it around in your pocket." His eyes lit up and he snapped his fingers. "That's it."

"What?"

"It won't be a surprise if I tell you," Linc teased. "I love surprising you."

"Will I end up with another broken bone?"

Linc snorted and pulled me to him as we made our way back to the bed. He rubbed his knuckles over my head like he did when we were kids. "You're never going to let me live that down."

"You ruined my chances at being the star quarterback."

I would've been insulted at how hard he laughed if it wasn't deserved. "You fucking hated football."

"I did, until I could appreciate how good you looked in those pants. My God, the jerk-off sessions I had. I could've earned league MVP for all the times I scored with you behind my closed eyelids." Then a smile spread slowly across my face as I looked at him from the opposite side of the bed. "Turned out I didn't need the skills to throw a football to make you my tight end."

"Ha ha ha," Linc said, sliding beneath the covers. He patted the bed beside him, the only place I wanted to spend my nights. "That was corny then, and it's corny now."

"Sorry," I said sheepishly, sliding between the sheets until I was pressed against him.

"But also very true." Linc kissed the top of my head where it lay resting over his heart. "What are you going to get me for our first Christmas?"

"Socks and underwear so you'll stop taking mine when you run out of clean laundry," I said.

"Practical, but boring," Linc said, nudging me. "An artist like you can come up with something more amazing."

"I'm a photographer, babe."

"That's a form of art."

"Nah, pretty sure I'll stick with the socks and underwear. Maybe some new aftershave if you're a really good boy between now and Christmas."

"I know better," Linc said, then hummed sleepily. "You're up to something. I can smell it."

"I think that's Brutus's fart you're smelling," I said then yawned. "Go to sleep. You need to find me the perfect gift."

Linc chuckled. "I'm revising my plan now. I was going to get you something amazing and grand, but you'd feel like utter shit if all you're going to get me is socks and underwear."

"Don't forget the aftershave." I tweaked his nipple playfully.

"Hey now," he said, sounding as affronted as he could when he was moments away from falling asleep. I doubted either of us would remember the ridiculous back-and-forth conversation in the morning.

I licked the afflicted nipple briefly and loved the way his arm tightened around me, like he would've done more if he wasn't so exhausted. Or perhaps, like me, he pulled me tighter because he worried he'd wake up to find it had only been a dream—one too beautiful to come true.

When the morning came, I knew he remembered everything when he rolled me to my back and tried to tickle me until I confessed to his real gift, as if I'd ruin the surprise I started planning before he even moved to Chicago. Instead, I yelled out every ridiculous thing that came to mind until I was so hot and horny from his hands on my body that I might've spilled the secret if he hadn't fucked me.

We had brunch at his favorite diner before we hit the small, independently owned stores near my house. We would go to the mall or the large chain stores if we needed to, but I wanted to support the small guys whenever I could. We split up for a bit so that we could shop separately then met for coffee and pastries at the café beside our favorite bodega.

"I don't see any bags in your hands," Linc said then offered a cute little pout.

"Couldn't find any socks and undies in your size," I quipped.

"Well, I'm pretty big," he said in a low voice, making me squirm in my chair.

"What about you? Any luck finding my perfect gift?"

"Nope, so it's a good thing you didn't want anything," Linc told me. I could tell by the ornery gleam in his eyes that he had found something for me. The owner was probably holding it for him to pick up later or shipping it to our house.

"Just give me your love," I repeated.

"Again? Right here?" Linc leaned closer to say something, but stopped to pull his vibrating phone out of his jeans pocket. "Hello, Phee. How's it going?" He listened intently to whatever his ex-wife said on the phone then the happiest smile split his face. "That's so amazing, Phee. Congratulations to you both."

I knew then what she was calling to tell him. Ophelia and Jackson wasted no time getting married after they got engaged over the summer. Then they immediately started the IVF process. According to Phee, it wouldn't happen quick. She had to undergo rigorous medical testing and take hormones for a few weeks before they would retrieve the eggs and fertilize them. Phee and Jackson were prepared for it to take a long time, but based on the sappy smile on Linc's face, the couple had conceived after the first try.

I was truly happy for them. Phee and I had grown very close, and Jackson was a good man. Still, I couldn't help but feel the tiniest sting of jealousy because there was nothing I wanted more than to become a father. Linc glanced over at me like he could sense my internal struggle, but I wasn't surprised. We'd always been in tune with one another.

I wanted to recant my statement about what I wanted for Christmas. Yes, I wanted Linc to give me love, but I also wanted him to give me a baby to love. I somehow doubted that Linc made those arrangements while shopping.

22—Time After Time

Lincoln

I NSTEAD OF ALL OF US FLYING TO SAN DIEGO, OPHELIA AND Jackson came to Chicago to spend the holidays with us. I would've known by her glow that Phee was pregnant, even if she hadn't told me a few weeks prior to her arrival. She was fortunate to avoid morning sickness when she carried Kennedy and Holden, so I hoped her luck carried over this time as well.

The kids picked them up at the airport and brought them over for dinner after they checked in at the hotel. We would be spending so much time together that I thought it was silly for them not to take advantage of our nice guest room, but Phee was adamant that they would be intruding.

"What's the point of having a guest room if we don't use it?" I told Phee as she helped me make dinner for the seven of us since

Mystic went everywhere that Holden did.

I'd initially thought their relationship would last a week or two, long enough for the excitement to wear off, but they seemed to be smitten with one another. Once Mystic relaxed around us, we got to see her true personality shine through, and we really liked her. She typically wore her long hair pulled back and kept her face free of makeup, which was much different than her supermodel persona.

"People don't have guest rooms because they want guests," Phee said, tapping the spoon against the pan of meat sauce.

"They don't?" I asked. Her parents were frequent guests at our old house, and I never minded. "We do want guests, Phee."

"Regardless, I say you put that room to a better use." She rolled her eyes when I continued to stare at her like she'd lost her mind.

"Home office?" I asked. "Hey, a sex room!"

"Nursery," she said slowly, drawing the word out and enunciating carefully like she was talking to an idiot. "Do I need to write it down too?"

"Since when did you get to be such a smartass?" I asked, but couldn't keep the grin off my face.

"When did you become so obtuse?" she rebutted. "Have you not seen the gleam of longing in your man's eyes every time one of us mentions *the baby*?"

"Of course, I've seen it," I told her.

"What are your intentions?" she asked, sounding just like her father did the first time I met him.

"Well, I can't get him pregnant, Phee, even if I weren't shooting blanks after you had me neutered."

She slapped my arm, but then threw her head back and laughed. It had been a joke between us for a long time. "I didn't have you neutered, moron." She sobered after a few minutes and said, "Seriously, Linc. None of us are getting any younger. Do not wait to make your dreams come true and give him the family he's dreamed of having with you. He crazy loves our kids, and they're so lucky to have two wonderful stepfathers in their lives, but Rush needs a baby."

"It'll happen, Phee. I promise." I kissed her cheek then said, "Even if I have to steal yours."

"Oh, you," she said, swinging at me again. "I'm serious, Linc."

"I am too," I told her. "Well, except for stealing your baby. I know how much Rush wants to be a father. It will happen." I would move heaven and earth to see his dreams come true. "Starting over with a newborn isn't something I would've entertained until I met him. I had my little minions and I didn't need anything more."

"It's a little scary," Phee admitted. "It's been so long since I've had to get up for midnight feedings and having to guess why they were crying. Is she hungry? Does he have a dirty diaper? Are they getting sick?"

"It'll be worth it to share that little miracle with Jackson," I told her.

"Just as it will be when you and Rush adopt a child." Then she tipped her head to the side and smiled. "You won't have to go six weeks without sex this time."

"Nope," I said smugly. "Good luck with that."

"Asshole."

"Bitch."

"I told you not to call me by my first name," Phee said sassily.

"I'm so glad you're spending the holiday with us," I told her, hugging her tight. "I love our extended family."

"It sure makes it easier for our kids," Phee agreed. "And I can't imagine a holiday without you, and now Rush, either. It doesn't matter if people think our dynamic is weird, because it works for us." I knew Phee was thinking about her family. They hadn't accepted my relationship with Rush as being healthy or a good influence for Kennedy and Holden. Phee only gave them one warning that she wouldn't tolerate any bullshit from them, especially in front of our kids. Their relationship was strained at best. I should've felt a little guilty about it, but I didn't. I was happier than I'd ever been in my life, and I wouldn't regret it.

"When are you seeing your mom?" Phee asked. "I hate to think of her being lonely."

I snorted. "I've never heard her sound so happy. She stays busy with her friends at the retirement village. I wanted her to come to Chicago and spend the holidays with all of us, but they're putting on a Christmas musical and she plays the piano." I smiled when I thought about the excitement in her voice when she told me that someone was recording it for me. "Rush and I are going back to Tennessee next week. We'll get to celebrate the holidays with her, and perhaps put some old ghosts to bed."

"Is Rush going to attempt to see his family?" Phee asked.

"I don't know, but I'll support whatever he decides. As far as I know, he considers Jules, Will, and Racheal to be his family. They're joining us for Christmas Eve, by the way."

"The more the merrier," Phee said, rubbing her stomach. "I'm starving, so let's get this lasagna put together."

"There's a plate of fruits and cheeses in the refrigerator. Take it to the living room so you can rest and have a snack."

"Sounds great, but do I have to share?" she asked with a cute pout.

"Nope. You just holler if they try to take your snack. I'll come out there and knock some heads together."

"I love you, Lincoln."

"I love you too, Phee."

When I joined the group after putting the lasagna in the oven, the snack was gone and they were deep into a game of Cards Against Humanity. Apparently, Rush's turn hadn't gone well because he hung his head like he was embarrassed.

"Are they picking on you, baby?" I asked, sitting on the arm of his chair.

"Yes, I'm totally shit at this game." He turned his face up for a kiss.

"I don't believe it," I said, kissing the slight pout from his lips.

"It's true," Kennedy said. "I love you, Rush, but you suck at this game." Rush smiled affectionately at my daughter.

"Aww, I love you too, Kennedy." It was obvious he chose to ignore the dig to focus on the adoration she expressed.

"He's not devious enough," Holden suggested. "I don't think it's necessarily a bad thing. Besides, he," Holden pointed to me, "sucks at it too. You guys make a great pair."

"What about me?" Phee asked, batting her eyelashes playfully.

"You're as devious as they come," Holden said without hesitation.

"Hey, I want to win at all costs."

"We know," Kennedy, Holden, and I said at once.

I exchanged smiles with Kennedy and Holden, knowing that they too were remembering family game nights that ran longer than the three of us wanted. Phee had been in her element whipping our asses, so we went along with it.

By the time dinner was ready, everyone was more than happy to throw down their cards and declare Phee the winner. Once everyone left, I was glad that no one took our offer to stay in the guest room. I just wanted to hold my man in my arms on the couch by the glow of the Christmas tree lights while staring at the dancing flames in the fireplace.

"I've never been this happy in my entire life, Rush. Not even when we were first discovering each other," I whispered into his hair. "I love you so much."

"Not even the first time I touched your dick? You were pretty damn happy." *Crack!* "Hey," he said rubbing his hand over his ass cheek that I'd just slapped. "How about the first time I let you put your dick in my mouth. I swallowed your happiness down my throat."

"I'm being serious, babe."

Rush crossed his hands over my chest and propped his chin on them. "I know you are, Linc. I'm happier than I ever dreamed possible too. When I boarded that bus for Chicago twenty-six years ago, I never expected to feel whole again. How could I when big chunks of my soul were missing?"

"They weren't missing," I whispered. "I held onto them for you, just as you did with the pieces of me you took on that bus with you." I ran my finger along his smooth jawline. "Can I give you an early present?"

"Does it involve nudity?" Rush asked, waggling his brows.

"Not this time."

"Darn, but okay." He sat up excitedly and waited for me to retrieve the gift from under the tree.

"I wasn't exactly sure what I was going to get you for our first Christmas together until I saw this in a window display."

Rush took the box from my hands and slowly unwrapped it, like he was savoring the moment. Resources were limited when we were kids, and I was only able to buy his favorite candies or maybe some film for his camera. He cherished each gift I gave him, just as he did more than two decades later. Only this time, I was able to come up with something a little better than Reese's Cups and film.

Rush studied the long, rectangular jeweler's box. I could tell he was trying to guess what was inside it. "Too big to be a necklace or any other type of jewelry." Was he disappointed it wasn't an engagement ring? I suddenly became nervous that my gift was frivolous and silly.

"Open it already," I said when he just stared down at it.

"So impatient," Rush said, but he lifted the lid off the box. He ran his finger over the soft, velvet pouch, feeling the shape of the items nestled inside.

"Open it."

Rush laughed at my squirming then put me out of my misery by loosening the drawstrings. "Oh," he said, pulling the gold pocket watch from the pouch. "Linc, it's stunning."

"Open it," I said again.

Rush opened the watch and read the inscription out loud. "Time after time, everything comes full circle to us."

"I wanted to give you something that would act as a reminder, not for the time we lost, but for every precious second we have now. When you look at your watch, you'll know that everything I own, and all that I am, belongs to you. I can give you my love, I can give you my name, but the most precious gift I can give you is my time. It's all yours, baby."

Rush took a shaky breath as he ran his finger over the inscription. Then he looked at me with tears shimmering in his eyes. "I should've gotten you something nicer than socks and underwear." I knew cracking jokes was his way of getting his emotions under control. "It's so beautiful and thoughtful, Linc. I love it." He gently set it back inside the box and leaned forward for a kiss. "I'll cherish it forever. Thank you."

"You're welcome," I said going in for another quick kiss. "Now it's my turn!" I clapped my hands excitedly. "There are no gifts from you under the tree, so where are you hiding my socks and underwear?"

Rush gently set the box on the coffee table and rose to his feet. "Okay, maybe I got you something a little nicer than socks and underwear. I've had to stash it away because I didn't want you snooping. Follow me." Rush led me downstairs to his office and pulled a large wrapped box out of the closet. It was at least four feet tall and just as long, but only six inches wide. It had to be artwork or a really large photo. "I hope you like it."

"Is it a naked portrait of you to hang in our bedroom?" I asked, waggling my brows.

"I don't think the artist would've appreciated that very much," Rush said wryly.

"You hired Holden to paint something for me?" I asked, resting my hands on top of the box. Who else would find it awkward to paint my nude, sexy-as-fuck boyfriend? "He agreed? He's so damn shy about sharing his work that I question what the hell he plans to do with his degree."

"Linc, open it."

I wasn't as patient as Rush, so I had the wrapping paper off and the box open in no time. I knew I would love whatever the gift was because Rush chose it and Holden created it. Still, I wasn't prepared for either the thoughtfulness of the gift or my son's talent as he captured my life with Rush—both past and present.

"I gave him a few of my favorite photos from when we were kids along with the ones we goofily recreated with the Polaroid camera you gave me when I visited you in San Diego the first time," Rush said softly. "Your son is remarkably gifted, so in response to your remark a minute ago, he can probably do anything he wants after he graduates."

I could only stare at the collage Holden created on the large canvas, my heart racing with joy and pride for both the love I saw smiling back at me from the painting, and the talent it took to make it feel so lifelike and real. "We're hanging this over the fireplace mantel," I announced. "I want to look at it every day of my life."

"I'm so happy you like it."

"It's stunning. I love it," I said as we made our way back upstairs. "It's the most thoughtful gift anyone has ever given me."

I helped Rush remove the existing piece of art over the fireplace and replace it with the story of us. There we were, as kids and grown men, with love and hope shining in our eyes. The boys had no idea of the pain and anguish they would face, the loneliness of missing the pieces that made them whole. The men knew, and they smiled brighter and loved harder because of it.

We made a nest of couch cushions and blankets on the floor next to the fireplace then stripped each other down and made slow, sweet love. Every touch, kiss, and slow glide of our damp bodies sliding together felt both familiar and new, just like the painting. The way I clung to Rush's body was familiar, but the gasp I emitted when he slid inside me sounded different. Old and new; new and old. Perfection.

23—A Thousand Years

Rush

AS WE DROVE PAST THE COUNTY LINE MINUTES AWAY FROM our childhood home, Lincoln reached over from the driver's seat to squeeze my hands. I thought it was ironic that John Denver's iconic song "Take Me Home, Country Roads" came on at that exact moment. *Home.* I had stopped thinking of it as home when my parents made it clear I was never welcomed back into the house I was raised in. Jules became my home, followed by Will and Racheal. I later adopted Nigel and Kent, and then Lincoln walked back into my life and brought several amazing people with him. As far as I was concerned, my family was complete, with the exception of the son or daughter I wanted to have with Linc. I didn't want, or need, a reconciliation with the man and woman who brought me into the world then rejected me for not being what they wanted. I refused to waste my time on conditional love when I knew how wonderful unconditional love felt.

"I love you, Rush."

I turned my hand over and linked our fingers. "I love you too."

"Listen, we don't have to stay if it becomes too much. Just say the word and we're gone."

I planned to tell him that I'd be fine, because I didn't anticipate feeling much of anything beyond indifference, but then Linc made the final turn that brought us to the edge of town. I expected the town to have changed in my absence, but it hadn't. It looked the exact same as the day Jules and I hitched a ride in the pouring rain to the bus station in the next town over. If the town looked the same, then would the same archaic ideals exist too? Just like that, I was back in the body of the scared kid who was afraid to walk or talk a certain way, or let anyone know how fucking much I loved the guy sitting next to me. I could've been bullied beyond belief, branded a pervert or deviant, and possibly beaten—or worse.

"Breathe, babe." Lincoln's voice calmed me and brought me back to the present. My eyes refocused, and I saw that we were stopped at the only traffic light. "They can't hurt us now."

"You're right."

"Even so, I'll turn this rental car right around. We'll change our flight plans to—"

"No," I said, cutting him off. "Your mom is eager to see us and show us the video of her performance last week."

Linc groaned. "Maybe she forgot about it already."

"Linc, that's so mean."

"Babe, I've sat through so many plays, concerts, and chorus performances for my kids. I never thought I'd do the same for my mom, but it's only fair after all my sporting events she sat through over the years."

I, for one, couldn't wait to see our child singing in their music programs or forgetting their line in the school plays. "You're going to do it all over again, you know," I said confidently.

"Yes, I do. It's good that you know now that I'm going to grumble about it, and you can find interesting ways for rewarding my good behavior."

"Yeah?" I asked. I glanced over and spotted our old favorite haunt. "Oh wow! Scoops is still in business."

"I stopped there the night before I reconnected with you. I thought about the way you used to stretch out your allowance to get as much penny candy as you could."

"I'll take five of these, ten of these, and five of those," I said, pretending to point at candy in a glass display. "How much money do I have left?"

"That's the memory," Linc said, chuckling.

"Damn, that feels like a thousand years ago. Hell, I forgot about that until now."

"You probably blocked out a lot of bullshit out of self-preservation. I'm just happy you didn't block me too." Linc released a shaky breath and said, "I ran into your father on my way out too."

I turned and looked at him in surprise. "You didn't say anything."

"At first, I was too focused on kissing you, then I thought there was no point in upsetting you."

"Why? Did he call me his fag son?"

"No," Linc said then told me about the encounter. "He and your mom will be the ones answering to God someday, Rush. I firmly believe that."

"Thank you for sticking up for me."

"You've always been the best part of me, Rush."

I wanted to say more, but Linc had pulled in front of his mom's condo at the retirement village, which appeared to be the only new thing about the town. I settled for giving him a kiss that lingered for a few seconds. When we pulled back, Lillian stood on the porch waving at us. I'd talked to her on the phone many times, but I half-expected our first face-to-face encounter to be a little awkward.

I was so wrong. Lillian met me with open arms and held on for a long time.

"Mom, let's go inside where it's warm to hug it out."

"Oh, you!" she said, waving the dish towel she held in her hands. "Just for that, Rush gets first pick of the fried chicken pieces."

Knowing how much Linc loved drumsticks, I licked my lips dramatically and said, "I think I want the drumsticks." Linc was too busy staring at my mouth and picturing other dirty things I could do with it to react.

"I made homemade biscuits too," she said, leading the way inside. "Lincoln, I upgraded the furniture package to include a sofa bed. I hope it's not too uncomfortable for you boys to sleep on tonight."

"It'll do, Mama," he said, his voice picking up a hint of his old Southern accent. "You'll fill my belly with your good cooking, and I'll sleep like a rock."

"You always did anyway," she said, patting his cheek. "Does he still sleep like the dead, Rush?"

"For the most part," I told her, not bothering to clarify that he sure seemed to wake up at my slightest touch. Regardless of how accepting of our relationship she was, I was certain she didn't want to hear about random blow jobs or hand jobs at two in the morning.

"Mmm hmmm," she said with a twinkle in her eye that let me know she knew exactly what I'd left unsaid. "Make yourselves comfortable while I pour you a glass of sweet tea."

"Oh, you always made the best sweet tea, Miss Lillian." I couldn't find sweet tea worth drinking in Chicago. "I hope you made a lot." I could drink a few gallons all by myself.

Lillian chuckled then said, "I made plenty. This one," she pointed to Linc, "told me that he can't get good tea either." She brought us both a tall glass. "At least I don't have to remind you to pee before bedtime so that you don't wet the bed."

"We outgrew bedwetting a few years ago," Linc teased. He leaned closer and put his lips to my ear when she walked back into the kitchen. "Our sheets have a different kind of wet spot these days."

I nearly choked on my sip of tea. "Be good," I demanded when I stopped sputtering. "Maybe you want me to choke to death so that you can have all the tea."

"I'd rather choke you with my big…"

"Here's some snacks, boys," Lillian said, completely unaware of the dirty things her son had just whispered in my ear.

I was going to make him pay for that. My mind had already started to formulate a plan of how I could draw out his pleasure and make him squirm on that damn sofa bed. I was sure I could find something in my overnight bag to use as a makeshift gag so he wouldn't wake his mother when he blew his wad.

"Mmmm, mixed nuts," Linc said cheerfully, accepting the bowl from Lillian. "Thanks, Mom." He immediately started digging around for his favorite kind. The phone rang and Lillian went into the kitchen to pick up the cordless phone off the counter.

"Stop eating all the cashews," I told him. "I like them too." I tried to reach for a handful, but he jerked the bowl away. "Real mature, Linc."

"Hey, they don't put many cashews in the mixed nuts and you know they're the only kind of nuts I like."

"I can think of another set of salty nuts that you can't get enough of," I reminded him. Linc loved playing with my balls, and there were a few times that he almost made me shoot just from sucking and rubbing them. "How would you like it if I jerked them away?"

"Here," Linc said, looking contrite. "I'll share my nuts with you."

"That would make really sweet wedding vows," I told him.

"Oh my!" Lillian said, returning to the living room in time to catch the tail end if our conversation. "You're getting married? Why didn't you tell me? Who proposed and how?"

"Ummm," Linc and I both said at the same time.

"Oh no," Linc's mom said, a look of horror washing over her sweet features. "I'm so sorry for jumping to conclusions like that."

"It's okay, Lillian," I assured her.

"Don't get me wrong, Mama. I don't see a future where I'm not married to Rush, but we haven't made any arrangements yet." Linc looped his arms around my shoulders and pulled me closer. I awarded his sweet gesture with a kiss on the cheek.

"I won't be one of those nagging mothers," she said. "You'll know when the time is right to get married."

"Who called?" Linc asked, changing the subject.

"Oh, um… a friend."

"What kind of friend?" Linc asked suspiciously after his mom blushed and looked flustered. "The male kind? Do you have a boyfriend?"

"What if I have a girlfriend?" she asked. "Ever think that the apple didn't fall far from the tree?"

"Really?" Linc and I asked at the same time.

"No," she said, snapping Linc in the leg with the damp towel.

"Ouch," he said, rubbing the spot above his knee.

"I'd expect two gay men to be a little more open-minded though and not assume that it was a gentleman calling on me."

"Mom, are you dating someone?"

"We're just friends," she said haughtily.

"Where have we heard that before?" I asked Linc, earning a crack on my leg with the towel too. "Ouch!"

"You're part of our family now and subject to the same punishments," Lillian told me. Damn, no wonder Linc liked to smack my ass when he was trying to prove a point. The apple *didn't* fall far from the tree.

"Yes, ma'am," I said contritely.

"Carl is a recent widower and we've formed a friendship, but that's all." Lillian ran a hand over her hair. "I'm too old to date."

"You're only sixty-seven, Mama. I'd hardly call that old. Why don't you invite Carl over for dinner so Rush and I can interrogate—I mean meet—him."

"Well, I'm not sure we're at that stage of our relationship yet, dear."

"Mama, you deserve to be happy wherever you can find it. Please call Carl and invite him to dinner."

"Well, okay." She started to turn back into the kitchen but thought better of it. "You'll behave yourself, right?"

"Define behave?" Linc asked.

"You won't tell embarrassing stories about me, will you?"

"What embarrassing stories?" Linc asked, looking and sounding like he couldn't think of a single incident.

"The time I nearly broke my neck getting out of the shower after a spider descended on its web in front of me."

"Oh yeah."

"You won't be telling him about that, right?"

"Nah," Linc said. "That's just one story."

"Or the time I locked my keys in the car and had to walk home two miles from the store in the dead of August because your dad turned the ringer off so it wouldn't disturb him while he was watching the Braves."

"Damn, how'd I forget that one? You were a hot, sweaty mess when you got home. One of your heels had broken off, and you walked up the driveway unevenly."

"I don't want Carl to know about that either."

"Okay," Linc said, holding up his hand. "I won't tell either of those."

Lillian looked at him suspiciously because we both recognized the orneriness shining in his dark eyes. "What will you talk about?"

"The usual stuff, like what kind of season we expect the Braves to have, what kind of chances the Vols have at winning a national championship, and whether or not the Titans will ever make it to the playoffs again."

"You're assuming the man likes sports," Lillian said.

"Well, does he?"

"Yes, but that's not the point. You're making assumptions based on gender again." She quirked her brow in disapproval.

"Mama, call the man and invite him for dinner," Linc said. "I'll let Carl guide the conversation."

"Well, okay. If you're sure."

"I am," Lincoln said.

"You better not embarrass your mom," I said when she went into the kitchen to call Carl. I knew damn well he was up to no good, regardless of that angelic face he made.

Carl turned out to be a really sweet guy. It was obvious he'd known about mine and Linc's relationship, and he seemed to be cool with it. As Linc promised, he let Carl steer the conversation while Lillian put the finishing touches on supper. I offered to help but Lillian wouldn't hear of it, so I remained tucked in close to Linc while we got to know her beau. Carl mostly talked about where he was from and why he chose this retirement community to live after his wife died.

"I guess it was fate," he said smiling up at Lillian. "I'm really happy here."

"We're happy that you're here too," Linc said kindly.

Lillian set an amazing table of fried chicken that was crispy on the outside but juicy and tender on the inside. She served it with mashed potatoes and homemade gravy that was better than any I'd found in a restaurant. I absolutely despised lima beans, but I ate some anyway since she went to the trouble. For me, the best part was snagging one of Linc's drumsticks and eating homemade biscuits until I felt like a brick had settled in my stomach. I had no regrets.

After we ate, we gathered in the living room with cups of coffee to talk some more. Carl was a really neat guy with so many different experiences over his seventy-two years. After about an hour, he looked at his watch and set his cup down on the coffee table.

"I should be heading back home." Carl stood up and offered his hand to Linc then me. "It was really nice meeting you boys. I look forward to getting to know you better."

"Likewise," I said to Carl.

"Any *friend* of Mama's is a friend of mine," Linc said good-naturedly, placing his hand on Carl's shoulder. I thought I had mistaken Linc's mischievous grin from earlier, and that Lillian was going to coast through the night without Carl learning any of her secrets, but I should've known better. "Say, Carl, did Mama ever tell you about the time that she snuck around the side of the house with the garden hose to spray me and drenched the mailman instead?"

"Lincoln Huxley!" she said, ringing her hands. I could tell she wanted to snatch that towel right off the table and whack him with it, but she wanted to be on her best behavior in front of her beau.

"Oh man," Linc said, laughing so hard he could barely catch his breath. "I was coming down the sidewalk and saw Mom creeping around the side of the house dragging the hose with her. She jumped around the corner and yelled, 'aha' and proceeded to hose old man Wilson down good. He looked like he jumped in a pool. I have no idea what possessed her."

"I do," Lillian said. "I was getting you back after you dropped the water balloon on me the day before when I was hanging clothes on the line."

"Sounds to me that you had it coming, son," Carl said. "Too bad Mr. Wilson was the innocent victim."

"Mama, does he still holler 'don't shoot' every time he sees you?" Linc asked his mom.

"Yes," she groaned. "I do everything I can to avoid him." Lillian got over her aversion to snapping Linc with the towel with Carl present. He got to witness Linc dodging left and right to avoid his mother's deadly aim, but it was obvious she'd had a lot of practice. She had nothing to worry about because Carl laughed heartily at mother and son horsing around.

Their shenanigans were interrupted when the doorbell rang. "I got it, Lillian. You keep giving Linc what he deserves."

"I can't imagine who in the world would stop over so late without calling ahead," Lillian said, straightening her wayward strands of hair.

"Someone needing a cup of sugar," I suggested as I headed for the door.

"The law," Lincoln said dramatically. "Someone turned you in for child abuse."

I didn't hear what Lillian's response was because I opened the door and looked into a familiar pair of green eyes. I stood rooted to the spot as I waited for my mother to say something, but she just stood there ringing her hands.

"Who is it?" Lillian said, coming up behind me. "Oh! Hello, Alice." Lillian sounded as surprised as I was.

"Hello, Lillian," my mother said, still not acknowledging me. Was it just a coincidence that she came to see Lillian on the day I arrived in town? It didn't feel like a coincidence, but why wouldn't she look at me again?"

"Lincoln, grab your coat. You're taking me and Carl to Scoops."

"What? Now?" Linc asked. "It's December."

"They serve hot cocoa and coffee along with some tasty baked treats. I forgot to make dessert."

"What's going on?" Linc asked. I didn't just hear him approaching behind me, I felt it. "Oh," he said when he looked over my shoulder to see my mother standing on the front porch. She looked up then and smiled slightly. "Hello, Lincoln."

"Mrs. Holden," he said firmly, placing his hand at the small of my back to offer comfort. "I think I'll stay here with Rush, Mom. You and Carl have a nice time."

"Now, Lincoln," Lillian said firmly.

I turned sideways to look at Linc. "It's okay. Take your mom and Carl to get hot cocoa and dessert. Maybe you'll be nice enough to bring me back something chocolatey."

"Are you sure?" he asked.

"Positive." I kissed him quickly on the lips and stepped back so my mom could enter.

"We won't be gone long," Linc said.

"Come on, Linc," Lillian said when her son lingered in the doorway. "I'm not getting any younger."

"You didn't seem to have any issues when you were chasing me around the living room a few minutes ago," Linc said before he closed the door and followed his mom and Carl.

My mother didn't say anything for several moments. She just stood looking at me like she was trying to compare the differences between the boy she raised and the man she didn't know. She offered me a small, awkward smile. "You look really well, Rush," she finally said.

I wished I could say the same, but time had not been kind to Alice Holden. She looked so much older than Lillian, but maybe the stress of turning her back on her children aged her. "Why did you come here?" I asked instead of commenting on her appearance. I thought it was best to get to the point, so I didn't offer to take her coat or suggest we have a seat in the living room or at the kitchen table.

"I heard it from Mary who heard it from Sarah that—"

"Mom," I interrupted her. "I didn't ask how you knew I was here; I asked why you came."

"You're not going to make this easy on me, are you?"

"Did you make it easy on me when I came to you with my heart in my hand and tears in my eyes, asking you to love me even though I wasn't the son you wanted?"

"No, I didn't." Her chin wobbled, and she looked at her feet to escape my accusing glare. "I was a horrible mother, a despicable human being."

I felt this little bud of hope start to unfurl in my heart like a rose, but I urged myself to proceed with caution. "Does *he* know that you're here with me right now?"

She didn't move or look at me, didn't acknowledge my question at all.

"Mom?"

"No," she whispered. "He thinks I ran to the market for laundry detergent." She looked up then, and I saw the silent tears running down her face. "I just wanted to see you and know that you're okay and happy. I don't deserve your forgiveness, so I won't ask for it. I have missed you and Jules every single day since you left town. There's nothing I regret more in life than not standing up for you, but I was…"

"Afraid."

"Yes." My mother pulled a tissue out of her coat pocket and dried her eyes. "That's no excuse because I at least was an adult. You were nothing more than a boy going off to a big city with your sister. I had nightmares about all the horrible things that could've happened to you and Julia. Your father tried to pretend that the two of you didn't exist, but I couldn't do it. He got so mad every time he found me crying in one of your bedrooms, but I found comfort being near your things. I fixed your favorite meals at the holidays and on your birthdays. I secretly donated money to charities that I thought you and Jules would support. Rush, I—"

I held up my hand to stop her. It didn't make me feel better to know that she missed us. It pissed me off. "You're talking about us like we had died. That's the kind of behavior I'd expect from a mother whose children were ripped away from her. You gave us up. You threw us away."

"I know what I did, Rush. I am sorry, whether you believe it or not."

"What did you hope to gain by coming here, Mom?"

"I didn't expect anything, Rush. I just wanted to see you."

"And now that you've seen me?" Did she feel better, because I sure as hell didn't.

"Too much time has passed for us to truly reconcile," she said.

"Time isn't the issue, Mom. It's intent. Do you think you're proving anything by sneaking around to see me? What do you plan on doing when I return to Chicago with Lincoln? Call me when Dad's bowling? I refuse to be your damn dirty secret."

She flinched, and I was sorry for raising my voice. "I'm sorry, Rush. I didn't mean to make things worse."

"I'm going to write down mine and Jules's phone numbers. You can call us once you're strong enough to stand up to Dad." I walked over to the notebook that Lillian kept by her phone. I jotted down the numbers and returned to my mom. "One more thing," I said. "I am not a pervert or a deviant. My love for Lincoln is just as pure as the love between any man and woman. If you ever call me, I'm going to assume you accept that too."

I extended the piece of paper to her. She stared at it for so long that I thought she would reject it, but she finally took it and slid it inside her pocket.

"You better get on to the store before Dad starts to wonder what you're up to. If you heard I was in town, so did he."

She only nodded and walked to the door. "Goodbye, Rush."

"Goodbye, Mom."

After she left, I collapsed on the couch and sat in stunned silence. I wasn't sure what to think about the interaction, and I refused to hope that my mom would stand up to my father and call Jules or me. I closed my eyes and leaned my head against the back of the couch and tried to think of happier things going on in my life, such as the man I loved and the ever-growing family of people who loved us. I thought about how badly I wanted to extend our family even more. All those things helped push the sadness from old and new hurts away.

A few minutes later, Linc and Lillian returned. Instead of sitting down beside me, Lincoln carried my jacket and scarf to me. He grabbed the throw blanket off the back of the couch and smiled seductively. "I know how I can make this night better for you."

"Something chocolatey would've been nice," I said with a little pout.

"I have hot chocolate and scrumptious brownies waiting for us in the car." Linc smiled when I shot to my feet and put on my coat.

I didn't bother to ask where we were going, because it didn't matter; I'd follow that man anywhere. I wasn't at all surprised when Lincoln drove to our old high school and parked as close as he could to the football stadium.

"Grab the goodies and I'll grab the blanket," he said.

I picked up the carrier that held two delicious-smelling hot chocolates and a small paper bag. I held it with my right hand and grabbed Lincoln's ass with my left hand when he rounded the car to join me.

"You told me to grab the goodies," I said, earning a hot kiss.

Lincoln hummed low in his throat when he pulled away. "I got to wondering after we reenacted our first dance with upgrades. What else would I do over with you, or do that I never got a chance to when we were in high school?"

"Ohhh, do you want to make out under the bleachers like all the other kids did?"

"I figured, with our advanced years, we might try to get a little more comfortable," Linc replied, holding up the blanket for me to see.

"Let's go."

During warm weather, a few lights around the stadium would've been on for people who liked to walk the track at night for exercise, but the school district kept the area dark in the winter to save on money, rather than invest in solar lights that would've been less expensive and discourage deviant behavior like what Linc and I had in mind.

The night sky was mostly clear with just a little cloud cover, so we used the light from the moon to make our way to the center of the bleachers. Linc laid the blanket down for us to sit on then we pulled the edges up and over so we could huddle beneath it.

Linc set the goodies down on the bleacher in front of us and cupped my face. I loved the way his eyes shone with love in the moonlight. He kissed me softly at first then let his lips linger against mine until my mouth parted so a sappy sigh could escape. Linc didn't use that to his advantage to push inside my mouth; instead, his tongue slowly circled just the tip of mine. I tightened my lips and sucked his tongue into my mouth, wanting more from him.

Linc's hands were in my hair, and I slid mine beneath his sweatshirt and scraped my nails against his tight abs. Sighs and moans quickly turned to groans of need, so we eased apart to catch our breath and get ourselves under control. As much as I wanted to jack Linc off beneath the blanket, it wouldn't be wise. I didn't want to think what would happen if we were caught making out or outright fucking on school property. Even though we probably wouldn't be the first couple to take advantage of the darkness, I somehow felt the local law would view two men fucking differently than a man and a woman.

"The things that you do to me, Lincoln Huxley." After one last, long kiss, I gestured to the goody bag. I refrained from making jokes about wishing I could have something salty to counterbalance the sweet, because it wouldn't take much for me to throw caution to the wind.

Lincoln pulled a brownie from the bag and held it up for me to take a bite. I moaned in delight when the brownie melted in my mouth. "Good," I said. "More." Linc smiled because they were the same words I grunted during sex when I was so close to coming that I couldn't form coherent thoughts. He leaned forward and kissed the crumbs from the corner of my mouth then held the brownie for me to take another bite.

"What about you?" I asked.

"I already ate mine with Mom and Carl. This is just for you." Linc leaned forward and said, "Besides, I get to taste the chocolate in your kiss."

"I could get used to this," I said then took another bite.

"Are you okay, babe?" Linc asked after I swallowed.

"I will be," I told him, unwilling to pretend that seeing my mother didn't hurt me.

"I've loved you for a thousand years," Linc said tenderly, "and I can promise you a million more."

"That's the kind of line you use in your wedding vows," I said then smiled. "Not the one about sharing nuts."

"Maybe we can have both public and private vows," Linc suggested. "Keep it clean while standing in front of our friends and family, but vow to always eat each other's asses once we're alone." He waggled his brows suggestively, but my mind was still stuck on his first suggestion. God, I wanted to marry this man and spend the rest of my life loving him.

"Last bite." Linc held it to my mouth, but then jerked it back when I parted my lips to devour the last morsel. Instead, he popped it into his mouth and began to chew.

Under the moon and stars, and surrounded by the warmth of Lincoln's love, I decided that the place where we'd experienced the greatest sorrows would become the place we experienced the greatest joy. "Marry me, Linc."

His eyes widened in surprise at first, but then a joyous smile spread across his handsome face.

"How does a week from tomorrow sound?"

"Perfect!" Yep, all was going to be right in my world—with or without my mother.

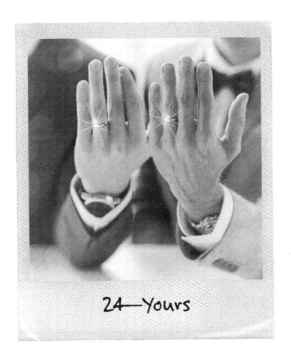

24—Yours

LINCOLN

A S MUCH AS I WANTED TO MARRY RUSH A WEEK AFTER HIS impromptu proposal, I thought it would be best to plan a wedding so that our family had time to prepare and attend. I mentioned that to him the morning after we returned home.

"Do you doubt my intentions?" Rush had asked me, filling his coffee cup while I kept a close eye on the waffle iron. "Did you think I asked because I was upset?"

"No, I saw the sincerity and love in your eyes," I answered honestly. "That's not the issue at all."

"I don't want a fancy wedding, Linc. I just want to be yours." His green eyes shone with fervor and love. "I adore our family, but this isn't about them; it's about us. Why can't we have a simple ceremony, and then have a big party to celebrate later?"

"Or we do this right the first time."

"Define right?" Rush asked.

"Think about all the dreams we had when we were younger? Did you dream of marrying me in a courthouse in front of a monotoned justice of the peace?"

"Linc, I never allowed myself to hope that someday we'd share a last name or be legally recognized as anything, let alone become husbands."

"Come on," I said, "I don't buy that for a minute. You always had your head in the clouds, Rush. You lived for the what if and what could be. You're a dreamer, a visionary, and a hopeless romantic. Be that little boy who looked at clouds and saw dinosaurs and bunnies when all I saw was mashed potatoes and cotton balls. Baby, tell me the kind of wedding you dreamed of having with me."

I could tell the moment that I won, the absolute second he realized a quickie wedding at the courthouse was not the way he wanted to start our lives together. "We wore matching white tuxedos with rainbow bowties and rode up to the altar on unicorns." *Or maybe not.*

"Be serious," I told him.

"I am serious. Madonna married us."

"Rush," I growled.

"Okay, fine!" He threw his hands in the air and paced away from me.

I couldn't take my eyes off the way his rounded ass looked with his sleep pants hanging low on his hips. He had those amazing little ass dimples that I loved to bite and paint with my cum, marking him as mine. *Mine. Yeah, yeah. We were talking about making him permanently mine.* "Quit distracting me with your perfect ass." He spun around and suddenly smiled diabolically. I pointed the spatula at him. "Pull your pants up too. Your ass dimples are playing peekaboo and my cock wants to play hide-and-seek with your sphincter. God, you're so fucking hot."

"Something smells hot," Rush said about the same time I noticed the smoke coming from the waffle iron.

"Dammit!" I lifted the lid and discovered my Sunday morning surprise had turned into a Sunday morning disaster. "I'd planned on serving you Belgian waffles with strawberries and whipped cream."

"Trying to sweeten me up before you break it to me that you aren't ready to get married after all?" Rush asked.

"You know better," I replied, unwilling to be deterred from the subject that I brought up. "If I was trying to pull a fast one then I would've waited until after I fed you a delicious breakfast." Rush looked at the charred waffle I removed from the iron. "Practice run," I said confidently. I dropped the waffle on a plate to cool before I threw it away. "Back to our conversation. Tell me about the kind of wedding you envisioned."

"It doesn't matter what I imagined when I was a kid; it only matters what I want now."

"It matters if you're settling. We only have one wedding, Rush." I ladled more batter onto the waffle iron and closed the lid. "Let's compromise, okay?"

"Maybe," he said, sounding slightly less stubborn.

"I'm not asking for a large, lavish affair. I'm not asking to wait a year, or even six months. Can you give me until March or April?"

"February," Rush said.

"Babe, that's weeks away. All the best venues or churches will be booked."

"We'll get married here."

"In the kitchen?" I asked.

"Or the living room," he said. "Look, we'll invite less than twenty people so why bother with a venue? We can hire a caterer to fix the meal."

"What caterer isn't booked in advance?"

"One who's just getting started and would love the opportunity to work with a photographer with connections," Rush replied.

"You sound like you have a plan in mind," I said.

"Of course, I have a plan, Linc. There's like six weeks until Valentine's Day. I know it's not much time for Phee and Jackson to make travel arrangements, but…"

"Phee wouldn't miss it unless she wasn't physically able to travel." I reached for his hand and pulled him closer until I felt the heat of his bare chest press through my T-shirt. "Valentine's Day?"

"You asked me what I had wanted as a kid, right? Well, Valentine's Day is supposed to be the ultimate day for love and romance. It was the day you openly declared your love for someone by saying 'Be Mine.' I dreamed of the day that I wouldn't have to sneak you the paper hearts I made or chocolates that I stole from the convenience store."

"You were so bad," I whispered against his lips. "It's kind of hot." This time, the rising temperature in the kitchen had nothing to do with the damn waffles. It was the sexy man in my arms. "I can live with Valentine's Day, as long as there's no gaudy cupid and red hearts for decorations."

"Don't insult me," Rush said. "I stage stunning scenes for a living, and I would never make our wedding look gauche and cheap."

Six weeks later, on a Wednesday, our living and dining rooms were rearranged for our wedding and reception. Just as I suspected, my romantic husband-to-be couldn't resist adding a cupid here or there, but at least they were in the form of gold, antique-looking candle holders. Instead of red hearts, we set the table with red and white roses in crystal vases. In fact, there wasn't a heart to be seen anywhere.

I was a tiny bit disappointed that I couldn't tease him about it, but that was forgotten when I looked into Rush's eyes as we recited the vows that would finally tie our lives together. It was impossible for me to be aware of our surroundings, or even the people who attended to celebrate our union, when those green eyes I loved so much shimmered with tears of love and joy. In fact, the pastor had to give me a little nudge when it was time to seal our vows with a kiss.

I cupped Rush's face with both hands, running my thumbs over his cheekbones while he wrapped his hands around my wrists to anchor himself. My husband's lips trembled and happy tears slid down his face, just as they did mine. The moment was too precious to hurry, hell, we'd waited for half of our lives to get here. I wanted to savor the first kiss with my husband.

"Go on and kiss him already, son," my mom whisper-shouted from the front row.

"Rush, will you be mine?" I asked

"I've always been yours."

I kissed him then, a long lingering press of lips made salty from our tears. It was a kiss unrivaled by any we'd shared, including the clumsy first kiss of discovery as teenagers, the sad goodbye kiss on prom night, or even the joyful kiss of rediscovery after so many years apart. Our first kiss as husband and husband was a promise. It said, "I will forever be yours."

We posed for pictures in front of the fireplace with our family, friends, and the pastor. I couldn't think of a better background for our photographs than the large painting showing the story of us—past, present, and future.

After the last photo was taken, we adjourned into the dining room for our wedding feast. On our way there, I wrapped my arms around my husband and pulled him tight against my side. "I have to admit, babe. I expected to see some sappy hearts tucked in amongst the decorations."

"There will be hearts," Rush said, grinning ruefully. "The top tier of the wedding cake is a heart."

"Seems appropriate to me."

"That's not all though." He stopped and turned into my arms. "I'm also wearing some."

"Where?" I asked, but my mind was already stripping him out of his navy-blue suit.

"You'll see for yourself after our guests leave," Rush said.

"They have an hour to eat and wish us much joy and happiness before I throw them out."

Rush threw his head back and laughed, loving how eager I was to touch, taste, and possess his body. I was the one that got the last laugh that night when we were finally alone. He expected a fast, hard fucking after I got my first look at him in his adorable, ass-hugging boxer briefs with candy hearts that urged me to suck him, rim him, and fuck him. I did each of those things as I took my sweet time drawing out our pleasure until he was the one shaking and begging. Only then did I give into the demands of my body to fuck, mate, and claim my *husband* for the first time.

"Forever yours," we both sighed once our bodies were joined.

Epilogue—With Arms Wide Open

Rush

ALMOST A YEAR TO THE DAY WE GOT MARRIED, LINC AND I welcomed our little bundle of joy into the world with arms wide open. "She's so tiny, Linc. So perfect." I knew that I would love the child we adopted, but I didn't expect it to be so immediate. I thought it might take a few days for the bond to form, but I knew that Gabriella belonged to us the minute we saw her through the nursery window at the hospital.

She was everything I dreamed she would be, and so much more. "Look at all that dark, curly hair," I whispered after I took off the knit hat for another quick peek. "That tiny button nose and that little mouth. I love her so much."

"You're our little perfect angel, aren't you?" Linc cooed softly to our daughter. Oh man, I didn't think I could possibly love him any more until that moment. "Big noises will come out of that little mouth," Linc warned. I didn't believe him, but our girl let it be known when she wasn't happy.

"Having second thoughts?" Linc asked on the car ride home from the hospital when Gabriella chose to express herself again.

"None," I said running a finger over her downy cheeks to calm her. "Thank you so much, Linc." My heart felt so full I thought it might bust.

"I didn't buy her at Target for you as a Valentine gift, babe," he quipped, trying to play it cool, but I heard his voice thicken with emotion.

"No, but you've made every dream I ever had come true."

"I bet you saw us bringing her home in a chariot pulled by unicorns though, right?" Linc asked.

"Yep," I agreed, "but my SUV worked out nicely."

Our large, boisterous Chicago family descended on us after we got home. I expected Gabriella to cry when so many people looked down at her, but she seemed to suck up the adoration like a sponge. She'd have these people eating out of the palm of her hand in no time at all. My favorite moment was when Brutus introduced himself. He was a dog who'd known great sorrow until he came into our lives, so we went out of our way to make sure Brutus knew he was still our best boy. He wanted nothing to do with us though; he only had eyes for Gabriella, and he hovered nearby like he was protecting her.

Of course, I snapped at least a hundred pictures that day of our friends and family holding our daughter. Holden, Mystic, and Kennedy tried to act like they were too old and cool to fuss over a baby sister, but Holden held the rattle over her head while Kennedy and Mystic took turns using baby-soft voices to tell Gabriella how perfect she was and how lucky she was to have such a loving family. Jules openly wept because she knew how long I had waited for the moment I became a father. Racheal looked a little put for a few minutes, until Uncle Linc reminded her that she was our girl first.

"Gabriella will be so lucky to have a big cousin like you looking out for her, Rach," Linc said. "Isn't that right, Uncle Rush?"

"That's right," I agreed. I beckoned for Racheal to come to me, and she climbed onto my lap like old times. "No one could ever replace you, Rach. You'll always be my first princess. Okay?"

"Okay." She hugged me tight, and I savored every second. "But you're still not riding my bike."

I threw my head back and laughed. I loved her sass so much and knew she'd be one hell of a force to be reckoned with someday. She would become a wonderful role model for Gabriella. Racheal sat on the couch between Linc and me so she could hold the baby. It wasn't long before Racheal kissed her forehead and sang the same lullabies she heard as a child. So far, our daughter hadn't found a heart she couldn't win over.

Nigel waited patiently for his turn to hold the baby, while Kent stood nearby scowling at me. I was on his shit list lately for two reasons: I'd hired an intern from SAIC that Kent felt was too sexy for Nigel to be around, and all my baby talk triggered Nigel's baby talk. Apparently, Kent wasn't quite ready for fatherhood yet, but I knew that would change the minute he saw Nigel with a baby in his arms.

Sure enough, Nigel scooped Gabriella into his eager arms and cradled her against his chest. "Oh, you're so warm and smell so pretty." Nigel took off her knit cap and fussed over her curls and her little fingers and toes while Kent sat beside him on the couch looking dazed. Nigel gently kissed Gabriella's forehead, and it was the exact minute Kent knew he was ready to be a father after all.

"Hey, I'll distract them while you steal the baby," Kent mock-whispered.

Nigel beamed with joy at his husband. "Or, we could just get our own."

"Okay," Kent relented. "What kind of weekend hours do these places keep?"

"It's not like an animal shelter, baby," Nigel said. "I'll call on Monday to make an appointment to get the adoption process started."

Once everyone left, we FaceTimed Lillian and Carl so they could see their beautiful granddaughter. "I can't wait to hold her next week," Lillian said. She seemed so much happier in her second marriage, and I knew how much it meant to Linc to see his mom in a healthy relationship.

"You saved the best for last didn't you," Phee said when we FaceTimed her next. Jackson sat beside her with little Micah on his lap.

"Of course," I agreed. "How are you doing? Looks like the big guy is doing great."

"I am," Jackson said, "thanks for noticing."

Phee laughed and rolled her eyes. "I cannot wait to hug all of you. We miss you so much. I'm glad it's your turn to travel and get the evil eye from airline passengers."

I groaned because I wasn't looking forward to that part of flying to San Diego during spring break with Kennedy and Holden. Kennedy was due to graduate in May and had accepted a job at Wright Creations in D.C., Holden would graduate soon and who knew where life would take him and Mystic. There might not be many more opportunities for us all to be together at the same time, so we were looking forward to it.

Micah started to kick up a fuss, which made Gabriella cry too. We said goodbye to Jackson and Phee then turned our attention to calming down our angel. Linc cradled her against his chest and talked to her soothingly while Brutus paced anxiously.

"She's just hungry, Brutus," I assured him. He didn't look like he believed me though.

I retrieved a bottle from the warmer and handed it to Lincoln. Gabriella's cries turned to grunts of joy as she drank from her bottle. Linc kissed her forehead and gently rocked her from side to side.

My heart felt like it would burst from the love swelling inside it. I couldn't find the words to express how much the moment meant to me, so I picked up my camera to capture more images from the next chapter in the story of us.

The End!

Other Books by
AIMEE NICOLE WALKER

Only You

The Fated Hearts Series
Chasing Mr. Wright, Book 1
Rhythm of Us, Book 2
Surrender Your Heart, Book 3
Perfect Fit, Book 4
Return to Me, Book 5
Always You, Book 6
Any Means Necessary, Book 7

Curl Up and Dye Mysteries
Dyeing to be Loved
Something to Dye For
Dyed and Gone to Heaven
I Do, or Dye Trying
A Dye Hard Holiday

Road to Blissville Series
Unscripted Love
Someone to Call My Own

The Lady is Mine
The Lady is a Thief

Coauthored with Nicholas Bella
Undisputed
Circle of Darkness (Genesis Circle, Book 1)

Acknowledgments

First, I need to thank my husband and children for their constant support and encouragement. It's not easy living with a writer who often disappears into a fictional world for long periods of time. They do so many things to help me out so that I can realize my dream. I love you guys more than words can ever express.

To my creative dream team, thanks seem hardly enough for all that you do. Miranda Vescio of V8 Editing and Proofreading, thank you for your tireless work, feedback, and many laughs while editing. Jay Aheer of Simply Defined art is an incredible artist, and I love how she brings my words to life. Stacey Blake of Champagne Formats is also an amazing artist who does incredible interior formatting, illustrating, and designing for e-books and paperbacks. Let's not forget Judy Zweifel of Judy's' Proofreading. She does an amazing job of finding the tiniest details that make a book shine. I need to give a special thank you to Wander Aguiar for the incredible photo shoot for the Second Wind cover and teaser images.

To my lovely PA, Michelle Slagan. I'm not sure how I ever did this without you. I love you to the moon and back!

Lastly, I am so grateful for my beta readers and the honest feedback they provide me. Thank you for all that you do, Racheal, Kim, Laurel, Michael, Brittany, and Jodie.

About

AIMEE NICOLE WALKER

Ever since she was a little girl, Aimee Nicole Walker entertained herself with stories that popped into her head. Now she gets paid to tell those stories to other people. She wears many titles—wife, mom, and animal lover are just a few of them. Her absolute favorite title is champion of the happily ever after. Love inspires everything she does, music keeps her sane, and coffee is the magic elixir that fuels her day.

I'd love to hear from you.

You can reach me at:

Twitter—twitter.com/AimeeNWalker

Facebook—www.facebook.com/aimeenicole.walker

Blog—AimeeNicoleWalker.blogspot.com

Made in the USA
Middletown, DE
08 April 2019